Praise for *Stranglehold*

"Rotenberg does rich work—full, and full-hearted, compelling and compassionate. And judging from *Stranglehold*'s final words, there's more of this good work to come."

London Free Press

"His fourth and best."

The Globe and Mail

"Readers of all descriptions will get off on *Stranglehold*'s courtroom drama. . . . The action is authoritatively presented . . . and as twisty as anything from Perry Mason's worst nightmares."

Toronto Star

"Author Robert Rotenberg was in the business of turning Toronto into fiction before Toronto became stranger than fiction."

Metro News

Praise for *Stray Bullets*

"A cracking good story."

Toronto Star

"Rotenberg really knows how to build legal suspense."

The Globe and Mail

"The entire unfolding and resolution of a tragic, sadly semi-familiar, crime-and-punishment tale shows a real pro of a writer, just getting better and better."

London Free Press

Praise for *The Guilty Plea*

"Rotenberg's . . . courtroom drama is terrific."

Ian Rankin, bestselling author of
the Inspector Rebus series

"A compulsive page-turner. . . . His humanizing of seemingly obvious killers raises doubts in the reader at the same pace as it does for the jury."

Maclean's

"It's a solid whodunit."

Winnipeg Free Press

"Rotenberg juggles the many plot elements with aplomb, unveiling each new surprise with care and patience."

Quill & Quire

Praise for *Old City Hall*

"Robert Rotenberg does for Toronto what Ian Rankin does for Edinburgh."

Jeffery Deaver, bestselling author of
The Bone Collector

"Clever, complex, and filled with an engaging cast of characters."

Kathy Reichs, bestselling author of
the Temperance Brennan series

"It's clear that *Old City Hall* has enough hidden motives and gumshoeing to make it a hard-boiled classic."

The Globe and Mail

"The book has wowed pretty much everyone who's read it. . . . A finely paced, intricately written plot is matched by a kaleidoscope of the multicultural city's locales and characters."

Maclean's

HEART
OF THE
CITY

ROBERT
ROTENBERG

Published by Simon & Schuster

NEW YORK   LONDON   TORONTO   SYDNEY   NEW DELHI

SIMON &
SCHUSTER
CANADA

Simon & Schuster Canada
A Division of Simon & Schuster, Inc.
166 King Street East, Suite 300
Toronto, Ontario M5A 1J3

This Simon & Schuster Canada edition August 2017

SIMON & SCHUSTER CANADA and colophon are registered trademarks of Simon & Schuster, Inc.

For information about special discounts for bulk purchases, please contact Simon & Schuster Special Sales at 1-800-268-3216 or CustomerService@simonandschuster.ca.

Manufactured in the United States of America

10   9   8   7   6   5   4   3   2   1

Library and Archives Canada Cataloguing in Publication

Rotenberg, Robert, 1953–, author
    Heart of the city / Robert Rotenberg.
        Issued in print and electronic formats.
        ISBN 978-1-4767-4057-7 (paperback). —ISBN 978-1-4767-4059-1 (html)
    I. Title.
    PS8635.O7367H43 2017   C813'.6   C2016-906517-0
                                     C2016-906518-9

ISBN 978-1-4767-4057-7
ISBN 978-1-4767-4059-1 (ebook)

For my long-time law partner and great friend
Alvin Shidlowski,
who has always had my back

Toronto will be a fine town, when it is finished.

Brendan Behan

DECEMBER

Ari Greene handed two passports to the customs officer and smiled at her. The passport on top was Canadian. It was his. The one underneath was British. It belonged to the young woman standing next to him.

"Where are you folks flying in from?" the officer asked, smiling back.

"London," Greene said.

"Ari Greene," the officer said, opening his passport. He could tell from her tone of voice that she recognized his name. He wasn't surprised.

A year earlier his name had been headline news: a top Toronto homicide detective charged with first-degree murder. And three months later he'd made front-page news again when the case against him was thrown out.

He watched her run his passport through the scanner on her little desk. She squinted at the screen above it. There'd be a special notation about him on file. She nodded, confirming something to herself.

"Welcome home, Detective." She flipped through the pages of his passport. "You've been out of Canada for quite a while."

"Twelve months, two weeks, and one day. But who's counting?"

She chuckled. "Not me."

She reached for the second passport. Her forehead crinkled when she saw it had a British cover.

"Your name is Alison Gilroy," she said, turning to the young woman at Greene's side.

"It is," Alison said in her English accent.

The officer examined the passport page by page. Most were empty. "You've never been to Canada before."

"Not for one minute until today."

The officer turned to Greene. "Sir, I know you're a homicide detective, and I appreciate that this might be police business. But you realize I'm required to ask every foreign visitor what the purpose is of their visit to Canada."

Greene nodded. "Go right ahead."

"Alison, what's the purpose of your visit to Canada?"

"Actually, I'm not a visitor."

"You're not?"

"No."

The officer looked at Greene. He shrugged. She turned back to Alison.

"Are you coming here on police business?"

Alison gave her a long, slow head shake. "Absolutely not."

The officer put Alison's passport squarely on top of Greene's and tapped it with her forefinger. "What are you going to be doing in Canada?"

"It appears I am coming here to live."

"To live? Then why are you travelling with Detective Greene?"

Alison closed her left hand and stuck out her thumb in a hitch-hiker's pose. "Well, it turns out," she said, jerking her wrist toward Greene without looking at him, "that Mr. Greene is my father."

JUNE

1

Every part of Greene's body hurt. His feet ached from the weight of the steel-toed boots he'd worn all week. His legs were sore from countless climbs up and down the newly poured concrete stairs of the condominium construction site. His arm muscles burned from the weight of the metal rebar he'd been hauling around since six-thirty this morning. And he had a blistering headache. He'd worked all day in the hot sun and during the afternoon coffee break he'd smoked a cigarette with one of his fellow workers. It was the third time since high school that he'd lit up.

"Okay, ladies, weekend's here. It's closing time," Claudio Bassante, the site superintendent, said as he wove his way through the clusters of workers. He was one of those people whose face falls into a natural smile.

Thirty-seven men all played their parts in a well-orchestrated ballet. The formers, who poured the concrete floors and walls. The carpenters, who created the wooden forms the concrete was poured into. The ironworkers, who handled the rebar that reinforced the concrete. The electricians and plumbers, who hopscotched around everyone else, securing the wiring and plumbing before the concrete was poured to seal everything in place. And the labourers, such as Greene, who scrambled through the two basement floors and the three storeys that had already been built, carrying an endless array of building materials. Above all this activity, a crane towered, in constant motion, swinging back and forth like a one-armed orchestra conductor, delivering all manner of supplies to the worker bees below.

In seconds the repetitive din of metal and concrete colliding, hammers banging, and circular saws whirling all ceased. It was as if the mute button had been pushed on a loud, surround-sound television, replacing the noise with silence. Hard hats were removed, tools were put away, and the bright orange safety vests everyone wore were ripped off and discarded.

This was the end of Greene's first week on the job, and despite all his aches and pains, he had enjoyed the simple pleasure of stacking two-by-fours, carrying cans of nails, hoisting the rebar onto his shoulder, trudging up and down the stairs, and laying them out in perfect order. The feel of his body straining and strengthening day by day. Using his muscles instead of his brain.

"Before you disappear for the weekend, we've got to get everything spic and span," Bassante said to the crew. "Boy Wonder will be here any minute. He's coming to kick the tires like he does every Friday afternoon, and I want this place to look as if the queen of England slept here last night."

Boy Wonder was Livingston Fox, a.k.a. Mr. Condo or Mr. Con Dough, depending on your point of view, the owner, CEO, and face of Fox Developments Inc. Love him or hate him, Fox was always in the news. A high school dropout, he'd rocketed to wealth and prominence by building well-designed condominium towers throughout the city core. He threw up buildings at breakneck speed, lived an over-the-top lifestyle, complete with a chauffeur-driven Rolls-Royce convertible, and in just ten years had played a key role in transforming the cityscape. He was thirty-four years old.

Greene had learned this first week that most of the workmen lived in suburbs and towns at least an hour's drive from Toronto. At three-thirty, the end of the workday, they were in a hurry to hit the road and avoid getting caught in rush-hour traffic. All hands pitched in, and in less than twenty minutes they were on their way.

Bassante had asked Greene to stick around after everyone left. They hadn't had time to talk all week. It was no problem for Greene. Unlike his commuting co-workers, he lived downtown and walked to work. Soon only the two of them were left.

They had met in high school, a multicultural mosaic of whites, blacks, Asians, Italians, Russians, Portuguese, Protestants, Catholics, Muslims, and Jews. In many ways, it had been a precursor of everything that modern-day Toronto had become.

When Bassante was in grade ten, his father, an electrician, was killed while working on a hydro project down in Niagara Falls. His mother fell into a disabling depression, and Bassante, the youngest child and the only one left at home, ended up practically living at Greene's house for the next three years of school.

Greene sat on the edge of the third floor facing south over Kensington Market, the hodgepodge of streets and stores and houses that had been the landing spot for new immigrants for more than a century. It was one of those Toronto blue-sky afternoons, when the sun was high and would be for many more hours. The first heat wave of the season had rolled in overnight, bringing with it stifling humidity, and it felt good to sit up here and take in the breeze.

Local residents, led by the high-profile lawyer Cassandra Amberlight, had formed the Save Kensington Coalition. They objected to this condominium being erected on the northern border of their neighbourhood, but they'd been powerless to stop the project. Instead they'd extracted concessions from the hated Mr. Con Dough and forced him to reduce his plans from eleven stories to seven. Fox, never one to be modest, named the building Kensington Gate and plastered photos of himself alongside happy-looking, athletic young people across the hoardings that flanked the site.

Last November, Fox announced plans for a second condominium high-rise down the street. He'd cheekily named it Kensington Gate 2 or, as he liked to call it, K2 and was promoting it as the "Peak of Luxury in Every Way." Some people thought he was doing this just to rub salt in Amberlight's wounds. The venom between the builder and the protest leader was public and palpable. She'd come up with the term Mr. Con Dough. He called her Ms. Red Light, because she opposed every development he proposed.

Amberlight had spent the last few weeks organizing a march that was going to take place in the market this afternoon to oppose what she called density creep. From his perch on the third floor, Greene could see television trucks already lined up along Augusta Avenue, the street next to the building, where groups of protesters were gathering. Most were young people, with a smattering of scruffy-looking veterans. A few of them had brought their dogs; others had babies in carriers. Many held aloft signs that read "Stop the Fox. Save the Market." Others had their phones on telescopic selfie sticks and were filming themselves and the cops standing by. One man was pounding away on a big African drum, whipping up the crowd.

Greene heard boots on the concrete behind him and turned to see Bassante walking over, carrying two Corona beers.

"You'll have to drink it without any lime," he said, sitting down and passing Greene one of the bottles.

"I think I can handle it." Greene laughed and took a sip.

"You've worked five days straight, Ari. How do you feel?"

"A little sore."

Bassante waved his bottle in the air. "You were always a lousy liar," he said, "even back in grade nine."

"Okay." Greene took a longer sip. The beer was sweet and cool. "I hurt like hell, all over."

"That's why God created the weekend. Rest up. Stay cool. Take your daughter to a movie where there's air conditioning or something."

Below them on Augusta Avenue, more and more protesters were crowding onto the narrow street, singing and dancing and chanting.

Greene looked at Bassante. "Why aren't you drinking your beer?"

"Boy Wonder will be here at four. Guy's never late. I have to play the corporate game." He flicked the bottom of his bottle out toward the commotion on the street. "Look at those kids there. What do they think? They have some special right to live down here and hang out in their trendy coffee shops all day while Mommy and Daddy pay the rent? My guys, with wives and kids to support, they're stuck out in the burbs and commuting two or three hours a day. I'd like to see just one of these protesters put in a real day's work."

He took one small sip of his beer, put the bottle by his side, pulled out a roll of Mentos mint, and popped a few in his mouth. He stretched his arms over his head. "Ari, look at this city," he said, pointing south. "Remember when we were kids, there wasn't one high-rise downtown? Now it's all condos and office towers. Condos, condos, and more condos. See those two new big ones down by the CN Tower?"

"They all look new."

"The one on the left, I moved in there last year. You'll have to come down and see it. View of the lake is amazing."

"And the view of the building cranes," Greene said. "They're everywhere."

"Toronto, it's a city of cranes. Cost us a fortune." Bassante pointed to the street below. "Every time we put up a building, there's some new lawyer acting for a neighbour I have to negotiate with and pay off. Then all we do is raise their property values. Good work if you can get it. You see that house on the other side of the alley?"

Greene followed his gaze. The house was an unremarkable two-storey brick building with a second-floor window on the north side covered by a heavy brown curtain. An alleyway ran between it and the building site, then turned south behind the homes facing west on Augusta Avenue and the restaurants and stores facing east on Spadina Avenue.

"What about it?" Greene asked.

"Because our crane casts a shadow when it passes over the house, we had to negotiate a crane swing agreement with the owners to pay for their *inconvenience*. This one cost us thirty thousand bucks. Some numbered company owns it, and the place is empty anyhow. Can you believe that? Happens every time we put up a building."

Bassante stood, and as he rose his leg nudged his beer bottle. It tumbled over the edge of the building and smashed onto the extended balcony of the floor below.

"Christ," Bassante said, chewing hard on a few more mints.

"I'll take care of it," Greene said. "You go meet young Mr. Condo."

"Thanks, pal. The broom and dustpan are in the work shed near the back gate." Bassante pulled out his phone. "Weird. He should be here by now. He usually calls as soon as he arrives. Maybe he's spending some private time with that gorgeous chauffeur of his."

Greene finished his beer and put the bottle in his pants pocket. He took his time descending the stairs. Walking down was harder on his sore legs than walking up.

The shed was past a pair of Johnny on the Spot portable toilets at the back corner of the site. Greene hadn't been inside it since his first day at work, when he'd been outfitted with a hard hat and safety gear.

He was sweating in the heat, and the air as he walked past the toilets reeked. When he got to the shed, it occurred to him how cut off it was from the rest of the work site. He pulled open the spring-loaded door and it slammed shut behind him.

The heat hit him first. It was furnace-hot inside. The sun streamed through a large south-facing window and blinded him for a moment. But all his years as a street cop and homicide detective had honed his instincts. Something about the stillness of the room wasn't right. He could feel, before he could see, that there was someone else in the shed.

As his eyes adjusted, he could see through the window the hoarding that surrounded the building site and above it the old house on the other side of the alley.

Then he looked down.

Livingston Fox was lying flat on his back, right in the middle of the floor.

He wasn't wearing one of his usual hand-tailored Italian suits, just a plain white cotton T-shirt and a pair of khaki shorts. His arms and his legs lay limply beside him, his hands and feet anchored by heavy concrete blocks. His head was slouched to one side. His eyes bulged open, unmoving. And his chest was pierced by a long steel rebar, plunged right through his heart.

2

I t was Friday afternoon and Homicide Detective Daniel Kennicott was glad the week was finally over. Even better, the murder trial he'd worked on for the last three months was finished and the court-house had emptied out, so he could be alone now in the Crown attorney's office storage room.

He stared at the evidence boxes stacked in three towers stretching up to the ceiling and at the piles of papers and folders scattered on the large desk in the corner. No matter how long it took, he was going to file every scrap of it away tonight. He wanted to be done with the case of Wainwright Campbell, the punk who'd killed Kyle Little, a hard-working young man who had stood up to Campbell's gang activity and had been shot in the back of his head for his troubles.

The case had concluded yesterday, and the jury was out for the night. Half an hour ago they'd come back with their verdict: Campbell was guilty of first-degree murder. To Kennicott it felt good. Very, very good.

Behind him, the door swung open. Albert Fernandez, the prosecutor, came in still wearing his crisply pressed court robes. Unlike some lawyers who grew progressively shabbier as a long trial dragged on, Fernandez was always well dressed. He wore a fresh white shirt every day, shined his black shoes to a high gloss, and no matter how tired he was he never let it show.

He put a bankers' box squarely on a corner of the crowded desk. "This is the last one," he said. "It contains all my trial notes." Fernandez was also one of the most organized people Kennicott had ever met. The contents of this box would be labelled and in perfect order.

"I must get home; my wife and kids have hardly seen me for months," Fernandez said. "I'll come in Sunday morning to help you pack everything up correctly."

"No problem," Kennicott said. "I've got this."

"Thanks. Very kind of you."

They looked at each other. For the last ten weeks, the two men had lived in the cocoon of this case, working around the clock. There had been no media coverage of the trial, and no one in the Crown's office had paid any attention to it. That didn't matter to either of them. They'd worked as hard on this trial as they would have done had it made the headlines.

The only spectators regularly in the court had been Kyle Little's bereaved mother and aunt. And now what did those two women have left? The emptiness of their lives without their son and nephew. But at least the killer had been convicted.

"You should be proud of the work you did," Fernandez said.

"You should be too."

They shook hands.

"Don't stay late."

"No worries."

Kennicott shut the door behind Fernandez. Back at the desk, he picked up a binder and filed it in a new empty box. There would almost certainly be an appeal, and he wasn't going to leave any stone unturned to make sure this verdict stuck.

Ari Greene, the detective who had brought Kennicott into the homicide squad and been his mentor, had taught him that it was best to pack up a file right away. You never knew what was going to happen next, and if you put the task off, you never knew when you'd get back to it.

Kennicott shook his head. Ari Greene. He kept trying to put the man out of his mind. For five years Greene had kept him under his wing, had shown him secret parts of the city, where he had contacts and hiding places. They'd often meet early in the morning at Caldense, a Portuguese bakery on Dundas Street West about a ten-minute walk from Kennicott's flat. Greene would question him about a case they were investigating. He'd been like a law professor, prodding Kennicott to think through things from a different angle.

Almost a year and a half ago, everything changed when Jennifer Raglan, the former head Crown attorney, was found strangled to death in a room at a sleazy motel. Kennicott had been the officer in charge of the case. It came to light that Greene had been her lover. He'd found her body but had run from the scene without calling 911 and had tried to hide their affair. Kennicott had been forced to charge the man who had been his mentor, then his partner, with first-degree murder.

Thirteen weeks later the case collapsed when Greene figured out who the real killer was—Hap Charlton, the former chief of police who had just been elected mayor of Toronto. Kennicott was left feeling a crosswind of emotions. He was angry with Greene for not being honest with him and furious at himself for arresting an innocent man. Greene left the country right after his charges were thrown out. He'd disappeared without saying goodbye. Rumour was that he'd gone somewhere in Europe, but nobody knew exactly where he was or if he was ever coming back. It would probably be best for everyone, Kennicott thought, if he stayed away.

The ceiling fan in the storage room clicked on, making a pleasant white noise. He could have propped the door open to let fresh air inside, but he didn't. He was in no hurry. He wasn't dying to go back to his apartment alone. The weather was hot, and the city was in bloom. It would be a beautiful night outside. Wonderful for normal people who led normal lives. But it meant nothing to Kennicott. So much for the romance of being a homicide detective.

His phone rang with the hotshot ring tone indicating an urgent call. That meant there had been another murder in the city. The detectives who had families had all booked off time for their vacations, so the homicide squad was short-staffed. Now that his trial was over, Kennicott was on the bubble.

He didn't move. Every ounce of his being wanted to ignore his phone.

He looked at the photos that he'd taken from the file. There was a picture of Kyle, a warm smile on his face, coming home from work in his Walmart uniform. Another of him playing soccer with the kids in the scrubby courtyard of the housing complex where he'd lived with his mother and aunt. And one of him with his family and friends, blowing out candles on his birthday cake last spring when he turned twenty-five.

The phone hit its third ring. Two more and it would go to voice mail.

Kennicott had learned that to be a great homicide detective you had to do more than just walk in the victim's shoes. You had to care for the victim with every ounce of your being. It was as if you were falling in love with someone you would never get to meet.

The phone rang for the fifth and final time.

He stabbed the answer button.

"Kennicott," he said, making sure he hid the fatigue in his voice. "What have we got?"

3

Greene stood and stared at Fox's body. Tongue hanging out. Eyes glazed. Limbs slack. The rebar sticking out of his chest and the heavy cement blocks pinning him to the floor like a dead butterfly on a scientist's presentation board. A thin rivulet of blood had slithered down his body and pooled on the floor beside him.

Greene didn't move. This was a crime scene. But even from this distance, he could see the blood had not yet congealed. In the oven-like heat of the room, blood would dry fast. This murder had happened a very short time ago.

He felt sick. He was sweating, and his mind was whirling back to that horrible morning when he'd found Jennifer strangled to death in a motel room. It had been the worst moment of his life. He'd been so excited that day, rushing to meet her for what was going to be their final covert rendezvous. Final because, at last, Jennifer had decided to leave her husband. There would be no more secrets. No more hiding. Finally, they could be together.

But Jennifer was gone. Gone. Sure, he had been arrested, put on trial, the case thrown out. But what did it really matter? Without Jennifer, did anything really matter?

Thank goodness he'd found his daughter, Alison. She and his dad were the only people he cared about now. He wanted to make a new life with her. What he didn't want was to be a cop anymore. To have to stare at dead bodies. And yet, here he was, his eyes fixed on Livingston Fox. Dead. Horribly murdered.

He knew he should run. Move. But his feet wouldn't budge.

He lifted his eyes from the body and scanned the room. The shed was small. There was no other door. The afternoon sunlight streamed in through the large, south-facing window. Two bare bulbs shone overhead. Neatly stacked papers on a makeshift desk were surrounded by a white jar filled with pens; a black jar filled with pencils; a stapler; a three-hole punch; two empty water bottles, one blue and one orange; and a pair of empty drinking glasses. Everything was perfectly in place. Greene looked at the walls and the plywood floor. There were no obvious signs of blood splatter anywhere. A stray pencil lay under the desk. He took in every detail. Memorized it.

He turned away and dug into his pocket for his phone. The biggest blunder he'd made when he found Jennifer's body in that horrid motel room had been not calling 911 right away. He wasn't going to make that mistake again. He tapped in the number.

"What is your emergency?" a calm female voice asked.

"A man has been murdered. I just came upon his body." He knew the operator had a standard set of questions, and he wanted to cut through them quickly. "The address is Kensington Gate Condominium on College Street west of Spadina, the south side. The place is under construction. I'm in the shed at the back."

"I've dispatched police and an ambulance," the operator said after a moment's silence. "I need a few more details. Who are you, sir?"

Greene paused. Who was he? Homicide Detective Ari Greene? *Former* Homicide Detective Ari Greene? Construction worker Ari Greene? Alison's father, Ari Greene?

"I work here. Construction," he said.

"Do you know the victim?"

Greene hesitated again. If he said Fox's name, there was a chance a media scanner would pick it up. If he said he didn't know, that would be a lie.

"Sir? You still there?"

"The dead man is Livingston Fox," he said. "The owner of the property." He hung up before she could ask more questions. He opened the shed door with his elbow and let it close on its own. He should tell Claudio right away what was going on, before the cops arrived.

Instead, he stopped. The blood beside the body was fresh. The shed had one door. Where had the killer gone?

Greene checked the ground outside the shed. No blood. How had the killer got onto the site? The only entrance, other than the main gate on College Street, was the gate in the chain link fence behind the shed, leading to the alleyway. It was a few steps away.

He shouldn't. He knew he shouldn't. This was the worst time in his life to get involved in a murder investigation. He was determined to keep out of the limelight, and Livingston Fox's murder would be headline news. He had to focus on his daughter. After six tough months, Alison seemed to be settling into life in Toronto.

But the killer might be close. Every second counted.

The chanting and drumming of the protesters on Augusta Avenue was growing louder. It would be easy for the killer to disappear into the crowd. The cops wouldn't arrive for a few more minutes, and by then it could be too late.

He walked quickly around the shed. Homicide detectives never run. He could trip and that would be a disaster. He had to stay calm, focused. The back gate was ajar. The combination lock was open, hanging from the handle. Whoever had entered either knew the combination or Fox had opened the gate for them.

Greene stopped to listen. No sirens yet. He had thirty seconds, maybe fewer.

The gate was open wide enough for him to slip through without touching it. He half-tiptoed through in his construction boots, searching the ground at his feet. Dry concrete. No footprints. Not a sign of blood anywhere. One step outside he stopped and looked around. Across from him was the old two-storey house at Augusta Avenue, and he could see the protesters and the TV trucks out on the street at the western end of the alley. Just outside the gate there was a puddle in the shade against the fence where one of the protesters' big dogs must have peed.

He wanted to walk over to where the alley turned south. Did he have time? He stopped to listen and couldn't hear a police siren yet. He moved fast and peered around the corner.

The back alley was similar to hundreds he'd seen in downtown Toronto. On the east side there were the back of the stores and restaurants that faced out onto Spadina. The west side was lined with wooden garages belonging to the houses on Augusta, their metal doors slathered with colourful graffiti. A rusted ball hockey net and a clutch of hockey sticks were propped against one door, and two bikes were locked to a wooden fence by a heavy chain. In back of one of the restaurants, cigarette butts were piled on the pavement beside a pair of overturned red milk crates.

He returned to the open gate for one last look. Turned to the two-storey house across the alley.

There had to be a clue.

Something.

Nothing.

4

Alison Gilroy had lost track. How many little cups of green tea had she drunk in the last half hour? Eight, maybe ten? She was sitting alone in the backroom of Huibing Gardens, a steamy Chinese restaurant on Spadina Avenue, staring at her empty notebook, thinking it made no sense.

Livingston Fox, the so-called King of Condos, was supposed to have met her here at three. She checked her phone for the time. It was three-fifteen and Fox still hadn't shown up. This was not like him. His life was scheduled into exact time slots. For the last month, she'd met him here at the same time every Friday afternoon for half an hour, and he'd always been on time.

Fox had been a terrific source of stories for *Kensington Confidential*, the blog she'd started two months earlier. Two weeks ago he'd given her a scoop: he was getting engaged. It had given her blog a huge boost. Last week he'd told her he had an even better story for her. He said it was going to make major headlines and send her numbers through the roof.

The man was obsessed with secrecy. Before their first meeting at the restaurant, he'd given her precise directions about how to get here, which she'd followed to a T. She walked along Oxford, one block south of College, then up a path to the alleyway at the back of the restaurant, where a red milk crate held the rear door open. Inside, behind a beaded curtain, was a room with two chairs and a table always already set with a pot of tea and a pair of little white porcelain cups.

Fox had insisted that she never go into the main restaurant and had told her that none of the staff would ever come into the room. She was to wait alone until he showed up.

So, where was he? Why hadn't he come?

This morning she'd awoken to her first taste of Canadian-style summer heat and humidity. Back home in England they didn't have anything like this. And to make matters worse, this room had no windows and no air conditioning. She had never been so hot.

It all felt like more bad luck in the worst year of her life. One night last August, two weeks before she was set to start her second year at university, her mother collapsed while cooking dinner. Alison had called emergency right away but it hadn't made any difference. Her mother had died before she hit the ground. A brain aneurism, the doctor said. Could happen to anyone at any time.

Alison was an only child, and her mother was the only family she had. She'd never met her father. Her mother had told her he'd left when she was a baby and was living somewhere in New Zealand with a new wife and kids. That's what Alison believed until a week after her mother died when David Joyce, the family solicitor, invited her to his office to discuss her mum's will.

"Alison, I have a rather large surprise for you," Joyce said when she walked in. A man she had never seen before was sitting in a chair across from the lawyer's desk. "This is Detective Ari Greene. He's Canadian."

Greene stood. He was tall and had a nice smile. Alison had no idea what he was doing there.

"Detective?" she said with a nervous laugh. "Is there something wrong?"

"No, not all," Greene said.

He had a quiet warmth, and there was something vaguely familiar about him. What was it?

"I'm from Toronto. I knew your mother years ago when she lived in Canada."

"I remember. Mum told me she liked the snow, and she said that the summers were beautiful but terribly humid."

She looked at Joyce. "I don't understand."

Joyce glanced down at some papers on his desk. "Your mother had planned to tell you about Mr. Greene next year, when you turned twenty-one. She left me specific instructions that if, in the unfortunate event that something happened to her before that time, I should contact both you and Mr. Greene."

"Contact us about what?"

She looked back at the stranger. "Sir. Can you explain this?"

"After your mother returned to England, she sent me a Christmas card every year with a picture of the two of you," Greene said.

"Those photos were so embarrassing. I hope you threw them out."

"No. I kept them all."

"Why would you do that?"

He gave her a blank look.

"Wait. What year did Mum leave Canada?"

"Nineteen ninety-five."

Her birthday was February 1, 1996. "When? What month?"

"April."

It wasn't hard to do the math. But it didn't make any sense. She turned to Joyce. "But Mum told me my father lives in New Zealand and . . ."

The lawyer shook his head. "I'm afraid she made that up."

Alison nodded. She started to rock from side to side. This was unbelievable.

She looked at Greene. Stared. It took a few seconds until he returned her gaze.

Yes, something about him was familiar. It was his eyes. He had the same grey-green eyes with flecks of yellow as she had.

"Did you know?" she demanded.

"I didn't. I had no idea."

"But you kept our Christmas cards?"

"I don't know why. I just did."

How could this be? In the last week she'd lost her mother and found a father.

"Do you . . . have a family or something?" she asked him.

"No. I've never been married. Never had children. Well, never thought I did until . . ." His voice drifted off.

"Your mother thought it was easier this way," Joyce said. "Like you, Detective Greene was gobsmacked when I informed him. I assure you she was going to tell both of you—"

"Toronto?" Now Alison was shaking her head.

"Yes, Toronto."

"You mean I'm half Canadian?"

"I guess you are." He laughed for the first time.

So did she.

"Well," she said, taking a few steps toward him, "I suppose we should shake hands or something."

It felt strange, but at the same time comforting, to touch him. He told her he was staying in a hotel near Russell Square and that he was in no hurry to leave. He wanted time to get to know her. She liked the idea.

She googled his name right after that first meeting. He was a top homicide detective and the only child of Holocaust survivors. The weird thing was, she loved P. D. James's mysteries, which featured an older detective who was single with no kids. Google turned up tons of articles about Jennifer Raglan, a Crown prosecutor who'd been murdered. Raglan, a married woman, had been Greene's lover. He'd been charged with murdering her, and while he was out on bail, he'd found the real killer.

Amazing.

At first their relationship was strained. She was a journalism student, and a few times a week he'd take her out to dinner after school. He was shy and awkward around her. She didn't know him well enough to hug or kiss him, but she liked his sly sense of humour and she'd give him a playful punch on his arm whenever she cracked a joke or he said something funny.

He rented a flat near her home and, bit by bit, he became the one steady person in her life while everything else was falling apart. Every place she went in London reminded her of her mother. She hated sitting in class and her mind kept wandering. Her friends' crises and concerns seemed trivial: you broke up with your boyfriend, well guess what? My mother just fell down dead, and this stranger from Canada showed up and he's my father. She called him Ari. There was no way she was going to call him Dad, and she wasn't going to call him Mr. Greene, so she'd settled on his first name.

After he'd been in England for about three months, she announced over dessert in a vegetarian restaurant in Soho, "I'm going to quit school."

She thought he wouldn't approve and he'd tell her that she should try to stick it out. But he understood right away.

"You can't concentrate, can you?" he said.

"How'd you guess?"

"Remember, I was a homicide detective for a long time. I've seen how hard it is for people to recover from the death of a loved one, especially a parent."

"I think I need to get out of London."

"Makes sense. Where do you want to go?"

"Well," she said, nervous around him for the first time and unsure how he would react to her idea. "How about I move to Canada with you?"

He almost choked on the rhubarb pie he was eating, before he broke out in a gigantic grin. A month later they were on a plane.

In Toronto she met his father, her grandfather Yitzhak, who was the opposite of Ari. Outgoing and fun, he hugged and kissed her all the time. Within days she was calling him Grandpa Y, and soon he started fixing up a room for her in the basement of Ari's house to give her some privacy. He took her to Kensington Market, where he'd lived when he first came to Canada. Kensington wasn't exactly Portobello, but it wasn't all modern and ordered like most parts of Toronto. It was the first place in the city where she felt at home.

Because Ari was Canadian, she had the automatic right to citizenship, but since he wasn't listed on her birth certificate, she was required to get a private DNA test for proof. Ari, being a homicide detective, had already had one done.

"It turns out I'm three-quarters Jewish," she told him and Grandpa Y when the results arrived. "There was always a bit of mystery about where Grammy, my mum's mum, came from."

"Do you think your mother knew?" Ari asked.

"I'll never know," she said.

"But now we know," Grandpa Y said, "where you got your sense of humour."

They all laughed. It was a warm moment.

She checked the time again on her phone. It was three forty-five. She'd been waiting for Fox for three-quarters of an hour and now the big story, the protest march, was about to start one block away. She was tempted to call Fox's assistant, Maxine. But he'd made her promise that, no matter what, even if he were late, she wouldn't ask anyone where he was. He wasn't late. He wasn't coming. She had to leave. But it was complicated.

In January, at Ari's suggestion—so she could meet people her age, get to know the city and further her career—Alison had enrolled in journalism school downtown. But it was the same as when she'd gone back to school in London after her mother died. She couldn't focus. She started skipping classes and hanging out in Kensington Market. She launched *Kensington Confidential* as an anonymous blog and wrote about the community and its growing conflicts with developers. People began to send her stories, and within weeks she had more than two thousand followers. Now thirty other bloggers wrote alongside her, including the organizer of today's protest march, Cassandra Amberlight, who posted five or six times a day. Managing the blog was taking up all her time, and two months ago she'd dropped out of school.

The problem was that she didn't have the heart to tell Ari what she was doing. He'd been supportive of her going back to school. Recently she'd been getting inquiries about buying ad space on her blog, and she wanted to wait until it was bringing in good money to break the news to him. In the meantime, she pretended she was still a student, and they'd text each other at four every afternoon when she'd supposedly finished her classes.

But then, last week, Ari got a job at the Kensington Gate construction site. Talk about bad timing. She had to cover the demonstration, but she couldn't risk his seeing her on the street or on TV. Before coming to the restaurant she'd gone to one of the second-hand shops in the market and bought a plain black T-shirt, a pair of white shorts, cheap sunglasses, a Toronto Blue Jays cap, and a small yellow backpack, and had changed into the new clothes. As long as she wore the baseball cap, Ari wouldn't be able to spot her in the crowd.

Ten to four. And she was so hot. That was it. She threw back the last of the tea and smacked the cup down on the Formica table. She put on the sunglasses and the baseball cap, slipped on the backpack, and headed out the back door.

Where the hell, she wondered, was Livingston Fox?

5

Kennicott ducked out of the Crown attorney storage room, sprinted down the criss-crossing courthouse escalators and ran out onto the street. After being indoors all day, he felt the heat and humidity hit him and immediately began to sweat. He jumped into a squad car that pulled up for him. A young female officer was at the wheel.

"Detective Kennicott," he said.

"PC Sheppard, 93615," she said, a big grin on her face. "You might want to do up your seat belt." She blasted her high-volume siren and gunned the engine.

"Good idea," he said, buckling up as the car lurched forward and threw him back against the seat. He grabbed the door handle to steady himself while she swerved through traffic.

With his free hand he pulled out his phone. Detective Kamil Darvesh, his newly assigned partner, had recently been promoted to Homicide and this would be his first major case. He would have gotten news of the murder and was probably waiting for Kennicott's call.

"It's Kennicott. You heard?"

"I did."

"Who found the body?"

"A worker at the site."

"Hit the computer right away. There will be a ton of press coverage on file about the victim. I want you to download everything you can find. And contacts. Family, co-workers, friends, girlfriends. We need to get ahead of this before it breaks."

"Already on it."

Darvesh's can-do attitude reminded Kennicott of how he used to work with Greene. He'd loved it when Ari would shoot him a list of things to do and he could say he'd already done them.

"Good. I'll call you from the scene." He hung up. Even though their line was almost certainly secure, they'd both made a point of not mentioning Fox by name, just in case.

Rush-hour traffic was building, but PC Sheppard bulldozed her way through the cars in front of her, zipped up to College Street, pulled a hard left at the lights, then executed a perfect U turn and screeched the cruiser to a halt parallel to the curb right in front of the main entrance to Kensington Gate. It was rare for a new recruit to be involved in a murder case, and she was doing all she could to make a good impression.

It had been less than ten minutes since he'd received the hotshot call. Pretty darn good.

"Nice work, Officer Sheppard," he said.

She was still grinning from ear to ear. "I love driving."

"Badge 93615," he said.

"That's right."

"I'll keep you in mind."

He jumped out of the car. An ambulance was already parked in front of the condo construction site. Traffic was backed up, stalling streetcars. Overheated drivers were leaning on their horns.

A few steps over, Augusta Avenue was clogged with protesters carrying signs and shouting "Stop the Fox. Save the market." A drummer was banging away, piling sound on sound. TV trucks, their satellite dishes aimed at the sky, lined the sidewalks while police cars were lined up on the near one, blocking the protesters from the construction site, which was now a crime scene in need of protection.

Kennicott watched several cameramen rush about. He knew the news that Fox had been murdered was bound to leak out soon and heighten tension on the street. An overweight cop was directing officers to string up police tape and keep the crowd back. Kennicott strode up to him. Greene had taught him how to do the homicide-detective walk: nice and slow. Make eye contact with the officer in charge. Be calm. Assert your authority at the start of a murder investigation but never overdo it.

As Kennicott approached, he realized he knew the cop. PC Lindsmore was an out-of-shape, never-promoted but street-smart constable and an old colleague of Greene's.

"We need back up," Lindsmore was saying into his radio. "Right now. I don't care about Friday-afternoon traffic. TV crews are all over this thing. We need to shut everything down."

Lindsmore nodded at Kennicott. "Detective, good to see you." He offered a firm handshake.

"You too, Officer Lindsmore. What have we got?"

"You heard it was Fox, the rich-kid developer?"

"That's all I know."

"So, you don't know who found him and called 911?"

"My partner told me it was one of the workers here."

"Hmm." Lindsmore pointed to a tall man wearing a hard hat, standing with his back to them. "There he is."

Kennicott walked up behind the worker. "Excuse me, sir," he said. "Toronto Police. My name is Detective Kennicott."

The man turned around. "Hello, Daniel," he said.

How did this guy know his name?

The worker extended his arm for a handshake and, with his other hand, peeled off his hard hat. It took a few seconds for Kennicott to process what was happening. He was shaking hands with Ari Greene.

6

The protest on Augusta Avenue was larger and more chaotic than Alison had expected. What was going on? Where was Cassandra Amberlight? The woman should be easy to spot as she was at least six feet tall. At most protests, she could be found shouting through an old leather megaphone.

Alison elbowed her way to the front of the line. There was no sign of her anywhere. That was strange.

Amberlight, a lawyer and activist in her late sixties whom the press had dubbed the Queen of Protests, had spent decades fighting for one cause or another: stopping the Spadina expressway from being built right through the middle of the city; protesting the city's amalgamation with its suburbs; stopping jets from using the airport on the Toronto Islands; stopping the city's garbage from being shipped to a native reserve. Name the protest, Amberlight would be there at the barricades, megaphone at the ready. Journalists liked to quip that she had never seen a TV camera or radio microphone she didn't love.

The Save Kensington Coalition was her latest cause. A year earlier she'd got press coverage when she moved into an apartment above a cheese shop in the middle of the market so she could be, in her words, "front and centre in the struggle for the heart of the city."

Alison had investigated Amberlight's history and found that not all was rosy. She'd blown through two marriages—with a man and a woman—had seven children she rarely saw, and owed thousands of dollars in support payments. Her law office had closed after two lawyers who worked for her had filed complaints with the Law Society about her "bullying and abusive behaviour," and in January she'd been suspended from practice for twelve months.

Alison saw a TV news reporter with a headset on standing near the police barrier. She shimmied over.

"I'm a freelance reporter," she said. "You might have seen some articles about this protest on my blog, *Kensington Confidential*." She touched the blog icon on her phone and showed it to the woman.

The reporter stared at the phone. "We've been trying to find you, but there's no contact information on your site."

"That's intentional."

The reporter put a finger in the air, cupped a hand over her headset, and bent forward to listen.

"Jesus," she said into the mic. "But you can't confirm that yet? Okay, okay, we're on standby."

She turned her attention back to Alison. "You're young. You a student?"

"No."

"What's your accent, English?"

"Afraid so."

"How long have you been in Canada?"

"Long enough to fall in love with the market."

"I've read some of your articles on your blog. They're good."

"Thanks."

"You sign them the Kensington Blogger. What's your real name?"

Alison shook her head. "Sorry. I have to be anonymous."

The reporter pulled out a business card and wrote some numbers on the back. She passed it over. Her name was Sheena Persad. "If you change your mind, text or email me any time. On the weekends try online first, but I might be tied up with my daughter. I've given you my home number. Don't share it with anyone else."

"Thanks. Have you seen Cassandra Amberlight?"

"The Queen of Protests? Everyone's looking for her. At first we thought she was the murder victim."

"Murder victim?"

"Didn't you see the ambulance up front?"

"No, I came from the back. Where was the murder?"

Persad pointed in the direction of the condo construction site. "At Kensington Gate."

"What?" Alison's first thought was of her father.

"The cops sealed off the top of Augusta. These protesters are getting squeezed."

Alison's mouth was so dry she could hardly talk. "Any ID?"

"Nothing official."

Persad glanced from side to side before she spoke. "It's unconfirmed. You can't publish a word on your blog until it is."

"Of course."

"Sounds like it was"—Persad flipped the microphone out of the way and brought her mouth next to Alison's ear—"the Condo King, Livingston Fox."

7

Greene saw the shock register on Daniel Kennicott's face as recognition set in. Lindsmore walked up to join the conversation.

"I work here," Greene said, speaking calmly to his former partner. "It's my first week on the job. Our shift ended at three-thirty, and I stayed behind to have a beer with my boss, an old friend of mine from high school, Claudio Bassante."

Kennicott didn't speak. Greene could tell he was tongue-tied.

Greene angled his body toward Kennicott so that Lindsmore couldn't see what he was about to do. He caught Kennicott's eye and made a subtle writing motion with his right hand.

"That's Bassante," he said. "B-A-S-S-A-N-T-E."

Kennicott's eyes came into focus. He gave Greene a subtle nod, reached for the pen he'd clipped to the last page he'd used in his notebook—the way Greene always had—and glanced at his watch.

"The time now is," Kennicott said, beginning to write, "four-twelve p.m.," he said.

"The 911 call came in at four-oh-one," Lindsmore said.

"Bassante and I were sitting up on the third floor looking south having a beer," Greene said. "He stood up and knocked his bottle over the edge and it landed on the second-floor balcony. I went down to the shed in back to get a dustpan and broom to clean it up."

"Where did Bassante go?" Kennicott asked, making notes.

"Out front. He was waiting for the owner, Livingston Fox, to arrive. Bassante told me Fox hadn't called ahead of time, which apparently was unusual."

Greene waited until Kennicott looked back at him. He felt as if they were two actors in an audition, neither of them sure what their character's motivation was or what their relationship was supposed to be.

"The shed is in the southwest corner, past the two Johnny on the Spots," Greene said. "They stink in this heat. I walked past them and when I opened the shed door, once my eyes adjusted, I saw the body lying face up in the middle of the floor."

"What did you do?" Kennicott asked, writing away.

"What I should have done when I found Jennifer. I called 911 on my cell."

It was his biggest regret. His biggest mistake. Not calling 911 had started all the problems between him and Daniel.

"Right away?" Kennicott asked.

"Immediately. Make sure that's clear in your notes."

"It's clear."

"I yelled to Bassante and ran to the front of the building. I told him what had happened, and he was stunned."

"Did you check the body for vital signs?"

It was the right question for a homicide detective to ask. "No. It was obvious he was dead. I didn't want to contaminate a crime scene, so I didn't step farther inside."

"How did you know it was Fox?"

"He's in the news all the time and his face is plastered over the hoardings surrounding this place and all his other projects in the city."

Kennicott was writing, taking his time, choosing his words with care.

"You ever met Fox?"

"Never. We don't exactly travel in the same social circles."

"Did you see him at the work site today?"

"No."

"Except for you and Bassante, who else was on site when you found the body?"

"I don't think anyone else was here. The shift ended at three-thirty, and the guys cleared out real fast."

Kennicott snapped his notebook shut. Unclicked his pen.

"I need to check what's going on with these protesters," Lindsmore said. "We've got to keep this under control."

Greene and Kennicott didn't say anything until he was gone.

"I'll get a car to take you to headquarters and you can give a full video statement," Kennicott said.

"Don't bother. It's not far. I'll walk over."

"You remember Kamil Darvesh? He's in Homicide now."

"Glad to hear that."

"I'll call and make sure he's the one to interview you. Then I'm going to need him for the rest of the day."

Greene stood aside to let Kennicott by. Two steps past Greene, he turned around.

"When did you come back?"

"Six months ago."

"Six months."

"I was going to call you soon, Daniel. Once I'd settled a few things." It was true, but Greene knew it sounded lame.

"How's your father?" Kennicott asked.

"Fine. Thanks for asking."

"He must be glad to have you home."

"Very." And even happier to have a granddaughter, Greene thought.

Kennicott hesitated. "Can I ask you what the hell are you doing working in construction?"

Greene put his hard hat back on. "I like it."

Kennicott stared at him.

Greene knew what he was thinking. "No, Daniel," he said. "I'm not undercover."

"What's your job then?"

"General labour. I haul stuff around all day."

"What in the world do you like about it?"

"I like that I don't have to think."

Greene wasn't going to tell Kennicott about Alison. Not yet. But Kennicott knew him well. Greene could sense he knew there was more to the story.

"Ari, you seem to stumble over a lot of dead bodies."

"Not of my choosing, believe me. This is the last thing I need right now."

Kennicott didn't move, didn't blink.

"Daniel, I'm sorry I misled you. I was in shock when I found her. I was desperate to find the killer."

They both knew he was talking about Jennifer.

"I'm sorry I charged you with her murder. I hope I never arrest another innocent person ever again," Kennicott said.

Greene thought about reaching out to shake his hand, but the wounds they'd inflicted on each other were too deep, too raw.

"Right now," Kennicott said, turning away, "I need to figure out who killed young Livingston Fox."

Greene watched him walk away. He knew Daniel wouldn't look back, and he didn't.

8

The sun was beating down, and Alison could feel herself break out into a sweat. She was trying to process the shocking news she'd just heard: Livingston Fox was dead. Murdered. How could that be? The story was unconfirmed, but in her gut she knew it was true. That's why Fox had missed their meeting at the restaurant. Things in her life just kept getting worse.

She knew Fox had many enemies. But who would want to kill him? What was the big story he'd wanted to tell her and why had it been such a secret? And where was Amberlight?

From behind her she heard a new chant arise from the crowd. "Cassandra, Cassandra, Cassandra!"

She turned and saw Amberlight striding up the middle of Augusta Avenue, her tall, gawky frame bobbing with enthusiasm. The protesters parted to clear a path. She had her megaphone raised in the air, and as she got to the middle of the crowd she used it to shout, "Stop the Fox! Save the market! Stop the Fox! Save our city!"

People started clapping and shouting and taking up the chant. Amberlight made it to the front, stopped at the police barricade at the top of Augusta, turned, and spread her arms out, like an old-fashioned preacher about to give a sermon. This quieted the raucous crowd.

"Friends," she shouted. "Your presence here today sends a message to the politicians, the media, the bankers, and most of all, to the out-of-control builders who are turning Toronto into Condo City!"

There were loud cheers.

She raised her arms higher. "Our message is clear. We need quality housing, accessible health care facilities, parks and playgrounds, modern sporting venues, and environmentally sustainable buildings that serve all the people, not just the wealthy."

She pointed down College Street to where Fox planned to build his second condo. "We are not going to let Livingston Fox K2 Kensington!"

This brought the biggest cheer yet.

Amberlight raised her megaphone and began another chant. "Keep the Fox out of our backyard! Keep the Fox out!"

The crowd was squeezing Alison on all sides, tighter and tighter, as newly arrived cops pushed people back. Clearly the news that Fox was dead hadn't leaked out yet. When it did, the protest could get out of hand and she could end up on TV, disguise or no disguise. She could even get arrested. Either way, Ari would find out what she was up to.

She had to escape. The protester beside her had a big dog with him that was in the way. It wasn't on a leash.

"Excuse me," she said. "Can I get by?"

"Sure," he said. "Fahrenheit, come here, come here."

The dog sidled up to him and she scooted through the gap. *Think, Alison*, she told herself, *think*, as she ducked her way among arms and legs and bodies. She had many unanswered questions: What time had Fox been murdered? Who knew about this? Had his family been informed? His fiancée? She would be devastated. Did Maxine or his chauffeur know about this awful news? What about the police? They would soon learn about her scheduled meeting with Fox, wouldn't they? Or maybe not. It had been a secret.

She inched her way through the crowd. The mood of the protesters was becoming less joyous, the chanting and singing giving way to an angry rumble. Everyone was jamming forward. She spotted a TV truck where a cameraman had climbed up the antennas tower to get a top-side view. She managed to squeeze through and shelter herself behind the truck. She peered around the corner and up the sidewalk.

Cops carrying Plexiglas shields were walking side by side toward her, herding people who had strayed onto the sidewalk back onto the street. It was clear they didn't want anyone going near the construction site or the alley behind it.

Should she talk to the police? Would they even care? And what about her father? Did he know about the murder? He was an ex-homicide detective. He might have been on site when it happened. Thank goodness, he was safe.

Across the sidewalk there was a path beside the last house before the alleyway. It had to lead to its backyard. This could be a perfect escape route. And maybe, if there was someone home, she could knock on the back door and convince them to let her in. If she could go upstairs, she'd be able to get some amazing photos of the protest march from the bedroom window that overlooked Augusta Avenue.

She had a few seconds. The trick was to not draw any attention to herself. If she ran, the police, and maybe one of the TV cameramen, would notice her.

Emerging from behind the truck, she rolled the backpack off her shoulder and pulled out her keys. She strolled casually toward the house as though she'd done this a thousand times. Passing the front porch, where neglected promotional flyers were piled in front of the door, she veered onto the path, thinking that she was out of luck and no one would be home. It had been that kind of day.

The flagstones beside the house were cracked and overgrown with weeds. She opened a creaky gate and walked into a tiny backyard. A garage occupied half of it and a large maple tree took up most of the rest. There was a concrete patio against the back wall of the house covered by a grapevine. She sat on a bench beside the door and made herself breathe. The noise from the street had almost disappeared.

The roof of the garage was sagging and the paint was peeling off. The bench she was on was uneven and tippy. No signs of recent life here. Beside her was a heavy-looking metal table in front of the kitchen window. If she wanted to look in, she'd have to move it out of the way.

She put her keys in her pocket, approached the back door, and knocked. "Anyone home?"

There was no response. She knocked again as loud as she could. Still no answer.

More out of habit than anything else, she turned the door handle, expecting it to be locked. It wasn't. She pushed the door open, took a tentative step inside, and found herself in the kitchen. The place looked as if no one had used it in years. The air was moist and hot.

"Hello?" she said, shutting the door behind her. "Is anyone home?"

She put her backpack on the kitchen counter and in a few steps she was in the dining room, then the living room. Both were filled with old, dusty furniture.

"Hello," she said again, louder. The bay window at the front of the house was curtained in see-through sheers. Outside, the cops had completely encircled the protesters. Some of them were now sitting in the street and a few were raising extra-long selfie sticks high in the air to take photos. She had to get upstairs. In a few steps she was standing in the empty second-floor hallway. There were four doors, three of them open.

"Anyone here?" Her voice was tentative. She could hear the drummer outside and the protesters were getting louder. She checked the rooms with open doors—two bedrooms and a bathroom. They were empty. She went up to the window of the room facing the street, kneeled down, and pulled out her phone. A scuffle broke out between some protesters and a female cop and she snapped away. This was great stuff. A bunch of cops rushed in and dragged away two protesters, then things seemed to calm down.

She still hadn't checked the room with the closed door. It was on the north side of the house, and its window would overlook the alley-way. She knocked, hard. "Hello! Anyone here?"

She could hear police sirens approaching. The cops were bringing in reinforcements. She opened the door.

The room was dark and seemed to be empty, but as her eyes ad-justed, she noticed a metal chair next to a curtained window. She walked across the wood floor, her footsteps echoing in the vacant space. Then, like a spy in a movie, she carefully pulled the curtain far enough aside to peek out. From up here, she had a clear view over the hoarding surrounding the construction site. She could see through the top of a large window into a work shed.

The chair. She climbed onto it and now she could see right in. Her eyes were drawn to a tall man with a hairnet on, wearing plastic gloves and slippers. He had to be a cop. Alison jerked back when she saw what he was looking at. It was the body of Livingston Fox lying face up on the floor, a long metal bar sticking right out of his chest.

Bile rose in her stomach. This was horrible. Horrible, horrible, hor-rible. She thought she was going to vomit.

It was also, she realized, an unbelievable opportunity. She raised her phone above her head and hit the shutter button, brought the phone to eye level and took a second shot, then bent down to take a third.

Before she could flip the phone around to see the photos, a hand-some man in a suit and an overweight cop walked out the back gate beside the shed. The handsome man was looking down the alleyway. If he looked up now, he'd see her.

She clutched the edge of the curtain. What should she do? As quickly as she dared, she let it roll back into place, praying that he hadn't noticed the movement. She turned the phone around and opened the photo gallery. She'd got good shots of the cops grabbing the protesters. But the TV crews and the protesters would all have similar pictures.

She scrolled to the last three photos. The first showed the top of the window and the roof of the shed. The second was too low. It had caught the bottom of the shed, the hoarding, and a bit of the alleyway below.

The last one was perfect. There it was, framed by the shed window: Livingston Fox's dead body on the floor. No other media outlet would have that shot. It was gruesome. But, she knew, it was journalistic gold.

9

When Kennicott was a kid, he and his older brother, Michael, used to sneak into construction sites. Back then, apartment buildings and office towers were going up in the suburbs, not downtown. On summer nights the two boys would ride their bikes to one of the towers being built not far from their neighbourhood. No one worried much about security in those days, and it was usually easy to find a gap in the fence or loose hoarding that surrounded the place, squeeze inside, and explore.

The workers often left their tools behind, and sometimes there were electric platform carts that the boys goofed around on for hours. Once, when they were playing tag on the sixth floor of a building, Daniel almost ran right into a gaping hole. Michael spotted it and grabbed him seconds before he could fall to what would have been an ugly death.

As he walked through the Kensington Gate site, it all came back to Kennicott. The clean rawness of freshly poured concrete, the spaciousness of rooms formed but empty, the excitement of something new being created. The air was filled with a sweet, sandy smell. Lindsmore joined him and started reading from his notebook, which, even unfolded, looked tiny in his big hand.

"The 911 call was received at exactly 4:01:23 this afternoon."

"What did Greene say?" Kennicott asked.

"He didn't identify himself. He just said he was a construction worker and that he'd come upon a dead body in the shed."

That sounds like Greene, Kennicott thought. Always keeping something secret. "What else did he say?"

"Very little. He identified the body as Livingston Fox, then he hung up. Call took sixteen seconds."

They got to the back of the building and the sunlight hit Kennicott in the eye. A few steps ahead, two Johnny on the Spot toilets let off a foul smell. Past them was the shed, its door closed. A young female officer stood in front of it, trying to look stoic but Kennicott could see she was distressed.

"Detective Kennicott," he said, reaching out his hand.

"PC Rozier." Her palm was sweaty.

"Where are the paramedics?"

She turned and Kennicott followed her line of sight. A man and a woman in uniform were sitting in the shade on a pile of two-by-fours.

"The smell from the portable toilets is pretty bad," Kennicott said.

"Yes it is, sir."

She stood aside to let them enter. Instead of going in, Kennicott pointed beyond the shed. "What's back there?"

"I don't know."

"The back gate," Lindsmore said. "It was open when we got here."

Kennicott hesitated. "Let's see that first," he said. "The body's not going anywhere."

He counted twelve steps to the gate. An unlatched combination lock hung from its handle. They passed through the gate and stepped into the alleyway. Kennicott kept his eyes on the ground for signs of blood on the concrete. There was nothing but dirt and a puddle of dog pee that Lindsmore almost stepped in. He'd have the forensic officers search it later, but he doubted they'd find anything.

He surveyed the scene. There was an old house across the alley with one curtained window up on the second floor. To his right he could see the protesters out on Augusta Avenue. To his left the alley turned the corner and ran south.

He played back in his mind the conversation he'd had minutes ago with Greene. He knew Ari. After he'd called 911, he probably couldn't resist coming out here and taking a quick look around. What had he seen?

Kennicott motioned to Lindsmore to follow him. They walked along the alley and peered around the corner. The killer could have come this way, unseen by the crowd on Augusta, had a private rendezvous with Fox in the shed, then walked back down the alley to escape.

Kennicott retraced his steps to the gate. Augusta Avenue was filling up fast with boisterous protesters. It was only a matter of time, and probably not much time, before word got out that Livingston Fox was dead, murdered. There was no way of knowing how the crowd would react when the news broke.

Lindsmore had strung police tape across the end of the alley where it joined Augusta and had posted two officers there to keep people out. But this was thin protection for a crime scene.

He reached for his radio. "It's Kennicott. Get me every available car here fast. I need more crowd control. I need to protect this crime scene. I need to keep the press away. And I need officers to check the alleyway, talk to the media people here and get their video files, interview any protesters who will cooperate with us, and go door to door along the houses in Augusta and the stores in the area." He clicked the radio off and turned to Lindsmore. "Who's the forensic officer?"

"Detective Ho. He should be here by now."

"Good," he said, taking one last look and not seeing anything else. "Let's go see the body."

10

reene had refused a lift to police headquarters because he didn't want to be photographed getting into a squad car. On foot, he could slip away, unseen by the press. Besides, it wasn't far and he wanted to walk. He headed up to College Street, crossed Spadina Avenue, and in seconds he'd left behind the chaos of the demonstration and the crime scene and entered a different world. This stretch of College Street was the southern edge of the University of Toronto, and the outdoor cafes and sidewalks were filled with backpack-wearing students engaged in fervent conversations. A long time ago, Greene had thought about becoming a history professor. How different his life would have been.

He had to get a hold of his daughter. He was still getting used to using the phrase "his daughter." He assumed that news of a murder at Kensington Gate would have already gotten out—even if the police managed to hold back Fox's name for a few hours—and he didn't want Alison to be worried about him.

He texted her as he walked. "Hi. Sorry for delay. Busy afternoon. If you heard the news about Kensington Gate, no worries. I'm fine. I'll be home in a few hours. You?"

Alison replied within seconds. "Just heard the news. Someone murdered at K. Gate?? So relieved u r okay!!"

He stared at Alison's message. *So relieved u r okay!!*

He had to keep reminding himself that it had been less than a year since they'd discovered each other, and the two of them were still feeling each other out. He'd made a point of holding back, of not putting any expectations on her. They were strangers from different worlds, and yet here they were, together adrift on the same life raft.

"Sad day. Talk later," he texted.

"K," she replied. "Shopping for a desk with Grandpa Y. Will c u at home."

Grandpa Y. That was the nickname she'd come up with for his father. *Home.* That's what he'd wanted to create for her ever since they'd met in the solicitor's office in London.

That moment. The first time they touched. When she'd come closer to him and taken his hand. It was the most awkward and most wonderful moment. All the hate he had for Hap Charlton for murdering Jennifer, all the emptiness in his life without her, all his anger at himself melted away. He had a daughter. He had something to live for again.

Greene's father had been there at the airport back in December when he'd brought Alison to Toronto. He'd had tears of joy in his eyes. The two were comfortable with each other from the get-go, and within days she was calling him Grandpa Y. Perhaps, it had occurred to Greene, it was because they had both experienced tragedy at a young age. Alison had just lost her mother, and as a teenager, his father had lost his whole family.

Three squad cars screamed past Greene, heading toward the protest. People stopped to watch them fly by. Greene kept walking. Alison loved going to Kensington Market, and he was glad she was in school this afternoon and not at the march. Tension would be high, and things could turn ugly.

Police headquarters, where the homicide squad was located, was a few more blocks away. Greene put his phone back in his pocket and kept his eye on the stunning blue sky as he walked. He wanted to enjoy these last few minutes outside before he entered the place where he'd worked for so many years, the place he'd hoped he'd never set foot in again.

11

Alison stood still in the dark room. Ari was safe. He'd been good to her, and she was grateful. Very grateful. And what had she done? She had lied to him about going to school, and now here she was in a stranger's house she'd snuck into. She had to get out of here, fast. The police could be on her any minute.

She headed down the stairs, walked through the deserted first floor and kitchen. She cracked the back door open, and as she stepped outside, she heard heavy footsteps coming up the steps to the front porch. The police. She was trapped. She tiptoed back inside and closed the door behind her. It had an old Yale lock. She flicked the catch and heard it click into place. She sat on the dusty kitchen floor, put her back to the sink under the window and waited.

Out on the front porch, she heard muted voices talking, then a loud knocking.

"Toronto Police. Is anyone home?"

Alison held her breath. They wouldn't be able to see her from the front door. But what if she hadn't closed the curtain of the upstairs window soon enough? Had she been seen? She put her head between her knees and rolled herself up into a tight ball. In a few seconds they'd be in the backyard and looking in the kitchen window.

She heard the cops go down the front steps and moments later she heard them on the patio behind her. One of them tried the back door.

"It's locked," a man's voice said.

"We don't have a warrant. Detective Kennicott said we should check all the windows," a female voice said. "Here, help me move this table."

Alison looked up. She remembered the metal table in front of the window. Once it was out of the way they'd be able to look inside, but they wouldn't be able to see her.

Then she spotted the yellow backpack she'd tossed on the counter. It was in clear view of the window. How could she have been so careless? It was too risky to grab it now. The police were going to find her.

She heard the scraping sound of the table being shoved across the patio. Oh no. She was trapped. What could she do?

Then it came to her. It was a crazy idea but it might work. She had to be fast. Grabbing her phone, she pulled up the photo of Fox's body, put a tag on it that said "Taken from a selfie stick," and uploaded it to her blog. She knew that many of the protesters were following her posts, and maybe, just maybe . . .

She heard the table hitting the stones.

"Jesus. This thing is heavy," a male voice said.

"That should be far enough," a female one said. "I think I can slip in."

Alison buried her head between her knees again, deeper this time, trying to make herself as small as she could.

"No, too tight," the female cop said. "We have to push it farther from the wall."

Alison closed her eyes and held her breath. *Come on, come on*, she prayed. Someone had to notice the incredible photo she'd just posted. She heard the cops grunt as they moved the table again.

There was a huge roar from the street and the sound of breaking glass.

One of the cop's police radio crackled. "All officers back to Augusta Avenue immediately! Red alert!"

"Roger," the male officer said.

She heard their footsteps rush away.

Alison exhaled. She stood up and peered out the window. The coast was clear. She looked at her backpack. What a fool she'd been to buy a yellow one that would stand out in the crowd. What if someone had seen her walk down the pathway, or she'd been captured on TV? She'd better not risk wearing it now. Same with the hat and sunglasses.

She quickly changed back into the clothes she'd worn this morning, tossed everything she'd bought into the backpack, opened the cupboard under the sink and threw it in.

Wait.

What had she done? Now the whole world was going to see that picture of Livingston she'd just posted. Including his family, his fiancée.

This was a nightmare. She had to get out of here.

She opened the back door. Should she lock it behind her or was it better to leave it unlocked, the way she'd found it?

She left it unlocked and walked through the little yard, past the garage and into the back alley. Luckily, no one was around. Making herself appear as calm as she could, she ran her fingers through her hair and strolled south, away from Kensington Gate. At the end of the alley, she followed a narrow path that took her to Oxford Street, cut over to Spadina Avenue, and got lost in the crowd of Friday afternoon shoppers.

12

Kennicott returned to the shed. The door was open now. Forensic Officer Ho was crouched beside the body, illuminated by the sunshine pouring in through the window opposite the door. He was wearing plastic booties over his running shoes, latex gloves on his hands, and a net over his hair.

"How the mighty have fallen," Ho said.

"You just get here?"

"A minute ago while you were out for your stroll in the alley. Cover up, cowboy, and come take a look."

Kennicott put on the protective gear and approached the body. It was a grotesque scene. Fox's hands and feet were held down by concrete blocks and a long steel bar pierced his heart. He was wearing a T-shirt, a pair of shorts, and sandals, like a hundred other young people in the city. His casual summer clothes made his murder seem even worse. He should have been out on a patio like everyone else his age, talking, laughing, living.

"First impressions?" he asked Ho.

Ho lifted his big shoulders. "The first cut is the deepest."

Kennicott had worked with Ho on a number of homicides. The man was smart and he wanted you to know it. He loved to hear himself talk—except for the time an innocent young boy had been killed by a stray bullet. That had shut him up.

"How heavy do you think that steel bar is?" Kennicott asked.

"Heavy enough. I worked construction in university and I carried stacks of rebar all over the place. We'll weigh it at the autopsy as well as those concrete blocks," he said, nodding at them. "Nasty, nasty."

"What else do you see?"

"The blood on the floor hasn't begun to dry, even in this heat."

Kennicott took a few steps closer. Blood had spilled out onto the floor from Fox's body and pooled into a small puddle.

"Don't jump to any conclusions about timing," Ho said. "There are many factors. Viscosity of his blood, quantity of the spatter, temperature, humidity, airflow. What surface is the blood on. This is a wood floor, and blood dries faster on concrete. My team is on the way. We'll take a sample of the blood and cut out a piece of the floor and replicate the temperature and humidity in the lab. See how long it would take to reach the exact same viscosity. But that will only be a best-guess estimate."

Kennicott looked squarely at Fox's body. "I don't see any other marks on him."

"No obvious defensive wounds. Looks like one and done."

"What about the back of his head?"

Ho took a closer look. Kennicott bent down beside him. "I don't see anything."

They both stood.

"Next steps?" Kennicott asked.

"The usual. We'll go through every inch of this room. Check for prints. If we find any hairs we'll DNA test them and those glasses and water bottles." He pointed to a pair of drinking glasses and two different-coloured water bottles on a long wooden table. "We'll heat scan the floor for footprints and spatter. Photograph and videotape everything. Do the same outside, especially that fence and gate in back. Killers always make a mistake and leave something behind. I can tell you one thing for sure."

"What's that?"

"Whoever it was, they were not very happy with the Condo King."

"You think?" Kennicott looked around the room. The walls were covered with architectural drawings and work schedules. On the table were labelled cans of pens, pencils, rulers, calculators, and stacks of graph paper. Everything in perfect order.

He walked gingerly over to the window and almost stepped on an errant pencil on the floor. There wasn't much to see outside except the back of the hoarding around the building site and the second floor of the house across the alley.

He heard glass breaking on the street, and the protesters' voices spiking. The police radio on Ho's hip squawked. "All officers back to Augusta Avenue immediately! Red alert!"

13

"How lovely to see you, Detective Greene," Francine Hughes said. A fixture in the Homicide office for years, she sat at her desk in the reception area in the same position she'd been in the last time he was here. The same position she'd been when he first came to Homicide. She rarely left her post to come back into the offices and was always cheerful, no matter what bad news walked in the door. Except for the day she'd learned that Jennifer was murdered.

"Lovely to see you as well," Greene said, leaning forward to kiss her on the cheek. "I'm only dropping in. How are those two dogs of yours?"

"Poor Fifi. Lost her last winter. Gigi really misses her." She eyed Greene's workboots, dirty jeans, and sweatshirt. "I heard you had a new job."

Kennicott must have called her already. Hughes never missed a trick.

"I'm swinging a hammer instead of chasing bad guys. It's a nice change."

"You deserve a break from all of this. Detective Darvesh said to send you right in. He's in the video room."

Greene took his time going down the hallway. It felt odd to be here as a civilian, not a cop. As he passed their offices, some detectives nodded but no one came out to greet him. Word travelled fast: Ari Greene was back in the city but hadn't come back to Homicide. No one knew quite how to react to him, this man they had once wrongly accused of murder—their colleague and erstwhile friend.

The video room was at the end of the hall. He opened the door.

Darvesh was seated at a large table, reading some notes in a blue folder with "LIVINGSTON FOX" written on the cover in block letters. He put it down when he saw Greene.

"Good afternoon, Detective Greene," he said, standing up.

"Ari," Greene said, shaking hands. "You're a detective now, I hear."

"Thanks to you."

"You did the work to get the job."

Darvesh looked away to hide his reaction, but Greene could see he was happy to be complimented.

"The camera's set up and ready to go. I'll get the commissioner of oaths to come swear you in."

Greene took a seat in front of the camera. The commissioner came in, had him swear to tell the truth, the whole truth, and nothing but the truth, then left. Darvesh was fiddling with the edges of the folder. Greene could see he was uneasy having to question his former boss.

"Just treat me as you would any witness to a crime scene," he said.

"Yes, sir."

Old habits die hard, Greene thought. Darvesh couldn't call him by his first name.

"Can you please identify yourself for the camera?" he asked.

"My name is Ari Greene. That's Greene with three e's. I'm a former homicide detective and now I work as a construction worker."

Greene answered Darvesh's questions succinctly, describing his movements throughout the day until he'd come upon Fox's body.

"What did you do next?" Darvesh asked.

"I could see that he was dead," Greene said. "Comes from all my years on the homicide squad. I didn't want to interfere with the crime scene, so I didn't go inside the shed. I immediately called 911 on my phone. My boss, Claudio Bassante, had gone out front, expecting to meet Fox. I yelled to him, then ran up and told him what had happened."

"What was his reaction?"

"Shock."

Darvesh was nodding. "Anything else?"

Greene hesitated. He didn't want anyone to know that he'd peeked out into the alley. He had nothing to hide, but once a detective always a detective. His instinct never to reveal anything about an investigation until he had to ran deep.

So he didn't.

14

"The name of the deceased will not be made public pending notification of the next of kin."

It was standard language for the press release the Toronto Police Service put out whenever there was a homicide. Kennicott made sure the media department published it as quickly as possible. The time stamp on it was 4:38 p.m.

And already it was out of date. The protesters yelling "Fox is dead!" had seen a photo of Fox's slain body that someone had posted online. Damn social media. He hadn't had time yet to call the family.

Darvesh had sent him the details of Fox's next of kin and he reviewed them now. Fox's parents, Karl and Kate Fox, lived north of the city, near the small town of Kleinberg, where they ran a wellness centre with their daughter, Fox's older sister, Gloria.

Kennicott walked as far away from the noisy protesters as he could get, parked himself behind a wide concrete pillar, and called the number Darvesh had given him. He made a notation in his notebook that it was 4:42 pm.

"Foxhole Wellness Centre," an older woman said, answering the phone on the first ring. "How can we assist you to improve your life and create a healthier planet?"

"May I please speak to Ms. Kate Fox?" Kennicott said.

"Who is this?" The woman was immediately suspicious.

"My name is Daniel Kennicott. I'm a detective with the Toronto Police Service." Greene had taught Kennicott to never identify himself as a homicide detective when he made his first contact with a victim's family.

There was a long pause.

"May I please speak with Ms. Fox?" he repeated.

"It's true then? Gloria told me she saw a grotesque photo of Livingston on her Facebook page a few minutes ago. I didn't want to believe it."

"Is this Ms. Kate Fox?"

"It is. The press has been calling already. Have they no shame?"

"I suggest you not talk to anyone else until we arrive. My partner and I are driving up to see you now and we can talk in person." He was careful not to confirm her suspicions.

"Who would have done this terrible thing? I mean, do you have any idea why?"

"I'm afraid we don't know that yet, Ms. Fox."

"We can't believe it. Livingston could be a handful, but . . . I have to tell Karl."

"Karl, your husband? Where is he now?"

"I have no idea."

"When was the last time you saw him?"

"This morning."

"What time was that?"

"He left about eight."

"Do you know where he went?"

"Of course I know where he went. We've been married for thirty-three years."

Kennicott took a deep breath. When people were in shock they were often scattered and aggressive like this.

"Where did your husband go?"

"It's Friday. He went to Toronto to have lunch with Livingston."

At last he was getting some useful information.

"Do you know where they ate?"

"They always eat at the same place. That's how Livingston is. Everything scheduled."

"Where and when was that?"

"Fresh, on Spadina, south of Queen."

Kennicott knew the place. It wasn't that far from Kensington Market.

"At what time?"

"From twelve-thirty to two. Always."

"Do you know where Karl is now?"

Kennicott intentionally repeated the husband's name to make her feel he was understanding.

"No idea."

Fox had lunch with his father a few hours before he was murdered, Kennicott thought. And the family didn't know where the elder Fox was now.

"Have you spoken to Karl this afternoon?"

"No. How could I?"

"Did he call?"

"Call? Of course not. All those gamma rays."

"I'm sorry?" Kennicott said.

"Cellular phones. Gamma rays. Surely you know about that."

Kennicott smiled. "I see. What kind of car does Karl drive?"

"We don't own a car. The average vehicle emits ninety-five hundred grams of carbon dioxide for every one hundred kilometers."

Families. You never knew what they would be like. Their son was a high-profile condo developer with a Rolls-Royce and a chauffeur, and his parents didn't believe in cellphones or cars.

"I wasn't aware of that," he said. "Did Karl take the train?"

"Officer Kenni . . ."

"Kennicott."

"A train ride still has a carbon footprint. He's on his bike. It's only forty kilometers each way from our house to downtown."

"Do you know which route he took?"

"He takes many different routes, depending on his mood. With luck, he'll be here when you arrive. Please don't speed, that just adds to the emissions."

He promised to drive at the speed limit and hung up.

Kennicott had learned never to allow first impressions to cloud his judgment of people. Often, when their whole world was thrown off kilter by a crime such as murder or a fatal injury to a loved one, they hyperfocused on the small things in their control.

He had to get up to Kleinberg fast. He ran out to College Street and got there just as Darvesh pulled the squad car up to the sidewalk. He jumped in and Darvesh handed him a thick folder. Kennicott dug right into it. There was a handwritten note on the first page. Darvesh had found Fox's chauffeur, who said she'd dropped him off in a school parking lot on Spadina Avenue north of College at 2:15 p.m. and not seen him after that. The rest was a collection of magazine and newspaper articles about the flamboyant and controversial young developer.

"I've started a list of suspects," Darvesh said, hitting the gas and blasting his siren to cut through the rush-hour traffic.

"Give me the *Reader's Digest* version," Kennicott said, as he leafed through the file.

"Fox had more enemies than I have friends. And I'm Punjabi. We live for our friends."

"Give me the top five."

"In no particular order, there's Carol Archer, an angry ex-girlfriend who's been ranting about him over social media ever since the story broke on a blog two weeks ago that he was engaged to another woman. Last week he got a peace bond to force her to stop contacting him and to stay five hundred meters away from him."

"And his fiancée?"

"Anita Nakamura. High school teacher. Apparently one hundred eighty degrees different from his usual supermodel girlfriends."

"We have to notify her after we talk to Fox's family."

"She already knows. She's in Japan, returning tomorrow. She's freaking out on her Facebook page."

"Oh no." Kennicott looked through the papers and saw Nakamura's Facebook profile picture. She was smiling at the camera while Fox was kissing her cheek and making bunny ears above her head.

"George Braithwaite is Fox's former business partner," Darvesh said. The traffic heading south on Spadina was bad, and he was doing a good job of making his way through it. "Guy's suing Fox for a hundred million dollars and telling anyone who will listen that Fox stole his company. I printed out some newspaper articles about it."

Kennicott read through the headlines.

"Then there's Fox's ex-financier, Charlie Hicks, who claimed Fox was late on a twenty-million-dollar loan repayment for stage one of Fox Harbour. It's an enormous project he was planning to build on the waterfront just west of Parliament Street. He's leveraged all the assets in his condo empire as collateral for the loan."

"What motive would he have to kill Fox?" Kennicott asked.

"Charlie is a she, one of the top private equity bankers in the country, calls Fox a 'build-a-holic' who can't stop building condos. With him gone, she can avoid a long legal battle to recover her money before he squanders it on a project that she thinks is spinning out of control."

They got to the Gardiner Expressway, and Darvesh cranked up the siren to full volume.

"Keep to the speed limit," Kennicott told him.

"Don't we have to get there as fast as we can?"

"We do. But at the speed limit."

A promise was a promise, and he wanted to be able to look Ms. Fox right in the eye and tell her they had not sped. It was important to do everything he could to gain the confidence of the victim's family.

Darvesh switched the siren off.

"What else have you got for me?" Kennicott asked.

"Drugs. Rumours swirled for years that Fox was a heavy cocaine user. Maybe he owed a dealer. I'll get a subpoena for his bank records."

"Doesn't sound as if he had a lot of friends."

"True. A number of condo boards are suing him for supposedly shoddy work on his buildings. Gary Edwards is a retired computer programmer who seems to have taken this on as his personal cause."

"That's four."

"Then there's Cassandra Amberlight, the lawyer who led today's protest march. They very publicly hate each other. She's got a history of unstable behaviour and both her ex-spouses, one male and one female, have had her arrested for assault. Both times, she beat the charges."

"She was at the protest march. Let's get the video from all of those TV stations that were parked on the street. See what time she got there. Find out if she has an alibi."

"Already on it. The footage will be delivered to Homicide by the time we get back."

"Well done," Kennicott said. He looked out the window at the vast suburbs they were passing through. There was one more person to add to the list of suspects. One of the last people to see Livingston Fox alive.

Karl, Fox's father.

15

Greene emerged from police headquarters a few minutes after five. The sidewalks were packed with people enjoying the great weather. Long, languid June evenings such as this were one of the joys of living in Toronto, and compensation for the dark, cold winter evenings past and yet to come.

It was about a forty-five-minute walk to his house. He needed the time to think, to replay in his head all that had happened from when Bassante tipped over the beer bottle until Greene had come upon the body in the shed.

He wended his way through the downtown office towers, then strolled along Dundas Street West. Ten years earlier it had been lined with hardware stores, used furniture places, and cheap appliance shops. Now there were yoga studios, cafes, restaurants, clothing boutiques, and fruit and vegetable markets. He passed four condo developments under construction, each with a building crane hovering overhead, before he turned onto his street.

The street followed the course of a stream that had been dammed up and paved over decades ago but was still discernible in the shape of the land. It was a cul-de-sac and his home was at the end, elevated high above his neighbours. A long set of switchback stairways led to his door.

He was beyond tired. He sat on one of the chairs on his front porch. The lilac overhanging the railing was in full bloom. Its sweet fragrance scented the air.

After living alone for years, it had taken him surprisingly little time to grow accustomed to his unexpected new role as a father to a twenty-year-old. One of the things he liked the most was sharing his house with her. Now when he came home and she wasn't there, it felt empty in ways it never had before. He was happy to sit outside and wait until Alison showed up instead of going inside alone.

Over the last few months, he'd grown closer to her. But it was slow progress. She was understandably cautious around him. The long, cold winter had been hard, and the challenge of starting school and trying to make new friends had been difficult. In the last month or two she'd seemed to take a step back from him, and he wasn't quite sure how to respond to her.

The good news was that she was close with Greene's father, and he'd given Greene his usual sage advice. Mostly he preached patience.

"Give her time," he'd said a few weeks earlier, one morning when she'd already left for school and his father was over at the house working on her room in the basement. "She's lost everything—her family, her country, her home."

Just as he had, Greene thought. He didn't need to say so out loud.

"You have to be like that big maple tree in the front yard of my house," his father said. "Solid in the wind. She needs to know you are there. That's all that matters. She'll reach out for you when she's ready."

Greene looked down his street. The sun was still hanging well above the horizon. It was still hot and the air was still heavy with humidity. Any minute now he'd see Alison walking toward him.

His phone rang. He looked at the caller ID. He had been half expecting this call.

"Good afternoon, Ted," he said.

"Sounds as if you've had quite a day, Ari."

"The first half was pretty normal. What can I do for you?"

Ted was Ted DiPaulo, the criminal lawyer who had defended Greene at his murder trial. He was one of the few people Greene had contacted when he came back to Toronto. Over the last few months, DiPaulo had frequently asked Greene for advice about a case, always on an informal basis. Greene refused to take any money, but DiPaulo insisted on paying him a hundred dollars for each case—the same amount DiPaulo took when he defended Greene, so that Ari was officially on retainer.

"There's someone I want you to meet," DiPaulo said. "Cassandra Amberlight, the lawyer who organized today's protest. She's been my client for a number of years."

Greene got up and started to pace across his porch. "When?"

"The sooner the better."

"Where?"

"I thought it might be best to avoid my office."

It was unspoken, but DiPaulo was experienced enough to know that if the police were looking for Amberlight, they'd stake out his office and try to catch her coming or going.

"I just got home," Greene said.

"Good. We're in my car. Less than ten minutes away."

No rest for the weary, Greene thought. "See you soon."

He hung up and looked over the porch railing. Alison was coming up his street. She saw Greene and waved.

He pulled down the lowest lilac branch, snapped off a deep purple blossom, and waved back at his daughter.

16

Almost every article written about Fox that Kennicott read, as Darvesh drove up the highway at exactly the speed limit, talked about the contemporary design of his buildings. A huge fan of Bauhaus architecture, he loved minimalist design and discreet signage on his buildings. He was quoted over and over saying how much he hated clutter.

It wasn't hard to see where his distaste of overwrought signage came from, Kennicott thought, when he saw the heart-shaped highway sign announcing the Foxhole Wellness Centre. It was hand-painted, with white doves flying above and pink flowers sprouting behind the letters. Farther along, a second hand-painted sign featured a woman in a white robe seated cross-legged and pointing to the driveway. The words "Turn Right and Relax" were printed underneath.

A long gravel road, which wound through a large perennial garden, led to a mauve-coloured converted farmhouse. A sign pointing to the parking lot was shaped like a cloud. It said, "Peacefully park your troubles this way."

Wind chimes hung above the paisley-decorated front door, tinkling in the breeze. Here, a sign shaped like a hand said, "Welcome to Foxhole. Please push the bell. Peace."

Kennicott rang the bell and heard a loud singsong chime inside. They waited. No one came.

"Should I knock?" Darvesh asked.

"Sure."

Kennicott turned and surveyed the grounds as Darvesh rapped on the door. There were no other cars in the parking lot. On closer inspection, the gardens, which had seemed lush from the car, looked weedy and untended.

The door opened.

"Gentlemen, welcome." Kate Fox stood in front of them. Kennicott recognized her from Darvesh's printout of the staff page on the centre's website. She was taller than she'd appeared in the photo. Almost his height at six foot one, she wore a flowing dress and sandals. Her long grey hair, tied in a tight braid, hung over one shoulder and across her chest. She held out her hand. Kennicott shook it. Her skin was soft. She seemed very composed.

"Ms. Fox. I'm Daniel Kennicott. This is my colleague Detective Kamil Darvesh."

She stared at them, then dropped Kennicott's hand and turned to Darvesh. "Hello," she said, shaking his hand. "Please come in."

They followed her along a narrow hallway to a bright, spacious room at the back of the house. There were two sofas in the corner, and a woman was seated on the one farthest from the door. Kennicott recognized Fox's older sister from her photo. Her face was red and swollen from crying.

"Gloria," Kate Fox said. "These are the police officers I told you were coming."

"Then it's true, isn't it?" Gloria asked.

Kennicott walked up to her, bent down to put himself at eye level and spoke. "I'm sorry. Yes, it is true. Someone has killed your brother."

She squeezed her lips so tight that her mouth seemed to collapse on itself. She began to shake and wail. It was a deep guttural sound. "No, no, no, no, no."

Her mother sat down beside her.

Darvesh looked frozen. It was his first time encountering a family who'd just received such devastating news. Kennicott sat on the second sofa and gestured for Darvesh to join him.

Fox's sister, not his mother, was the most upset, Kennicott thought. It was difficult to watch someone in such pain. He looked away. Outside the bay window, another set of the wind chimes rang in the breeze.

"Detective," Mrs. Fox said. "Please tell us exactly what happened to Livingston."

She had remarkably dark eyes, which contrasted sharply with her pale skin and grey hair.

"Your son's body was found late this afternoon at the Kensington Gate building site," he said.

No reaction.

Gloria was curled into herself, hugging her knees, rocking back and forth like a child. "No, no, no," she kept repeating, whispering now.

"The police and ambulance arrived within minutes of the 911 call," Kennicott said. "Unfortunately, there was nothing they could do. A full autopsy will be performed later this evening. I wish I had more to say, but that is all I can tell you right now."

"I don't understand," Mrs. Fox said. "What happened?"

"I know how difficult this is," Kennicott said.

"This is ridiculous. You just said it's murder. You're the police."

"I understand it's frustrating, believe me. We are working flat out on this investigation."

"What about that horrible picture on the Internet? Who took that?"

"We don't know yet, but we're determined to find out. That should never have happened."

He looked over at Darvesh. It was good experience for him to see how challenging these initial meetings with the victim's family could be.

The back door of the house slammed, and everyone looked up. Karl Fox stomped into the room.

He was a small man, probably six inches shorter than his wife. He held a battered bicycle helmet in one hand, a pair of frayed bike panniers in the other. The bottoms of his pant legs were crimped to his legs by bicycle clips.

"Kate, what is happening?" he asked his wife. "Why is there a police car in the lot?" He turned to Kennicott and Darvesh. "Who are these men?"

Kennicott rose. "Mr. Fox, my name is Detective Daniel Kennicott. I'm afraid I have some terrible news about your son."

"Livingston?" He looked genuinely surprised. "What nonsense is he up to now?"

"I'm a homicide detective," Kennicott said.

"Homicide?" Karl looked over at his wife and daughter, seeing for the first time the grief in his daughter's face. He spun back to Kennicott.

"What? What happened?"

"I'm afraid that your son has been killed."

"Killed? Livingston? That's impossible. I just had lunch with him."

17

God, it feels good to be home, Alison thought as she climbed the steep staircase to Ari's house. After the chaos of the afternoon, it was a huge relief to come back here. Until a few months ago she'd never seen a dead body. And now. First her mother, then Livingston Fox. It was too much. Way too much. And she was so hot.

Ari looked tired. Maybe it was time to finally give him a hug. After all, he was her father, and in her head she was starting to think of him as Dad.

"Are you okay?" she asked, standing close to him.

"Bad day. I was the one who found the body."

"You were? That's horrible." This made everything even worse.

He gave her the lilac blossom that was in his hand. "A present for you," he said.

She wrapped her fingers around his hand and held it while she brought the flower to her nose. "It smells heavenly," she said. "Today must have been awful for you."

"I was a homicide detective for many years, but you never get used to it."

She let go of his hand as she took the flower from him, keeping it in front of her. "I don't know how you did it."

"I like to think I helped a lot of people."

"I'm sure you did. Do you miss it?"

He smiled. "Miss being a detective? Not for one minute," he said.

Had he hesitated for a moment, or was that her imagination?

"When I heard someone had been killed at the building site, I was worried."

He was speechless. Just as he had been that first day when they met back in London. She gave him a punch on his arm. "Hey, I don't want to lose you."

"Lucky you were in school and not in Kensington Market," Greene said. "The protest got out of hand."

Now is the time, she thought. She had to tell him the truth. That she'd taken the photo of Fox's dead body and posted it online. That she knew it was a terrible thing to do, but she'd been trapped in the house and she'd panicked. That she'd been lying to him for two months, pretending to still be in school. That today she'd put on a disguise to make sure he wouldn't see her at the protest march. That she was the Kensington Blogger everyone was looking for.

"You've probably heard about the photo of Livingston Fox's body that someone took with a selfie stick and put up online," he said. "Unbelievable."

Oh no, she thought. I can't tell him. No, I can't. Thank goodness she had the lilac to cover her face. "I saw something about it on Twitter."

"Can you imagine how the family feels seeing that?"

How could she have been such a complete and utter idiot? And to think that only a month ago she'd been congratulating herself for being resourceful enough to snag an interview with Fox. It had been a real coup. She'd sent him a letter saying she was a journalism student looking for her first big story, and he'd written her back a handwritten letter that said, "I have time to meet at my office, next Tuesday from 4:15 to 4:30 p.m. Email Maxine to confirm. Fox."

Maxine Daley had turned out to be an older woman from Newfoundland who'd worked for him for years. She seemed to run everything in his life and was friendly and helpful.

"What does Mr. Fox like to talk about besides his work?" Alison asked her when she set up that first meeting.

"Oh, that's an easy one," Maxine said. "The Bauhaus Movement. He loves their architecture and design. You should see his book collection."

She'd met Fox for the first time at his beautifully designed modern office. He was much shorter than she'd imagined. He shook her hand, had her sit in one of two matching chairs by the floor-to-ceiling window, pulled out his phone and made a call. She waited until he hung up and watched him turn his phone off.

He sat down beside her.

"Hello." He looked into her eyes, as if there were no one else in the world he'd rather speak to. "I talk to Maxine for one minute before each meeting, then go offline for the next fourteen minutes. Do you mind turning off your phone?"

"Of course not." She fished it out of her bag, turned it off, and looked up. He was staring straight through her. It could have been disarming but it wasn't.

"What should we talk about?" he asked.

"Maxine told me you love Bauhaus architecture, and I've been reading about it."

He grinned, keeping his eyes on hers. They talked about architecture and design and furniture and colour choices and the texture of marble, granite, and oak. Time flew by. Before she knew it, a quiet alarm went off.

"Time to go," he said, standing up.

She stood too.

He shook her hand and headed for the door, already back on his phone, talking to Maxine about his next appointment, leaving Alison feeling strangely elated and bereft.

After that, they met weekly on Friday afternoons in the backroom of Huibing Gardens on Spadina, and bit by bit, Fox started to confide in her.

"My parents run this bullshit wellness centre north of the city," he told her one time. "They say what I do is bad for the environment, but who do you think is paying to keep them in business?"

"I've never had a real friend," he said the next week. "It might sound funny, but my sister, who's twelve years older than me, and Maxine are my closest friends. Maxine was my nanny when I was growing up. Isn't that pathetic?"

"I think it's quite charming," she said.

"What about you?" he asked, fixing her with that all-encompassing stare of his. "What's your story, Ms. English Accent?"

He'd never asked her about herself before. She told him everything: her mother's sudden death; Ari Greene, her surprise father; her move to Toronto; going to journalism school; dropping out; keeping it secret from her father and grandfather.

"And that's when you became the Kensington Blogger," he said as nonchalantly as if he were asking a waitress for the dessert menu.

She flushed. "You knew?"

"I suspected. I didn't know for certain until now. Don't worry, I won't tell anyone. I like secrets."

Two weeks ago, he'd given Alison her first scoop.

"Headline news for you. And exclusive," he said. "I'm engaged."

"That's wonderful."

He showed her a picture of a Japanese woman dressed in a plain blue skirt and white blouse. She looked older than he was.

"You think people will be surprised? She's not my usual type."

"She looks nice."

"Her name is Anita Nakamura. She's a totally normal person from a totally normal family."

The minute Alison left the restaurant, she used her phone to post the news on her blog. By the time she got home, she had ten times the usual number of hits.

She twirled the lilac away from her nose and looked at Ari. "I'm going to put this in water. It will make my room smell lovely."

He grinned.

She felt like a total fraud.

He pointed to the street below them. "I've got visitors."

An expensive-looking vehicle had just parked on the street, and Ari's lawyer friend Ted DiPaulo, whom she'd met a few times, got out the driver's side. He walked around to the front passenger door, opened it, and Cassandra Amberlight stepped out of the car.

What was going on? She let the lilac slip out of her hand, then bent down to pick it up so that Ari couldn't see the shock on her face.

18

"**D**addy!" Gloria cried, and ran across the room to hug her father.

Kennicott watched Karl Fox hold her. Nobody else in the room moved. Father and daughter walked to the couch, and he sat down between his wife and his daughter. He took his wife's hand.

"I'm very sorry," Kennicott said. "Your son's body was found at the Kensington Gate building site late this afternoon."

"But why? How? Who?"

Kennicott watched Karl's reactions carefully. "We don't know yet."

Tears flooded the man's eyes. "He's my only son."

This was why the first few hours of a homicide investigation were so difficult. You had to deliver the worst possible news to people who were most likely victims but could possibly be killers. You'd never met them before and there was no foolproof way to gauge their reactions, which could be anything. A stoic mother; an emotional father. Kennicott had developed a detective's double vision, which meant eyeing people with both compassion and suspicion at the same time.

Fox didn't seem to have any clue that he was a possible suspect, and Kennicott didn't want him to think that he was.

"What can you tell us, Detective?" he asked.

"As I explained to your wife and daughter, at this early stage I'm afraid we can't tell you very much. We know how frustrating that is. Hopefully it won't be for long. Right now it's crucial that we trace your son's whereabouts throughout the day. You said you had lunch with Livingston."

It was important to use Livingston's name to make his father feel that his son was a real person to Kennicott. Not just a victim.

"Yes, at Fresh. We eat there every Friday. The food is all organic."

"What time did you meet?"

"Our regular time. Twelve-thirty. He always has a million meetings booked in a day. It drives him nuts that I'm such a slow eater."

Fox was still talking about his son in the present tense, as if he were still alive.

"Do you know where he went after your lunch?"

"I have no idea. He never tells me a thing. As usual, he had his Rolls-Royce convertible parked up the street, with that woman chauffeur of his waiting to take him to his next appointment. And he was drinking from one of his silly colour-coded water bottles. Said he needed to hydrate because of the heat."

"What did you two talk about?"

Fox clenched his jaw. "With Livingston, there's one topic: his business. How much money he's making. That didn't stop him from spending half the lunch flirting with the waitress."

Most of the articles about Fox had mentioned his womanizing. Perhaps that hadn't stopped, even though he was engaged.

"And now this crazy wedding plan of his. Marrying some older woman he hardly knows."

Fox glanced at his wife. Kennicott caught the scorn on both their faces.

"Did he mention that someone had threatened him, anything of that sort?" Kennicott asked.

"The last few weeks he's been acting real paranoid. He kept saying that someone was following him. Trying to steal an idea he was working on. He didn't know who it was."

"Anything else you talked about? It's important."

"He said he has a new concept for a building. He wanted us to move Foxhole down to the city. As if we'd do that."

"Move from here?" Kate Fox said, not shy to interject. "Never."

"Apparently this idea of his was top secret," Karl said. "He kept telling me how crucial it was to keep it hush-hush."

"Did he say where it would be built?"

"No. He said he drew up the plans himself. I said, 'Great. Show them to me.' But typical Livingston, he had all sorts of excuses. I know he's ruthless in business, and I'm sure he's made a lot of enemies."

Kennicott heard the sound of a door being flung open.

"Gloria! Gloria!" A stout middle-aged woman dressed in an old-fashioned business suit burst into the room, leaving the door open behind her.

Gloria lifted her head. "Maxine!"

"I can't believe it, I can't believe it," Maxine said. She rushed to the sofa and pulled Gloria into her arms. The two of them broke down in tears.

Kate Fox addressed Kennicott. "Maxine was our nanny when the children were growing up. We called her the third parent. She's been Livingston's executive assistant for years."

"I see," Kennicott said. There was something cold about Kate. She still hadn't cried. She was less upset about her son's murder than his nanny-turned-assistant.

Kennicott turned to Darvesh and nodded at the door. It was time to leave. Let the family grieve. He told Maxine that he'd need to speak to her as soon as possible.

"Is tomorrow morning too late?" she asked, fighting to compose herself.

"No. That would be perfect."

"I'm always in early. Can you come to the office at nine?"

"Yes," he said. "I appreciate it. And I understand Livingston had a chauffeur."

"Sherani."

"We want to talk to her right away."

"Certainly." She opened her purse and pulled out a well-worn pencil and a pad of Post-its, wrote out a phone number, and passed the note to Kennicott. "Here's her number. She's extremely upset. I'm sure she'll be most helpful. I'll have her there tomorrow morning if you like. She can show you where she spent the day with Livingston."

"That would be excellent," Kennicott said.

He and Darvesh shook hands all around and walked out. When they were back in the police car, Kennicott asked, "Are you okay?"

Darvesh put the keys in the ignition but didn't turn the car on. "It's very difficult to tell a family their child has been murdered."

"It's probably the toughest part of the job," Kennicott said. "And it never gets easier."

Kennicott could still remember the ashen look on the face of the police officer who had informed him his brother Michael had been murdered. The cop had been Detective Ari Greene.

"Tell me your impressions of the Fox family," Kennicott said.

"What's with the mother?" Darvesh said, putting the car in gear. "Madame Ice Queen or what?"

"I thought so too. Drive real slow until you get to the entrance."

Kennicott looked out the window at the grounds. The grass hadn't been cut recently, and the garden beds were filled with weeds. The parking lot was empty, and there was no sign of any clients. Meanwhile, their son was chauffeured about town in a Rolls-Royce. Making millions. Maybe that was why they thought his wedding plans were crazy. Livingston might have been about to sign away his fortune and leave them and their crumbling business in the lurch. Now he was dead, where would all his money go?

"After the funeral is over, we're going to have to get a look at Livingston Fox's will. Follow the money trail, see if it leads back here."

"Good idea." Darvesh stopped the car at the end of the driveway. "Should I still follow the speed limit back?"

"Hell no," Kennicott said. "Floor it."

19

"Ari, thanks for seeing us right away," Ted DiPaulo said when he got up to the porch. As usual, he was impeccably dressed. Despite the heat, the suit he was wearing looked crisp. "Meet Cassandra Amberlight."

Amberlight was the opposite. She wore an old, shapeless dress. A big woman with wide shoulders and long arms, she was breathing hard from the exertion of climbing the staircase.

Greene shook her hand. It was sweaty. "Can I get you anything? A glass of water?"

"A seat is all I need," Amberlight said, as she plunked herself down on a chair. "You do that climb every day?"

"A few times a day," Greene said. "You get used to it."

"Maybe you, not me."

DiPaulo chuckled. "Cassandra and I went to law school together. She always sat in the front row and I always sat in the back."

"This is my daughter, Alison," Greene said.

"Young lady," Amberlight said to Alison, "I hope you don't want to be a lawyer or a cop."

"I don't know what I want to do," Alison said. She'd picked up the lilac that she'd dropped and was smelling it again. "Presently I'm in journalism school."

"Probably a good idea," DiPaulo said. "For once in her life, Cassandra doesn't want to talk to the press."

Everyone laughed. Thank goodness for Ted, Greene thought. He was good at cracking jokes, getting people to relax.

"Especially after someone posted that dreadful photo of Livingston

Fox's body online," Amberlight said. "This social media stuff is totally out of control. Who would do such a thing? They should charge the person. There has to be some kind of legislation." She turned to Alison. "Young lady, this is your generation. All these cellphones and selfie shots. What do you think?"

DiPaulo grinned. "At law school, not a day went by when Cassandra didn't have a new cause to champion."

"I guess sometimes people just get carried away," Alison said.

"To say the least," Amberlight said.

"Well, have a good meeting. I'm not accustomed to this humidity and I've got homework to do." Alison waved her lilac and walked inside.

When the door closed, Amberlight gave Greene a quizzical look. "Can I ask where she picked up that charming English accent?"

"It's a long story." Greene crossed his arms. "I think I know, but what brings you two here?"

"Livingston Fox," DiPaulo said. "I fear Cassandra's going to be a suspect. The police will want to speak to her soon, and I need you to help me prepare her."

"I had nothing to do with his murder," Amberlight said, sitting upright.

"I assume you're a suspect because you're leading the opposition to Fox's new condo project," Greene said.

"That's not all," she said.

"What am I missing here?" Greene asked DiPaulo.

"Tell him, Cassandra."

"Maybe I will take that glass of water," Amberlight said.

Greene could see she was stalling and that she wanted to talk to DiPaulo alone. He took his time going inside to get her the water.

"The first thing the detectives will ask you," he said, once he was back outside and sitting across from her, "will be to account for your whereabouts earlier today."

She took a long swig. "I met with Fox at two-thirty this afternoon," she said.

No wonder she was nervous. He'd found the body at about four o'clock.

"Where?" Greene asked.

"At the back of the Kensington Gate work site, in the work shed where he was killed."

DiPaulo was still standing, his face expressionless, as hard to read as an expert poker player's.

"How did you get into the yard?"

"Fox had unlocked the gate and left it open for me."

"How long was your meeting?"

"I'm not sure. About half an hour."

"Then what happened?"

"I left."

"And Fox?"

"He stayed there."

And when you left, did you leave the gate open or did you lock it? Greene wondered. That was the key question, but now was not the time to ask.

"What was the meeting about?"

"We'd been meeting for a few weeks in secret. Fox wanted to make a deal. He was prepared to turn the Kensington Gate 2 into a rental building with affordable apartments for artists and the disabled. The main floor would include a medical clinic, a common kitchen, a gym, and a public swimming pool. He planned to set up a non-profit organization called the Fox Cityscape Foundation and make me the director and I was going to get a penthouse apartment in the building."

"What did he want from you in return?"

"We planned to do a joint press conference tomorrow morning. He was going to say he'd been persuaded by the protest today and had done a one-eighty. He wanted me to invite the protesters to work with me in the foundation. He had the building all planned out. He'd done his own architectural drawings, and he showed them to me today."

"Did you touch them?"

"Did I touch them? Yes, I touched them. And his desk. The door handle. Why wouldn't I?"

This meant her fingerprints and maybe even her DNA would soon be found in the shed. Greene and DiPaulo had to get this information to the police fast, so it couldn't be said she'd only admitted to being in the shed with Fox after she was presented with the evidence.

"What did you say to Fox's offer?"

She hesitated. Looked at Ted. Took another sip of water.

It was bad when a witness hesitated this way. "Let me be clear about something that is very important," Greene said. "When the police question you, they watch for things witnesses do to stall for time. Hesitation is a sign of guilt. Looking around the room. Taking a sip of water."

She put her glass down. "Okay."

Amberlight was smart, he thought. Maybe too smart?

"I've been meeting with Fox every Friday for the last month. The protest was his idea. He told me about this new blog, *Kensington Confidential*, and I began posting on it to get support."

"Wait a minute. You're saying Fox orchestrated the demonstration against himself?"

"I have to admit he was brilliant. He knew this would get him maximum press for his public about-face. Look, the government is set to spend millions in public housing and he wanted in on that money. There was no way he'd get a cent without a sea change to his image."

"You heard he was getting married?"

"To a schoolteacher. New life. New image. New man. I actually thought Fox was being sincere. This afternoon we worked out the final details. He poured water for both of us and we toasted our deal. He could be very charming."

Greene thought back to the water bottles and glasses he'd seen in the shed. Her DNA would be on the lip of the glass for sure.

DiPaulo, who had been silent until now, couldn't restrain himself. "See. Cassandra left evidence all over the place that she'd been in the shed with Fox. She wasn't hiding the fact that she'd been there," he said. "Just the opposite."

This was Ted being Ted. Always looking for the best legal argument. Finding ways to turn a negative into a positive.

"I had nothing to hide," Amberlight said.

"The police will collect your DNA and prints from the crime scene," Greene said, "but right now they won't know who they belong to because you won't be on file."

Amberlight's and DiPaulo's eyes met.

"What?" Greene asked.

"This is not the first time Cassandra has been arrested," DiPaulo said.

All the more reason why we have to get her to make a statement to the police, Greene thought.

"I didn't think of that. You've been arrested at many of your protests. They'll have your fingerprints, but they won't have your DNA."

Amberlight and DiPaulo were still looking at each other. Something else was going on here.

"Ted?" Greene asked.

He sighed. "Last year Cassandra was convicted of assault with a weapon. One of her young male employees was the victim. She's on probation. As part of the deal, she gave a DNA sample. I've managed to keep this out of the papers."

Not for much longer. Greene knew the press would figure this out in no time once they heard she was a suspect in Fox's murder.

"What kind of weapon?"

DiPaulo rolled his eyes.

This keeps getting worse, Greene thought.

"A baseball bat. Cassandra's a big Blue Jays fan. She had a bat signed by José Bautista in her old office and, well, you can probably fill in the rest."

This was a disaster.

"Any other bad news I need to know about? Tell me now, not later."

"That's it," she said. "All my dirty laundry."

"It better be," Greene said. He thought back to the shed. The gate. The alleyway.

"What happened after you and Fox toasted your agreement?"

"I said goodbye. And I left."

"Which way did you go?"

She put her hands out as if to state the obvious. "Back out the gate."

"Did you leave the gate open?" Greene kept his tone even. He was getting to the crucial question.

"Like I said, Fox had left it open for me when I got there. When I was leaving, he told me to be sure to close it behind me but not to lock it because he'd be leaving soon, and that's what I did."

Her tone wasn't strident at all. She seemed totally unaware of the import of her answer, and that made her believable.

DiPaulo looked concerned but he shouldn't have been. He didn't know that the gate was open when Greene got there. Kennicott would notice this detail. If Amberlight was telling the truth when she said that she'd closed that gate behind her, it was evidence that someone came in after she left. The killer or killers had left the gate open when they fled the scene.

Kennicott would make sure this fact was not released to the public. The only people who knew it were the culprits and the police and Greene. If Amberlight's seemingly candid answer was believed, it might exonerate her. But he didn't want to tip her off to how important this was. Her not knowing was the best way to ensure she'd answer Kennicott in the same sincere way when he asked her the same key question.

"Then what did you do?" he asked.

"I went home and lay down for a while. It was so hot, I suddenly felt very tired. This was a big life decision for me and I knew a lot of people were going to think I'd sold out and made a deal with the devils."

"Did you see or talk to anyone on your way there?"

"No. I walked down the back alley to Oxford Street. I didn't want anyone to see me leaving Fox's building."

"How long were you at home?"

"I don't know. I fell asleep for a while."

Greene looked at DiPaulo. They were both thinking the same thing. She had no one to back up her alibi for the crucial time when Fox was killed. This was not good at all.

"What did you do when you woke up?"

"I got my megaphone and rushed up to the protest. It was already in full swing. I got up to the front and was leading things when we heard that Fox was dead, and then everything went haywire. I knew I'd just been with him and it would look bad, so I called Ted, and here we are."

"You've got a decision to make, Ted," Greene said. "If she says nothing to the police, she'll almost certainly be arrested."

DiPaulo frowned.

Greene knew that lawyers hate letting their clients talk to the police.

"And if she gives a statement? Admits to being there but maintains her innocence?" DiPaulo asked.

Amberlight looked shell-shocked. Greene had to snap her back to reality. And to action.

"If the police believe you, that will hold them back for a while. Maybe they'll keep investigating and find the real killer. But if you're going to talk to them, you need to do it in the next day or two. You and Ted will be stuck with your statement forever more. That means every word better damn well be true. And nothing but nothing left out."

20

Even though Grandpa Y hadn't finished the basement renovations, Alison's bedroom was in good-enough shape for her to move into it last week. Just in time, now that she desperately needed the privacy. And it was nice and cool down there.

She'd been surprised by the weather in Canada. Everyone had warned her about the winter, and they were right, but when it snowed the city took on a wonderful, almost fairy-tale quality. She hadn't anticipated the intense blue of the clear winter sky. And she was amazed that sometimes at night she could sit out on the front porch and see the stars.

One weekend in February, Ari had taken her up north for the day to a town called Haliburton. The drive was exhilarating. All the open space, snow blanketing the land for as far as she could see. They stopped at a Mennonite food stand and purchased grass-fed beef from two young women in traditional dress, then drove to a nearby field where men in black hats were taking turns being pulled along on wooden skis by a horse-drawn buggy.

Next they'd eaten at a roadside restaurant called the Hardscrabble Café. Ari knew the owner, though he wouldn't say how, an older woman who was very glad to see him. He seemed to know people wherever they went. She served them delicious French toast made with homemade bread and topped with local maple syrup. The afternoon was the highlight, when they went dogsledding through a deep forest and across a frozen lake.

On the way home, Ari draped her under a thick Hudson Bay blanket he'd bought in town. As she drifted off to sleep, she smiled. Though it was unspoken, they both knew he'd planned the day as a way to get her excited about living here.

She hopped on the bed in her new room, stacked pillows against the headboard, tucked her feet under the duvet, and opened her laptop. Her blog was on fire. Thousands of hits. She checked Twitter. Fox's murder was the number one trending story out of Toronto. This was spinning out of control.

She picked up the TV remote and clicked on TO-TV. The news had just started, and the reporter Sheena Persad was talking to the camera. "The city has been shocked by the gruesome murder of thirty-four-year-old Livingston Fox. Just who was the dynamic young developer? We've prepared this special report."

Persad continued to talk over high-school-yearbook photos of Fox, where he was tagged as "most likely to get rich," then pictures of him on a rainy day in a hard hat at his first building site with his sister and Maxine, his assistant, all holding the same shovel.

"Fox's empire grew," Persad said over rolling photographs of Fox with well-known models and actresses, his Rolls-Royce convertible, and a beautiful chauffeur, "as did his reputation as a larger-than-life personality.

"But in the last year, he seemed to change," Persad continued. "Much to the surprise of everyone, two weeks ago the anonymous new blog *Kensington Confidential* broke the story that Fox was engaged to a schoolteacher."

A screenshot of Alison's blog appeared with the headline that she'd written. "Fox Finds Fidelity? Builder Livingston Fox to Marry Local Teacher."

Alison felt ill.

"The blog has carried a number of breaking stories about Fox," Persad said when she was back on camera.

Alison tensed. Was Persad going to mention that she'd met the Kensington Blogger? It felt as if the reporter were looking right at her.

"I encourage anyone who has information about Fox to contact me directly." As Persad spoke, her email address and work number scrolled across the screen. The camera moved in on her for a tight close-up. "Of course, if you have any information about this case, go straight to the police."

Alison wanted to scream at the TV set: *I don't know anything about the murder!*

But was that true? She was supposed to have met with Fox this afternoon and he hadn't shown up. Did that matter?

"Not everyone was impressed with Livingston Fox's meteoric career," Persad said. "Earlier today, a large rally was held in historic Kensington Market, outside Fox's newest condominium project. TO-TV News was there."

Alison froze as she watched the screen.

Persad disappeared again, replaced by footage of chanting protesters holding up signs and of Cassandra Amberlight jumping up in front of the crowd, shouting through her megaphone, "Stop the Fox, Save the Market!"

"Then came the shocking news that Livingston Fox had been murdered," Persad said. "A note of caution: the photograph you are about to see is not appropriate for young children."

There it was, Alison's photo of Fox lying on the floor of the shed. They had blurred out his face and the rebar stuck through his chest, but the image was still powerful.

"Police have asked anyone with any information about the identity of the Kensington Blogger to contact them immediately," Persad said, then she signed off.

Her message was clear: *Alison, get hold of me soon, or I'll have no choice but to go to the cops and tell them I met you.*

21

Kennicott was thankful he lived just four blocks from a Metro supermarket that was open twenty-four hours and glad that at 4:30 a.m. it was almost empty. An exhausted-looking security guard wearing thick-sole shoes stood by the sliding front door. The store's lights were so bright they hurt Kennicott's tired eyes. The sound system was playing Barry Manilow's "Mandy" as he waited in line. Now Tony Orlando was playing and Kennicott wished he had a yellow ribbon to stuff down the singer's throat.

He liked to cook, but after weeks at the murder trial, his food supplies had dwindled to almost nothing. He desperately needed to shower, shave, eat, and get an hour or two of rest before the long day ahead. But even more than sleep, he needed time to think through everything he'd learned in the last twelve hours.

He looked at the tomatoes and picked through them for the ripest one. He selected a white onion, some cremini mushrooms, and two skimpy packages of fresh basil. He had some good pasta at home, and all he had to do now was pick up some chicken—he'd need the protein—to make a decent meal.

At the checkout, there was one customer in front of him. Kennicott closed his eyes for a moment. At least Tony Orlando wasn't singing anymore, but now it was Whitney Houston. She'd decided long ago never to walk in anyone's shadow. That's what he was trying to do— walk in Livingston Fox's shadow.

This afternoon, after they left Foxhole, Kennicott and Darvesh had sped back to police headquarters. Darvesh researched Fox while Kennicott sifted through the field reports that had come in from the officers on the scene. They'd knocked on every door on Augusta Avenue, talked to store owners on Spadina and College and to a few protesters who were prepared to cooperate, and come up empty. Some people weren't home, and those who were had been entirely focused on the protest. No one had been in the alleyway or seen anyone come in or out of the rear gate of the Kensington Gate construction site.

The area had been searched for video surveillance cameras. Unfortunately, most of the market was stuck in the 1960s, and few stores had them.

Detective Ho went with Kennicott to the autopsy, where Fox's organs were examined, samples of his blood and urine were sent out for analysis that would take the usual four to six weeks, and the body cavity was sewn back up. The pathologist confirmed Ho's initial hunch. There were no signs of trauma anywhere other than the hole in his chest. He had no defensive wounds on his hands. No scratches. No skin under his fingernails. It was as if Fox had voluntarily lain down and let someone spear him through the heart.

When Kennicott got back to headquarters, Darvesh was excited. They'd lifted a clean set of prints from the empty glasses on the worktable and he'd run them through the database.

"We got a match," he said.

"Tell me."

"Cassandra Amberlight."

Kennicott let out a long, slow whistle.

"Yep. Looks like we've got ourselves a prime suspect."

Darvesh had already gone through the TV footage of the protest. Amberlight hadn't shown up until it was in full swing. According to the timer on the tape, she'd arrived at 3:49:01. As a precaution, he'd sent a squad car to watch her apartment in Kensington Market. The officers reported that it was dark and they could see no movement inside. They'd located her car, an old Subaru with the license plate "PROTEST", parked on a side street. Darvesh had checked Facebook and Twitter and found that she was usually active online, but she hadn't posted anything after 2:00 p.m.

He'd run her criminal record and found she had a recent conviction. He'd also retrieved some older ones that she'd got expunged. And he'd sent copies of her photograph to every police division in the city with an alert to be on the lookout for her.

Kennicott was now so exhausted that the small bag of groceries felt heavy. It was still dark outside. Fatigue was pulling him down. He had to get home before the sun rose. If he hurried, he'd have enough time to make himself a meal, eat, and sleep for a while.

The Federicos, his landlords, had left the light on over the side entrance to the house on Clinton Street where he lived. A piece of folded paper was wedged in the door handle. Kennicott put the groceries down and tugged it out. This could only be from one person.

"Daniel," the handwritten note read. "Meet me at Caldense Bakery at 5:00 a.m. Ari."

22

At five in the morning, Dundas Street West was almost empty. A 505 streetcar, carrying early-morning workers, rumbled by, and the moon was tipping down to the horizon. It cast a grey shadow in front of Kennicott as he walked along the deserted sidewalk.

This was so like Ari Greene to get hold of Kennicott by leaving a note in his door, avoiding a traceable text, email, or phone call. His few words carried multiple meanings: Greene would know that Kennicott had been up all night working the case; he would know that Kennicott was too keyed up to sleep; and he would know that no matter how tired Kennicott was, he wouldn't resist his invitation.

The Caldense was a Portuguese bakery that opened early to serve construction workers who stopped in for an espresso and croissant before heading off to their job sites. Kennicott had met Greene here many times, and this morning he found him sitting in the window seat where he always sat, laughing with the same squat bald man dressed in the same black vest and black shirt as on all their previous meetings here.

Greene stood up when Kennicott came in.

Kennicott thought about shaking his hand, but he didn't.

"Daniel, you remember Miguel Caldas, proprietor extraordinaire?"

"Nice to see you again, sir," Kennicott said, reaching out to shake the owner's hand.

"My pleasure, Detective," Caldas replied. "Ari told me to get you a double espresso and a croissant when you arrived. I'll be right back."

Greene sat back down, and Kennicott took the other chair.

"You're not going to make me eat their croissants again," Kennicott said, glancing at the half-eaten one on Greene's plate. It was a long-standing joke between them. The croissants at the Caldense, unlike their light, buttery French counterparts, were dry and hard. Greene hated them.

"This time I'll eat yours," Greene said.

Kennicott didn't smile. "It's five in the morning. You know I have to be back at work in an hour. What do you want to talk about?"

Greene took another bite of croissant and grimaced. "These seem to get harder every year," he whispered.

"Here's your café, Detective Kennicott," Caldas said, moving in with a tray before Kennicott could reply. "And a fresh croissant. Enjoy."

Kennicott could smell the coffee and felt his stomach churn. Once Caldas left, he passed the croissant to Greene and turned away. At the counter, a group of men in workboots were trading jokes. On the far wall a TV was playing a European soccer game, and the fans in the stands were cheering wildly.

"This afternoon, when I told you I was planning to get in touch with you soon, you didn't believe me, did you?" Greene asked.

"Was it the truth?"

"It was."

Kennicott downed his espresso in one gulp.

"Thanks for the coffee, Ari," he said, with no enthusiasm. He stood up.

Greene grabbed his wrist. "There's something I need to tell you."

Kennicott thought about breaking out of Greene's grip. Basic training. Grab his bound hand with his free one and pull it toward Greene's fingers, which would not be strong enough to hold a moving arm.

"What?" he said, still standing.

Greene let go of his wrist. "I sometimes work as a consultant for Ted DiPaulo, my former defence lawyer."

"I thought you were happy being a construction worker."

"It's part time. Please sit down, Daniel."

Kennicott took a deep breath and sat. "Why?"

"Cassandra Amberlight."

Kennicott met Greene's eyes. "We've been looking for her. She's not answering her door at her apartment. Her office is closed. No one in the market has seen her. We don't even know if she's alive or dead."

"She's alive."

"Where is she?"

Greene shook his head.

"Ari, come on. If she has an alibi, I need to hear it sooner rather than later."

"I know."

"We want to talk to her."

"I hope to bring her in to headquarters."

"Today?"

"Tomorrow. Ted needs more time with her. Say three o'clock. You don't have grounds to arrest her."

"Not yet, but I may have very soon. Is she going to give us a statement?"

"You know the drill. Her lawyer doesn't want her to talk to you."

"And you?"

"I think she should."

"Why?"

"I don't think she did it. Daniel, I'm asking you not to arrest her."

"Tell me you're kidding."

"Don't arrest her . . . yet."

Kennicott stared out the window. At the traffic light a group of cyclists on road bikes dressed in matching gear adjusted their helmets and drank from their water bottles.

"You don't exactly have a lot of credibility on this kind of thing anymore," he said.

"*Mea culpa*. Amberlight's not to blame for my transgressions. Just hear her out."

He turned back to Greene. "You know we found her prints in the shed?"

"Yes."

"You know she's got a criminal record?"

"I heard she assaulted an employee last year."

One thing Kennicott had learned in his previous life as a lawyer was that your clients never tell you everything, and he doubted that Amberlight had told DiPaulo and Greene her full record. "Did you know that fifteen years ago she stabbed her husband with a kitchen knife? Or that she slashed her wife with a screwdriver two years later?"

Greene took a final bite of his croissant. He was stalling.

"She got the records expunged, but Darvesh was able to retrieve them. Amberlight didn't mention those convictions, did she?"

"That's covered by solicitor–client privilege."

"Ari, you are starting to sound like a lawyer."

"Ha! You know I dropped out of law school after the first year."

Despite himself, Kennicott laughed. "Okay, tell me again exactly what you did after you saw Fox's body in the shed."

"As I told you before, I called 911 right away."

"And after that?"

"What do you think I did, Daniel?"

Answering a question with a question. It was a classic delay tactic. "I think you couldn't resist looking in the alley out back. It was a few steps away. You could have got back in less than a minute. You were careful in your statement to Darvesh. You didn't lie. You just left things out." He didn't say "again," but he was thinking it.

"Don't worry. I didn't touch the gate. It was open wide enough for me to get through easily."

He'd been right about Greene. He *had* checked the alley. The guy always had a secret.

"What did you see?"

"I didn't see a suspect running away, if that's what you are asking."

It was a subtle dig. But he hadn't answered the question. Kennicott shook his head.

"Daniel," Greene said, "I saw the same thing you saw, a typical Toronto back alley."

"And?"

"And nothing."

Greene could be incredibly frustrating.

"More café for the young detective?" Caldas said, appearing out of nowhere.

"No thanks," Kennicott said. "I've got to get to work. Bring Ari another croissant."

"My pleasure." Caldas pivoted on his heels and was gone.

Through the window, Kennicott could see the street brightening with the rising sun. "I assume that if you uncover material evidence, you'll hand it over to me right away."

"You know I will."

"Amberlight," Kennicott said. "You really think she's innocent?"

"Her past plays both ways. It makes her a prime suspect, but it also makes her a perfect target for a set-up. I don't think she's guilty, and you don't want to make the same mistake twice."

This was Greene twisting the knife.

Caldas arrived with the second croissant. "Enjoy, Detective," he said placing it in front of Greene.

"He loves them," Kennicott said.

"Thanks a lot, Daniel," Greene said, once Caldas was gone.

Kennicott shrugged. He took a deep breath. "Ari, get Amberlight to talk to me," he said, standing to leave. This time, Greene didn't try to stop him.

23

Alison had hardly slept all night, and this morning she was having trouble concentrating. And keeping her hands steady. She was tucked away on the back patio of Jimmy's Café, one of her favourite places in Kensington Market, drinking an iced tea, but the tighter she gripped the tall glass, the more it shook.

Tea. It was another thing that reminded Alison of her mother, who was passionate about tea and how to make it properly. One particularly cold February morning this past winter, Alison had woken up early and found Ari in the kitchen, boiling water, a teapot set on the counter. She stopped in the doorway. He didn't know she was there.

She watched him monitor the kettle and take it off the stove just before it boiled—the same way her mother had taught Alison to do—so as not to boil the oxygen out of the water. He poured some into the teapot, swirled it around to heat the pot, tossed the water in the sink, and put in two bags of white tea. He poured the hot water down the inside of the pot. "Never pour the water directly on the tea," her mother had always said. "Let the bag come to the water."

She watched him place the lid across the opening, not covering it completely. "Always let it steep for five minutes," Mummy had instructed her, "but let it breathe a little."

Ari turned to get a mug and noticed Alison for the first time.

In the two months since she'd come to Canada, they'd slowly gotten to know each other. The one topic that they'd never broached was his relationship with her mother. She knew he was waiting for her to talk about it. He was respectful that way. Suddenly, it felt as if Mum was in the room with the two of them. It was time.

"It was like watching Mum, the way you made the tea," she said.

"She was a good teacher."

"How long were you together?"

"A year."

A thought occurred to her that she'd never thought of before. "Where did you two live?"

He hesitated. Shrugged. "I was lucky. I got into the real estate market early. I bought this house twenty-five years ago."

She took her head and laughed. "Well then, maybe this really is my home. Did mum like living here?"

He nodded. "She did. In the end she needed to go back to England. I respected her decision, but I couldn't leave."

"Your parents?"

He shrugged. "Your mother and I, we never fought."

"Did you love her?"

"I don't know if either of us was capable of love back then. We were good to each other."

"You didn't really answer my question."

He opened a cupboard, got out a second mug, slid the lid in place on the teapot, poured two cups, and passed one to her.

"Of course I loved her," he said at last. "And I was a fool not to realize it in time."

That cup of tea had been comforting on such a cold winter morning. Now the iced tea in her hand felt cool. The humidity hadn't let up, and even in the shade she was hot.

She had copies of the city's four newspapers on the table in front of her. They all had stories about Livingston Fox's murder, and the *Toronto Sun* featured the photo she'd taken of the body in the shed, with the rebar in his chest blurred out, on its front page. The image had gone viral online, and her blog was now trending on Twitter.

No one knew who'd taken the picture and who the Kensington Blogger was. Just her luck. She'd gotten an amazing scoop, a story that could make her journalism career, but she couldn't put her name to it. What was she supposed to do now? Go to the police? With what? She didn't have any evidence that would help them find the murderer. And she would probably be charged with breaking into the house on Augusta, maybe even for posting the picture online.

From her seat at the rear of the courtyard, she could see everyone who entered the cafe through the open back door. There was the usual morning mix of hipsters and aging hippies and other local regulars. A handsome man in a well-tailored suit came in, went straight to the counter, and talked to the barista. She recognized him. He was the police officer who'd come out of the gate by the shed when she was looking out the second-floor window. She looked down at the *Toronto Star*, at a photo of him giving a news conference yesterday: Detective Daniel Kennicott, the officer in charge of the case.

He must be looking for her. But how did he know she was here? Maybe the reporter, Persad, had given the police a description of her? Maybe someone tipped them off that she was a regular here? She could feel her heart pounding. There was nothing she could do to get away. She was stuck.

She opened the newspaper at a random page and held it up to hide her face. She was staring at what Canadians called the Sports Section. Sports, not sport, the way it was called in England. Just one of many little differences in language she was trying to get accustomed to. Most of the stories were about ice hockey, which Canadians simply called hockey. There weren't many at all about soccer, their name for football, but there were lots about baseball. Ari had taken her and Grandpa Y to a game at the domed stadium, and she'd found it entirely bewildering.

Why hadn't Kennicott come over to her yet? She lowered the newspaper enough to peer over the top. To her great relief, she saw he was walking out of the cafe carrying a paper coffee cup in his hand and two more in a cardboard carrier. Maybe he wasn't looking for her. The crime scene was two blocks away. He must be headed over there.

She put the newspaper down and picked up her drink. Her hands were shaking more than ever, but she managed to take a sip. She couldn't let herself get paranoid. That would freeze her. She wished she could talk to her mother about what to do. Here she was stranded in this strange city with a new but strange family. Ari. Grandpa Y. And who was she really? Was she the same Alison she'd been before her mother died? Or was she now the Kensington Blogger, the kind of person who could take a photo of a murdered man and post it for the world to see?

She had to get hold of Persad. She pulled out the reporter's business card, then hesitated. How could she contact Persad without giving away her identity or her phone number or her email address?

She looked around and noticed for the first time the vines and petunias in containers lining the patio and the cut flowers on every table. The winter had been long and cold, but her mother was right about the humidity. Good for the flowers though.

Flowers.

That would work. Go low-tech.

Alison laughed out loud at the thought, and a young man who was reading a textbook at the table next to hers looked up. She grinned at him.

Ha! she thought. I guess I am Ari's daughter after all. He'd be proud of me for this idea.

24

Greene knew the Tim Hortons coffee shop on Elm Street all too well. A few years earlier, a stray bullet had killed a four-year-old boy who was walking with his father through the parking lot of the coffee shop. He and Kennicott had been the detectives on the case, which had galvanized the city.

Greene had gotten to know the owners of the franchise, Mr. and Ms. Yuen, immigrants from Hong Kong who had put their life savings and years of work into the business. Fortunately for them, after the shooting the lure of coffee and doughnuts had proved stronger than people's aversion to visiting the site of the tragedy, and the Yuens' business had survived.

Whenever Greene visited, they offered him free tea or coffee, as Ms. Yuen did now.

"We're happy always to see you, Detective," she said.

"Happy to see you too."

"You drink coffee now, or still tea?"

"Tea."

"Free today," she said.

"Thanks." As always, he insisted on paying her two dollars and stuffed a five-dollar bill in the jar for a summer-camp fund. "My friend will be here soon. A police officer in uniform."

"No problem," Ms. Yuen said, putting the toonie into the cash register.

Greene took his cup and walked around to the tiny lunchroom in back. The Yuens had reserved it for him when he'd called half an hour earlier to let them know he needed to use it. He'd arranged to meet PC

Lindsmore, whom he'd known since their days together in police col-lege. The years of trust between them had broken apart after Greene was charged with murder. It was time to repair it.

Lindsmore came in, carrying two doughnuts in one of his meaty hands and a large coffee in the other. Greene pulled a chair back for him.

"Ari, good to see you. You surprised the heck out of me yesterday when you turned up at the building site."

"I think I shocked Kennicott even more."

Lindsmore plunked himself down. "How many more years can I do this crazy job?"

"How many more years of support payments do you have to make?"

"Don't ask." He pried the plastic top off his coffee and drank half of it in one gulp.

"How old is Carl now? Ten?"

"Good memory, Ari. Eleven. I see him Wednesday nights for two hours and every other Saturday for six, if his mother hasn't made other plans for him or he doesn't have a sore throat or any other excuse she can dream up to keep him away from me."

Few cops made it through their careers without getting divorced, and Lindsmore's had been particularly nasty.

"Hang in there."

"You helped me a lot back then. I won't forget it. I'm glad you're back in the city."

"Kennicott's mad that I didn't get in touch with him earlier."

"He's young."

Greene reached over and took one of the doughnuts.

"Since when did you start eating doughnuts?"

"There's an exception to every rule." Greene tore the doughnut in two and took a bite from the smaller piece. Then he sipped his tea, let-ting the silence between them settle in.

Lindsmore still hadn't touched his food, which had to be some kind of record, Greene thought.

"Shit, Ari. Look." Lindsmore sighed. "I didn't mean to fuck you over before, when you were on bail. I knew in my heart you would never have killed Jennifer. I feel terrible about it. I know Kennicott does too."

Greene chose his words carefully. "It was a bad time for all of us."

He hadn't entirely accepted Lindsmore's apology. They both knew there was still a debt to be repaid.

Lindsmore picked up his doughnut and demolished it in three bites.

"I'm not just working construction," Greene said.

Lindsmore eyed the half doughnut Greene hadn't eaten yet. "You're undercover, aren't you, Ari?"

"No. I have no ties to the force. My old lawyer, Ted DiPaulo, has asked me to help out a suspect in the Fox murder."

"Ari Greene, a PI?"

Greene grinned. "Nothing official."

Lindsmore laughed. "Ari Greene doing community service."

"Because he doesn't want to see the wrong person charged or convicted."

Lindsmore rubbed his large hands together. "Understood. You of all people know what it's like."

"Problem is I don't have any access to police information."

Lindsmore lowered his voice. "You know I'd do anything for you. But if I get fired, I got no salary, no pension, no support payments. That's it, I'll never see Carl again."

"I know."

"I want to help. But . . ."

"I need answers to a few simple questions." Greene pointed to his unfinished doughnut. "You want that? I'm done."

Lindsmore took a napkin and wrapped it up.

"Thanks," he said. "What simple questions?"

"Fox. Was he on the police radar? Did he have a criminal record? Had he ever been investigated?"

"Okay. He didn't have a record. There were rumours he was a coke-head. But that was a few years ago. Nothing ever added up to an arrest. Tax guys from Ottawa audited him a few years ago and apparently he was clean as a whistle, down to the last penny."

"What about Cassandra Amberlight?"

"Shit. Ari." He took a second swig of his coffee, not quite as big as the last.

This was going to be the hard part. Greene had to push him.

"Kennicott told me you lifted her prints from the work shed where they found the body."

"She's your client?"

"I assume she's one of the prime suspects."

"As in *the* prime suspect," Lindsmore said.

"I'm taking her to headquarters tomorrow afternoon to be inter-viewed by Kennicott. I think she might be innocent. Someone could have set her up."

"The way Hap Charlton set you up?"

Greene looked Lindsmore in the eye and nodded. Slowly.

"Let's not dwell in the past," he said. "Amberlight's problem is that she's got a lot of baggage. Kennicott told me she has some old convic-tions that she'd got expunged. I need to see everything she did."

"I get it. You want to make sure she's not leaving anything out when Kennicott has her on tape and under oath, so the interview doesn't blow up in her face at the trial." Lindsmore, for all his down-on-his-luck trappings, was street smart in the way a cop could be only after years on the force.

"We've both seen it," Greene said. "Someone misleads the cops about some small thing, and the prosecutors hang them out to dry in front of the jury on a stupid, irrelevant lie."

Lindsmore finished his coffee and plopped his empty cup down. "She's telling you she's innocent as the fallen snow and you're not sure, are you?"

Greene didn't answer. His old colleague was right. He wasn't sure.

Lindsmore broke the silence. "Last Wednesday night, I took Carl to the St. Louis Grill for wings, and he asked if he could come live with me. You told me a long time ago to hang in and he'd come back to me—best advice I ever got. I need an hour. Where do you want me to leave this brown envelope?"

"My car is an old reconditioned black Mercedes with a wood steering wheel. I'll park it two blocks north of your station and leave the back passenger-side window open a crack. Here's my licence number."

Greene wrote it down on a napkin.

Lindsmore picked up the napkin, looked at it, tore it in half, then in half again. He stuffed it into his empty paper cup, crushed it, and passed it to Greene.

"Don't get up," he said, lumbering to his feet. "Just get rid of that cup."

25

Kennicott had learned from Greene how important it was to go back to the crime scene the day after a murder and walk around it again. Think about it. Try to visualize what happened.

Augusta Avenue was coming to life as Kennicott walked along, sipping one of the lattes he'd just bought from Jimmy's Café. In such a modern, well-ordered city Kensington Market was a throwback to an earlier time. Its streets were packed with specialty stores, whose wares spilled out onto crowded sidewalks. They sold everything from fish, meat, and chicken to bread, nuts, cheese, and spices. He strolled past used-clothing boutiques, bicycle repair shops, cheap open-air restaurants, and graffiti-filled back alleys. The pervasive smell of marijuana hung lightly in the air.

But was the market worth being preserved the way the protesters were demanding? He wasn't sure. Some of the buildings looked so dilapidated that, with the price of real estate in the city exploding, he couldn't imagine they'd be standing in ten, even five years.

The construction site was still sealed off with police tape, and officers were posted outside the front gate as he'd ordered. He showed his badge and walked through to the shed. Detective Ho, wearing plastic booties and gloves and a hairnet, was waiting for him outside, chatting with Darvesh.

"Lattes. Double shots," Kennicott said, passing a cup to each of them.

"Just what the doctor ordered." Ho peeled back the lid and took a drink. "Been a long night."

"Thank you," Darvesh said.

"How did it go?" Kennicott asked Ho.

"We combed through the whole building site. Except for the shed where the body was, we didn't find a drop of blood anywhere." He looked at Darvesh. "You two suit up. Then I can take you inside."

Darvesh produced two sets of protective gear, and he and Kennicott quickly slipped them on. Inside the shed, the body was gone and it was even hotter than yesterday. LED lights had been set up in the corners, flooding the room with a harsh white luminance. Two technicians were on their hands and knees on the floor. A third was examining a side wall, inch by inch. On the floor, thin yellow arrows pointed at tiny dots of blood nearby. Every item in the room had been tagged and labeled.

"No sign of struggle anywhere, is there?" Kennicott said.

"Not a thing," Ho said. "Only in Toronto would a developer get murdered with construction materials and not even put up a fight."

Kennicott laughed, then caught the look on Darvesh's face. They both knew Ho would be happy to keep talking, and they had things to do.

"We're going to look around the alley."

Outside the shed, they took off their protective gear and left through the back gate, where two other police officers were standing guard. Kennicott had ordered that the gate not be touched and was happy to see it was still open the way he'd found it yesterday.

"You interviewed the site superintendent," he said to Darvesh. "He confirmed there were no surveillance cameras back here, didn't he?"

"Yes. Claudio Bassante. He said Fox didn't want any."

They walked to where the alley turned south and Kennicott peered up at the buildings lining the east side. "And there are no cameras in the alleyway."

"None. The places that face Spadina would have a camera out front, if they have one at all. On the west side, it's mostly rundown rooming houses."

"Hiding in plain sight," Kennicott said. "It's a perfect spot for Fox to meet someone in secret."

"Right. Someone such as Cassandra Amberlight. Her fingerprints were on one of the glasses inside Fox's shed. Rebar is heavy, but she's a big woman. She and Fox hated each other, and she'd just organized the rally against him."

"True," Kennicott said.

"To which she showed up at late. And Fox went to great lengths yesterday to make sure no one knew where he was. Maybe he'd arranged a secret meeting with Amberlight and things went wrong. They struggled. Maybe he fell and knocked himself out when he hit the ground. And then maybe . . ."

"Maybe."

"She had motive and opportunity," Darvesh said.

"I know," Kennicott said.

Damned if he was going to rush to a conclusion and arrest the wrong person again. He looked down the alley.

"How did Amberlight get here unseen?" he asked. "Everyone in Kensington knows her. She'd tower over half the crowd. She must have come this way, but it looks like a dead end."

He started walking down the south leg of the alley. Darvesh followed him. Kennicott mentally counted his strides. It took one hundred and twenty to get to the fence at the bottom. It had a hole in it, large enough for even a big person to step through. There, a small path to his right took them to Oxford, the east-west street between Spadina and Augusta. Directly across Oxford, there was another alley leading south to Nassau Street, where Amberlight lived above a cheese shop.

This must have been her route, Kennicott thought. She had walked through her home turf unseen. But why would Cassandra Amberlight, of all people, have met with Livingston Fox?

And how could she have got into the construction site if Fox hadn't opened the back gate for her?

26

"**G**ood morning, Cassandra," Greene said as he walked into Ted DiPaulo's spacious kitchen, which overlooked his backyard and the lush valley below. DiPaulo, who was an excellent cook, was making a large omelette filled with asparagus, spinach, and goat cheese. It smelled wonderful.

Amberlight sat in a corner by the sliding glass doors, slumped in a soft chair. She looked worn down, exposed, and vulnerable, like a performer who'd taken off her wig and makeup after a show.

"Hello." Her voice was flat.

Last night, after the three of them had met on Greene's front porch, they'd come here and talked for hours, until Amberlight was exhausted. Greene told her to get some rest, and she'd slept over in DiPaulo's guest bedroom.

Amberlight stared at the floor. She was a defence lawyer's nightmare: arrogant, defensive, suspicious, evasive, self-absorbed, confrontational. But was she a killer?

"I just spoke to Detective Kennicott, the officer in charge of the case," he told her.

"What?" She slammed her hand on the armrest and sat up straight. "Why the hell did you do that?"

"They're looking for you."

"I thought you were working for us."

"I thought they should know that whoever killed Fox hadn't killed you too."

"Oh," Amberlight said. "As if the cops care."

"Now Kennicott knows you're getting legal advice and that you're not on the run."

"I'm hardly on the run, more like a prisoner," she snapped.

"Kennicott wants to talk to you. He wants to hear your alibi and why you disappeared after the demonstration. I said I hoped to bring you into the Homicide office soon."

"Soon, what does soon mean?"

"I said tomorrow afternoon. I assumed Ted needed more time to prepare you."

"I'd like to have a week," DiPaulo said, jumping into the conversation. "If she's going to give a sworn statement, this is not a simple matter."

"I know. But the longer you wait, the weaker her alibi becomes."

"What did you promise him?" DiPaulo asked.

"I told him I think Cassandra is innocent and that she should make a statement. It planted a seed of doubt. But I warned him that her lawyer would try to shut her up."

DiPaulo chuckled. "On very rare occasions I tell my clients it would be best if they talked to the police. Very, very rare."

"I don't get it," Cassandra said, her face red with anger. "Why should I tell the police anything if they want to arrest me?"

"Because," Greene said, keeping his tone measured, "your prints are in the shed."

"Of course my prints are in the shed," Amberlight shouted, jumping to her feet. "I had nothing to hide. I didn't kill him. I told both of you that already."

She started to pace around the kitchen. "I bet the police aren't even going to investigate anyone else. I'm an easy target because I put myself out there. I challenge the establishment, and this is what happens every time."

Greene tried to catch DiPaulo's eye, but he was busy cooking.

"Don't you see, this is a classic case of tunnel vision? Cops." She said the word with total disdain. "What if I make a statement and this detective friend of yours doesn't believe me?"

They were almost the same height. Greene looked her in the eye. "If he doesn't believe you, he'll arrest you. But if you don't make a state-ment, he'll arrest you anyhow, and then the jury will wonder why you didn't go to the police to help out by telling them you met with Fox just before he was killed. Add to that the fact that you don't have a witness to your alibi, and you'll probably lose at trial."

He turned to DiPaulo, who had dished the omelette out onto three plates.

"Sorry, Cassandra. Ari is right."

"This is unbelievable," she shouted. She stomped back to her chair and flopped down. Deflated.

DiPaulo put the plates down on the table. "Cassandra, come on, eat."

She shot him an angry glare but pulled herself up. They all sat at the table. No one spoke.

Greene's legs were tired from working all week and from too little sleep. He was suddenly starving. He took a bite of the omelette. It tasted delicious.

Amberlight didn't touch her food. "What if I went to visit my sister in Vermont this afternoon?" she asked.

"That would be a disaster," DiPaulo said. "You're a lawyer. You know about post-offence conduct, consciousness of guilt. Every little thing you've done since you met with Fox, and every little thing that you do until you give them a statement, will be put under a microscope."

"I feel like a rat in a cage." She rested her head in her hand. "You're a former homicide detective. What would it take for you to arrest me?"

Greene coughed and straightened his shirt collar.

She laughed. "And you were the one last night who told me not to hesitate when I was asked a tough question."

He laughed with her. There was something vulnerable and likeable about Amberlight, once you got past her natural aggression.

"I wouldn't arrest you yet," Greene said.

"Well, that's reassuring."

"I'd check out every other possible suspect first. And if none of them panned out—"

"You'd slap the cuffs on me, wouldn't you?"

"First I'd check you out head to toe."

"Wonderful. I'll look like the bitch queen of the year to a jury. They'll despise me from day one of the trial."

"I have the feeling that if you testify, they'd believe you, but only if you do one thing."

"What's that?"

"Tell the whole truth."

"I've told you everything that happened yesterday afternoon," Amberlight said. "Everything." She took up her knife and fork and cut into the omelette.

"Everything? You didn't tell us that twenty years ago you were convicted for stabbing your husband, then two years later for assaulting your wife. Nor did you mention that as soon as you could you had your criminal record expunged."

She dropped her fork. "I thought that when it was expunged it was gone forever."

"No such luck." Greene shook his head. He reached into his briefcase and pulled out the package that Lindsmore had slipped through the window of his car. He tossed it on the table in front of DiPaulo.

"This is a complete list of all your client's police contacts, arrests, charges that have been withdrawn, and convictions. I suggest you go over every one of them before she says a word to the police."

Greene stood to leave. "The easiest way to talk yourself into a conviction is to lie or leave something out."

DiPaulo looked tense.

Amberlight looked ashen. "But I didn't mean to—"

Greene put his hand up to stop her. "No. You didn't think we'd find out. You have twenty-four hours with Ted to get your story straight."

He was dying to finish his omelette, but instead he walked out.

27

Every article Kennicott had read about Fox last night and this morning had mentioned his five-storey office building on Front Street East. Fox had saved one of the city's historic buildings from destruction, preserved its gorgeous facade, and had designed and supervised the renovation himself down to the last detail. His spectacular personal office, which took up most of the top floor, had been used many times as a TV and movie set and was regularly rented out for high-fashion photo shoots.

A sleek elevator whisked Kennicott up to a minimally furnished reception area on the fifth floor, where sunlight flooded in from every direction through floor-to-ceiling windows. A young woman with half of her hair shaved off and the other half in braids was perched on a spindly chair in front of a sleek rectangular table. Her eyes were puffy. She'd been crying.

"Detective Kennicott," he said. "I'm here to see Maxine."

"She's expecting you. Maxine's amazing. She was here before anyone else this morning."

"This must be terrible for her."

"I can't even imagine. If you go to your right, that column you see is Mr. Fox's private elevator. There's a glass door on the other side. In ten seconds I'll buzz you in. Maxine's office is on the left across from Mr. Fox's."

He walked around the elevator shaft and opened the frosted glass door when he heard a soft buzz. He entered a hallway. To his right was an enormous glassed-in office, sparsely furnished with long flat tables and cabinets, architect's drawing boards and easels, and two chairs facing each other by the window. Everything was square and clean. There were no blinds, and the view of the harbour and the lake beyond was stunning.

On the other side of the hallway was a traditional wooden door that seemed laughably out of place. A cheap-looking brass label on it read "Maxine Daley, Executive Assistant to Mr. Fox," and underneath the handle a sticker with a smiley face read "I'm a Newfoundlander. My door is always open."

Sure enough, the door was half open. Kennicott knocked. He heard a chair squeak, then footsteps. Maxine opened the door the rest of the way. She was wearing a brown long-sleeved dress and a green scarf around her neck. Her graying hair was pulled back and her eyes were red. He hadn't noticed yesterday how short she was.

"Come in, Detective Kennicott. Thank you for getting here early," she said in her lilting accent.

One wall of her small office was covered with a mishmash of photos, all of them seemingly taken on the same wharf in a harbour packed with multicoloured fishing boats. He looked closely at one of the photographs of several couples and families bunched together. Maxine was standing to one side, a smile on her face but no one beside her. A painting of a large house up on a cliff, with a sign reading Daley Youth Shelter, dominated the space behind her sturdy wooden desk. The south wall featured a garish map of Newfoundland in a plastic frame beside a window with a view of the lake.

On one side of her desk there was a wooden box with the words "Please Donate to Our Youth Shelter" stencilled on the side. On the other side was a box of tissues and a telephone.

"I've never liked the expression 'sorry for your loss,'" Kennicott said as he reached in his jacket for his wallet. "It seems to trivialize things."

She didn't wear a wedding ring. There was a bulge of tissues in the cuff of her sleeve. "I was Livingston's nanny before I came here to work for him," she said. "I still remember how hard it rained the day he poured concrete for his first building. Gloria and I were there. We were so nervous and so excited."

Without saying a word, Kennicott pulled out a twenty-dollar bill and put it in the donation box.

"Did you know that a third of the homeless people back home are youth?" she said. "The children thank you for your generosity."

"It's the least I can do."

"Detective, who would do this awful thing to my boy?"

"That's why I'm here. I'm hoping you can help me trace Mr. Fox's movements yesterday. It's vital we know where he went, who he met with, what he did."

She half smiled. "Livingston was always on the move, even as a little baby. If I put him in the crib, he'd go stir-crazy. He never bothered to crawl. No, no, not my Livingston. He was walking at seven months. You believe that?"

Be patient, Kennicott told himself, the way Greene was with witnesses. People in shock need time to cope and to pour out their memories of the recently dead. He was hoping she had some kind of day planner for Fox. Probably not a digital one, as he couldn't see any sign of a computer in this old-fashioned office.

She walked around her desk and sat on a high-backed chair that was much too big for her. He wondered if her feet even touched the floor. She turned over a folder. A label with the words "Detective Kennicott" was squarely placed in the middle. The folder looked used, and he could see the label had been placed over at least one other one.

She noticed him staring at the folder. "I've used this folder five times now," she said with a light laugh. "I was the oldest of seven. Waste not, want not, that's what my mother always said."

"Can't argue with that."

"I prepared this chart for you. I hope it is what you require."

"Thank you." He opened the file. There were several documents, each held together by a staple in the top left corner. The first one was a printout of Fox's day planner, one page per day, for the last month. "This is extremely helpful."

He looked at the back of the pages and saw they were filled with print. Nothing relevant. She'd reused the paper.

"We were poor growing up. You get used to not throwing anything away," she said with a chuckle. "Father was lost at sea a month after my youngest sister was born. My uncle Horace tried to help out, but he had six of his own to feed."

She turned to the window, her eyes fixed on the water. "I told Livingston when he designed this office that I needed to be able to see the harbour from my desk. It reminds me of when I was a girl, how I used to go down to the wharf in the mornings hoping that Daddy had come home."

Kennicott said nothing. He knew how one tragedy could trigger memories of an earlier one. His parents were killed in a suspicious car accident four years before Michael was murdered, leaving him with no family, and in his mind the two losses were always linked. A year after his brother's death, when the murderer still hadn't been found, he'd quit his job as a lawyer and become a policeman, with the goal of doing just this—being a homicide detective.

"For a young man you are very patient," Maxine said, returning her attention to him.

She reached under her desk and a pop-up stand brought up a laptop. "Livingston got this for me so I could keep my desk clean."

She tapped the keyboard and turned the screen to show him an open spreadsheet. "Here's the contact information for every name mentioned. It's all in your file."

Kennicott looked through the papers for the printout. Maxine had highlighted phone numbers in yellow, email addresses in red.

"Perfect."

"I send Livingston a draft itinerary at seven every night, and the next morning we go over it at our daily eight o'clock meeting. Livingston believes in starting work early."

"Tell me about your morning meetings," he said.

"We meet in here. It might surprise you, but Livingston likes my old-fashioned office. I give him his healthy snacks for the day that his chef has made him and the bottles of water that his nutritionist has prepared. Three for the morning and three for the afternoon. Blue, orange, and yellow, that way he can remember the proper order to drink them in. I always have his gym bag ready to go with freshly laundered gear for his next workout. At nine-thirty, Sherani takes Livingston's elevator up here to get her assignment of where she's driving him that day."

Kennicott looked at Fox's schedule for yesterday. He'd started the day with a workout, had a series of fifteen-minute meetings at the office, then a meeting at eleven at a place called Omni Jewelcrafters, and lunch with his father, which ended at two o'clock. There were no appointments for the rest of the day.

"Do you know where he went after two o'clock?"

"No. Every week there are blanks in his schedule. Livingston calls them his alone times."

Kennicott could tell from the look on her face that Maxine didn't approve. She probably assumed that alone time meant time Fox had booked to slip off with one of his girlfriends.

"You have no idea where he went after two o'clock?"

"You can ask Sherani. She's got the car all ready to go. Just take Livingston's private elevator down to B1, it goes right to his parking spot. She can drive you everywhere she took him yesterday."

Her eyes misted over. She glanced at the tissue box.

"How about texts, emails, phone calls? Did he touch base with you after two?"

"No. He took Friday afternoons off. Even turned his phone off. Unless he had some kind of an emergency, I'd never hear from him again until Saturday morning."

"And yesterday?"

She shook her head.

He looked out the window. Give her some time, he thought.

"Take a close look, Detective," she said at last. "We're building Fox Harbour right there on the waterfront. I walk down there sometimes before I come to work. I went there this morning, and it was peaceful."

Kennicott looked where she was pointing. "It's a large piece of land."

"Oh my. It's such a huge development, our biggest project ever. It will take years to build. Then it's going to block my view of the water, but I suppose that's the price you pay for success."

Kennicott nodded. Not wanting to break her train of thought.

"Well, we *were* going to build it," she said, her voice trailing off.

He turned back to her. "You must have been very proud of him," he said as gently as he could.

She tucked another tissue into her sleeve. "He was my boy," she said.

He stood up. "You can't imagine how helpful this is."

She did her best to smile. "Please leave the door open on your way out. I like the fresh air. It comes from growing up by the sea."

28

Alison trotted down the steps to the outdoor subway platform at the midtown Rosedale station. Sheena Persad, the TV reporter, was standing at the far end with her back against the wall, reading a copy of *People*, just as Alison had instructed her to do. She had a small backpack slung over one shoulder. There was no breeze, and the air was thick and hot.

Alison was wearing a new Blue Jays baseball cap and cheap sunglasses that she'd just bought. She didn't turn her head as she passed Persad. Ten paces away she pulled a copy of the *Toronto Star* from a new backpack she'd bought at the same place she'd got the sunglasses. This one was black, *not* yellow. She opened the newspaper and started to read. When the train arrived, they both entered the last car through different doors. There were three people inside, sitting near the front. Alison motioned toward the back. Persad followed and sat down beside her.

"Thanks for the flowers," Persad said when the train started up. "Very smart way to get a message to me in the greeting card."

"Safer than text or email."

"You got half the newsroom guessing the identity of my secret admirer." She laughed lightly.

"It worked. I'm here, and no one knows."

Alison pointed at Persad's phone. "Do you mind? Please turn it off. No recordings. And erase the last two minutes. With my English accent, I stand out."

Persad hesitated. "Okay. But I need to take notes."

"Get rid of my voice on the tape first."

Persad erased the recording and handed the phone to Alison. "Here. Take it as a show of good faith."

"Okay, keep your phone," Alison said. "You can take notes."

Persad pulled out a notebook and a pen. "Can I get your name?"

"No."

"How old are you?"

Alison shook her head.

"Do you have a background in journalism?"

Alison kept shaking her head.

"At least tell me how you got that photo of Fox."

"I need to know I can trust you first."

"What do you want me to do?"

"Get me a copy of all the footage your cameraman shot yesterday at the demonstration."

Alison needed to find out if she could be picked out of the crowd, and whether she'd been filmed cutting out of the march and walking behind the house on Augusta.

The tinny sound of the train's speaker came on. "Next stop Summerhill Station," a bland female voice said.

"This is a murder investigation," Persad said. "If you have any information that might help the police, you should—"

"I don't," Alison said.

The train was slowing. She stood up. Persad stood up with her.

"Why should I give you that footage?" she asked.

"Because you'll have a headline story if you get an exclusive interview with the Kensington Blogger."

"The raw footage is about two hours long."

"I need to see it all."

"The police already have it."

"I'm sure the station kept a copy. It's all digital. Won't take you long to download it onto a stick for me."

"You seem to know a lot about how journalists work."

Alison pulled out a plastic bag containing a flash drive that she'd also bought this morning. Persad held out her hand and Alison dropped the drive into it. She kept the bag, and stuffed it back into her pocket. This way, no fingerprints. After all, she was the daughter of a detective.

"Thanks," Alison said, "for not outing me last night on TV."

The doors slid open and several people entered the car. Alison and Persad moved to the side to let them pass.

"I need a few hours," Persad said.

A chime sounded and the doors began to close.

"I'll be back on the platform at four. Same spot," Alison said. She hopped out onto the platform an instant before the doors closed firmly behind her.

29

Fox's private elevator whisked Kennicott down to B1 in seconds. The door opened onto a parking garage like nothing he'd ever seen before. Fox's Rolls-Royce finned convertible was the only car there, resting on a rubberized floor. Spotlights shone down on it as if the vehicle were a star performer on stage. It was so highly polished it glimmered.

Sherani, a striking young woman with black hair that cascaded to her waist, was standing at the passenger door, which she opened as he approached.

"Welcome, Detective," she said in a cool, detached voice.

"Thank you for touring me around. I'm sure this is very difficult for you."

"Mr. Fox was an excellent employer."

"Interesting vehicle."

"Mr. Fox loved this car. He bought it for himself on his thirtieth birthday. It's a reconditioned 1958 Rolls-Royce Silver Cloud, a model nicknamed the Honeymoon Express because it has only two seats. The company just made two of them. Mr. Fox never wanted to sit in the back."

Fox sure knew how to promote himself as a rich and successful developer, Kennicott thought. But who was he really, behind the image he tried so hard to cultivate?

"Must be fun to drive."

"It was enjoyable with Mr. Fox."

Kennicott climbed in. She shut the door behind him, got in the driver's seat, and put the Rolls in gear. A garage door opened silently, and in moments they were on the street. Kennicott had never been in a car that rode this smoothly or a leather seat that felt this luxurious.

"How long have you been working for Mr. Fox?"

"Eleven months. Mr. Fox hires his chauffeurs for one year. He pays us very well so that we can pay off our student loans. Then he helps us find employment elsewhere."

Despite her cool manner, Kennicott sensed she was more upset by Fox's death than she was letting on.

"What will you do for work now?"

"Everyone says I should go into modeling or acting. But my mother wants me to go to medical school. Mr. Fox set up interviews for me with three female doctors."

"That was nice of him."

"Mr. Fox was kind to me."

Kennicott took out his copy of Fox's itinerary. "Your first stop yesterday was Omni Jewelcrafters."

"We're heading there now."

"Do you know what he was going there to buy?"

She gave him a questioning look. "He goes to Omni every Friday at eleven to meet with other people in the business. They meet there to discuss their deals. You really don't know a lot about real-estate development do you?"

The man had inspired loyalty. She was protective of Fox.

"I'm learning quickly," he said.

Sherani drove in silence, steering the Rolls through a warren of wealthy streets. In fifteen minutes she stopped beside a converted bank. What once must have been a lovely stone corner building was now adorned with a gaudy sign that announced "OMNI^2 JEWEL-CRAFTERS JEWELS & JAVA." Two more signs on either side of the front door blared: "CA$H for GOLD *We Also Buy* Gems, Watches, Diamonds."

"Really?" he asked. "The developers meet here?"

"Apparently the coffee is good, and the owner's wife makes excellent mushroom soup."

"Apparently? You've never been inside?"

"I never leave the car. You going in?"

Kennicott checked his watch. It was 10:59. "I'm not used to having a chauffeur. I'll be back." He reached for the door handle.

"Please do not exit until I open the passenger door for you. That's the way I always did it for Mr. Fox."

Kennicott felt foolish waiting for her to walk around the big car to open his door.

"Thanks. See you in a while," he said as he climbed out.

Inside Omni Jewelcrafters, he was surprised to find a functioning restaurant. Two waitresses were scurrying about, serving diners at tables set beside the windows on the south side of the building. The jewellery store was on the north side, where Kennicott imagined that years ago patrons once lined up to speak to bank tellers. A young couple were trying on diamond rings.

A thin man with a long menu in his hand approached Kennicott.

"Table for one?" he asked.

"I'm not here to eat."

"You looking for a diamond?" He glanced at Kennicott's hands to confirm he wasn't wearing a wedding band.

"No." He kept his voice low. "I'm a police officer and I'm looking to speak to the owner."

"I thought I recognized you from TV last night." The man whirled around. "Adam!" he yelled loud enough for everyone in the noisy restaurant to hear. "The detective on Foxie's murder is here for you!"

A group of men and one woman were seated at a round table in the middle of the restaurant, engaged in animated conversation. The wide-shouldered man sitting closest to the aisle sprang up and rushed over in a few quick, confident steps. He wore a sports jacket, a white shirt with a brown stain on it, and a *kippah* on his nearly bald head.

"Detective Kennicott, what a pleasure to meet you. Adam Lewis, but everyone calls me Ad Man. I'm sure you've seen my commercials on TV. You are most welcome. We all got together today to talk about Foxie. No one can believe it. Come. Come join us."

He put an arm around Kennicott and walked him across the tile floor. "You have to try my wife's mushroom soup. People come for it from Mississauga, Oshawa, you name it. And for the jewellery, of course."

"Thanks. I'm not hungry."

Detective 101: Never eat with your witnesses.

"Thirty-three years of marriage, I've learned: your wife makes soup, you eat her soup."

Lewis waited for Kennicott to laugh, but he didn't oblige.

"I've got some questions for you," Kennicott said.

"And I've got some answers. But please, try the soup," Lewis said. "Everyone, this is Detective Daniel Kennicott, the one we all saw on TV last night."

Interesting. Kennicott hadn't told Lewis his first name and on TV he'd only been identified by his last name. Lewis had been expecting him to show up.

"Detective, sitting here in front of you is the whole history of real-estate development in this city." Lewis pointed to a handsome older man closest to them. "Sid Fream. Sophisticated veteran of the group. Sidney built half of the homes north of Wilson in the fifties and sixties." Fream gave Kennicott a firm handshake.

"Tony Mantelli. Three-quarters of those high-rises on the outskirts of the city, Tony built them. Developers. Builders. First the Jews, then the Italians. These guys are the pioneers, they started by spending their last penny on concrete they poured on weekends. Unbelievable."

Mantelli was a slight man but his grip was like iron.

"Next is Arthur Locke. Banker and token WASP. We joke that he's the ethnic one. Used to be the bankers wouldn't lend a nickel to anyone they didn't go to private school with. Boy, the city has changed."

Locke was the only one in a suit and tie. His handshake was weak.

"Amresh Singh. I like to say he's got me topped. I wear a *kippah* that barely covers half my bald spot. He wears a turban and says he's got a full head of hair. Who knows? He's Mr. Trucking. You want to build in this city, you have to have trucks.

"Next comes beauty before age. And brains and *chutzpah*, Jamaican style. Odessa Breaker, marathon runner, whiz-bang accountant turned low-income housing czar."

Breaker wore bright red lipstick and stylish glasses, which she took off before reaching over to take his hand. He nodded instead of shaking hands.

"Pleasure," she said, meeting his eyes.

"Finally, the empty seat. Foxie's chair," Lewis said. "We can't believe it. Right, guys? Please, please, Detective, sit there. We gathered here today to remember our good friend. I can't stand to see his seat empty."

Kennicott sat down and began to question each of them about their involvement with the young developer, their whereabouts on Friday afternoon and any ideas they had about who might have had a bone to pick with Fox. The conversation was lively. A bowl of mushroom soup arrived and he ate a spoonful to be polite. It was delicious.

He tried to spend no more time talking to Breaker than to any of the others, but her chair was next to his.

"Where were you yesterday afternoon?" he asked her.

"Yesterday afternoon?" She looked him square in the eye, then broke out into a broad grin and laughed. "I was running down by the lake. You look fit. You a runner?"

"I used to be, when I had a job with more regular hours."

"You think my job is easy? You just have to stop making excuses for yourself."

Cell phone alarms started ringing all around the table. Lewis put his hand up.

"It's our five-minute warning," he said to Kennicott, as they all reached for their phones. "It was Foxie's idea. We all turn our phones off at eleven and set our alarms for eleven fifty-five."

Lewis balled his hands into fists and brought them down hard on the table. "Detective, everyone here will do absolutely everything in our power to help you find the bastard who did this to our friend."

He stood and raised his phone. "Okay, group photo time." He brought out a extendable selfie stick, put his phone on it, and pulled it out a long way. "These things are amazing. I could use this to spy on my neighbours if I wanted to, not that I'd want to, Detective."

This provoked a round of laughter.

"This was Foxie's idea. A group photo every week," he said to Kennicott as he snapped away. "Now it's a tradition."

When he was done, Kennicott took out a pen and a small stack of his business cards. "I'm giving all of you my personal cell number," he said, writing on the back of each card. "Don't hesitate to contact me directly if anything else occurs to you."

Everyone reached into their wallets and pulled out cards that they passed to him.

The last card Kennicott prepared was for Breaker and, along with his number, he wrote: *We should talk.*

He gave it to her. She looked at it and didn't flinch. While the others were busy packing up, she quickly took out a second card, wrote something on the back, and passed it to him under the table.

Everyone stood. "My partner, Detective Kamil Darvesh, will contact each of you for individual interviews," he said as he shook each of their hands. Breaker was the last to leave.

"Maybe I'll see you later," she said, keeping her voice low enough that only he could hear. She shook his hand, holding it longer than he expected.

"What did you think of my wife's soup?" Lewis asked, when everyone was gone.

"You're right, it's very good," Kennicott said, spotting a fresh soup stain on Lewis's shirt. "You take a photo of the group every Friday. Can I see the one you took yesterday?"

"Of course. Foxie was wearing a cool linen suit from Italy, a real beauty. He was such a sharp dresser."

Lewis started tapping on his phone. "Let's see," he said. "No, not that one, Foxie's got his eyes closed. That one too. Here he woke up for this one."

He turned his phone for Kennicott to see. There was Livingston wearing a light grey suit with a blue shirt and a thin dark green tie. The photo was taken at noon yesterday. At four in the afternoon when his body was found, he was wearing shorts and a T-shirt.

Where had Fox changed out of his suit, and where had he left it before he went to the shed at Kensington Gate? And why?

30

Claudio Bassante stood at the elevator doors on the thirty-third floor of his downtown condo building, and for one of the few times since Greene had known him, he wasn't smiling. He looked grim.

"Ari," he said, extending his arm as Greene stepped out of the elevator. "I'm glad you called."

Greene grasped his hand. "You sleep last night?"

"Not much. They had me at the station giving a statement for a few hours. You're a cop. You're used to this kind of thing. Not me."

Greene put his free hand on Bassante's shoulder. They walked down the hall to his front door and Bassante ushered him inside. Floor-to-ceiling windows gave on to a breathtaking view of a forest of new high-rise buildings and the blue harbour beyond. Everything was modern, from the grey hardwood floors, marble countertops, and an expansive kitchen island to the spanking-new high-end appliances and plush leather furniture.

It was not the kind of place Greene had expected Claudio to live in. Bassante grew up a suburban kid. When he was sixteen, he bought a used truck and spent most of his weekends fixing it up. He got married when he was twenty-one, bought a new truck and a bungalow three blocks north of his mother's house. Every few years after that, he bought a bigger house and a bigger truck until he got divorced.

"Nice spot," Greene said. "Where do you park your truck?"

Bassante laughed. "It's long gone. My ex took the house, and I had nowhere to park it. You remember my parent's little house. Every other place on the street got turned into a monster home. When Mom passed, I cashed in. I thought, the girls are gone, my wife is gone, what the hell, Claudio, live a little."

"You like it downtown?"

"Love it. In the winter I can walk underground to the ACC to watch the Leafs or the Raptors. The gym is great, and half the people here are divorced. It's not exactly lonely."

Bassante went to his brushed-steel fridge and opened it. "You want a juice or smoothie or anything? I've got these hand-pressed juices they sell downstairs."

"I'm fine."

Bassante took out a small glass bottle of green liquid. "Livingston was a genius. He was always way ahead of the curve. Everyone thought he was out of his mind when he put up a condo tower down here. Prices in this city are nuts. My unit's gone up twenty-five percent since I bought it a year ago. Same thing with his Fox Harbour development. He was taking that huge piece of scrap land by the water and building a whole frickin' neighbourhood."

Greene ran his hands along the marble countertop on the island. It was cool and smooth.

Bassante unscrewed the cap. "I'm seeing this Pilates instructor. She's got me into these. Twelve bucks for this little bottle. Crazy, eh?" He drank half of the bottle, recapped it, and put it on the counter.

He was stalling.

Greene waited.

"Ari, I didn't see you for a long time. When Sylvia left me, I was a mess. I couldn't eat. I lost forty pounds. Me losing weight! I lost my job. I was sleeping all day, up all night."

Ari could read between the lines. "Coke?" he asked.

"Coke. Meth. You name it. If I could pop it, shoot it, sniff it. Money went *puff*. Everyone knows everyone in this business and soon my name was mud. Then out of nowhere three years ago Maxine, Fox's assistant, calls me. She recommended me to Fox, and he hired me to put up a three-storey condo in the West End. Wood-frame construction and no underground parking. Forty-five-million-dollar job. Easy. I got it finished six weeks early. Right on budget too."

"Let me guess." Greene leaned on the island. "He gave you a cash bonus."

"Fox? No way. Okay, everyone in this crazy business throws around cash like it was candy, but not Livingston. He was the exception to the rule. Everything with him was by the book. You don't know how rare that is in this town."

"And you, Claudio?"

"Shit, Ari. Look, it's construction. Everyone hates the taxman. You don't want to know how much cash is floating around. I had two girls to put through college. The alimony I was paying . . ."

He put the bottle back in the fridge and slammed the door. "You see this? It's a fancy French fridge. Retail it's five thousand. And that Italian stove? You don't want to know what people pay for one of them retail. I get things. I do people favours. They do me favours."

"But not Fox?"

"I'm telling you no, never. Never."

Greene pulled up a stool and sat down.

"Ari, what do you want to talk to me about? I thought you weren't a cop anymore."

"I've been hired to help the lawyer of one of the suspects, and I think his client is innocent. If I can't find out who killed Fox, I'm afraid the client will be arrested."

"You know what that feels like."

Greene nodded. "How was Fox's business doing?" he asked. "Really."

"Being a developer is like being a shark. You can't ever sleep. It takes forever to get a project up and paying, at least seven years. The banks are up our asses all the time. Insurance. Unions. Condo boards. City inspectors. Politicians. Planners. That crane at Kensington Gate is costing us thirty thousand a month to rent. We get a windy day, there's the two crane operators who we have to pay while they twiddle their thumbs, the formers can't work without the crane and the interest keeps ticking on the bank line. Banks get paid no matter what, even if the site is idle. That's about five G's a day. This winter, with the cold and the high winds, we got shut down for seventeen workdays. Cost us a fortune."

Greene walked over to the window. A plane was leaving from the Island Airport. Beyond the harbour, Lake Ontario stretched out to the horizon, a huge pool of blue.

"The Rolls-Royce, the chauffeur, the ultra-modern office. All just image?"

"Smoke and mirrors. It was as if Fox was stuck in that role. Maxine was always telling him to cut expenses. It drove her crazy how he'd keep on spending." Bassante came up beside Greene and pointed to a piece of vacant land on the waterfront. "See the hoarding around that big empty lot? He was taking on an insane amount of debt. He couldn't stop."

"You think this had to do with someone he owed money?"

"All I know is that this business is a fucking fistfight. Every hour of every day someone's in your pocket. If you're not tough, you'll get squashed like a bug."

"Or murdered. You notice anything different about him lately?"

"The last month or so, I could tell something was up. He was being more secretive than ever. Then boom, two weeks ago he's engaged. He changed."

"How?"

"Calmer. Happier. But more guarded. He told me a few weeks ago he thought someone was trying to steal some new idea he was working on but he couldn't figure out who it was. Fox was obsessed with his privacy."

Greene started counting building cranes. It took him a few seconds to get to fifteen. "You ever see Fox with Cassandra Amberlight?"

"The protest lady? She your client?"

Greene shrugged.

"Fox and Amberlight together? You must be joking."

"He ever mention her to you?"

"All the time. She drove him berserk."

Bassante joined Greene at the window and waved his arm across the sky. "The city's out of control. Look. Condos are going up faster than the interest on my Visa card. Most people have no idea what's really going on. Prices are so crazy, how will my daughters be able to live here? Everyone is getting pushed out of town and the politicians? Useless. They can't stop it. You know thirty percent of new units are empty. Iranians, Russians, Chinese investors, they're all dumping their cash here. Third World dictators, human traffickers, and drug dealers. Some of them buy a condo so they can deal indoors instead of out on the street. It's a fucking cash-flow laundromat out there."

"What did you know about Fox's plans for the K2 condos in Kensington Market?"

This made Bassante pause. "Nothing. I kept asking him about it, and he kept putting me off. I couldn't figure it out. But he was up to something, and I'm sure it pissed somebody off."

Greene took a close look at his old friend. Bassante always put on a jolly face, but he looked frazzled.

"What about the back gate on your building site? I didn't see any video cameras."

"Fox wouldn't allow it."

"Did you know he was meeting people there?"

"No, just that for the last four weeks he told me to be sure nobody went back there on Fridays after two-thirty."

They stood in silence looking out at the water. Greene and Bassante had known each other for so long they didn't have to speak all the time.

"I'm thinking of getting a boat," Bassante said at last. "I'd get the girls to come down here. See them more."

"Claudio," Greene said, "if you were me, where would you look for the killer?"

"Fox had a lot of enemies. We were throwing up buildings faster, and for less money, than most of the old farts who ran this town for years. Our places were better. Look how beautiful this condo is. No one could compete with us."

"You think one of his competitors wanted him out of the way?"

"A builder, a banker, a candlestick maker. It's construction, Ari. Follow the money."

Bassante leaned against the window. He looked as if he was about to collapse.

"You okay, Claudio?"

"No. They killed Fox. Whoever did this probably thinks I know something. I could be next."

"I understand."

"No, Ari," Bassante said, "I don't think you do."

31

Sherani was waiting for Kennicott on the street outside Omni Jewelcrafters, standing beside the Rolls-Royce. She saw him approach and swung open the passenger door and closed it once he was seated.

Imagine living like this all the time, he thought, as he watched her walk around the car and get into the driver's seat.

"You try the mushroom soup?" she asked.

"It was excellent."

"Told you."

He reached into his pocket and peeked at the card Breaker had slipped him. The front read "Odessa Breaker, Planning Consultant." On the back, her handwriting was precise: "7:00 tonight at the Fox Harbour bldg. site. Bring running shoes. Tell no one."

He slid the card back in his pocket. Yesterday Fox had lunched with his father at Fresh. That was their next stop. While Sherani drove, Kennicott called and asked to speak to the owner.

"Etai here, how can I help you?"

"My name is Daniel Kennicott. I'm a homicide detective. I understand that Mr. Livingston Fox ate lunch there yesterday."

"We're all very sad about what happened to Mr. Fox," Etai said.

"I'd like to talk to the person who served him."

"Adrianna. She's working today."

"We are on our way there now. No need to tell her I'm coming."

When they arrived, the restaurant's west-facing patio was packed with diners soaking up the sun. Inside, Kennicott introduced himself to Etai, who seated him at a table by the back wall. Adrianna came in a minute later. She was a slight young woman with a red-and-black tattoo snaking down her right arm.

"Etai said you wanted to speak to me?"

"I'm Detective Daniel Kennicott, Toronto Police. Have a seat."

She looked around to check that there was no one nearby.

He showed her a picture of Fox. "Did you serve this man yesterday at lunch?"

She put her hands behind her back, as if she were afraid to touch the photo, and nodded. "I heard what happened. I can't believe Livingston is dead."

She called him Livingston, Kennicott thought.

"How well did you know him?"

Kennicott saw a flash of fear in her eyes.

"He ate lunch here on Fridays."

"Do you remember who he was with yesterday?"

"His father. As usual. Table eight. Twelve-thirty. They were fighting like they do all the time."

"Did you hear what they were arguing about?"

"Not really, but I know what the problem was."

Kennicott sat still. Fox's father had complained about his son flirting with the waitress.

"He's engaged, you know," she said. "I don't want to hurt anyone."

Kennicott leaned forward and lowered his voice. "I understand. How often did you see each other?"

"Tuesday mornings. We'd do a hot yoga class before my lunch shift. I live around the corner from the studio. He'd come back to my place for an hour. A month ago, he stopped. He said he was afraid his fiancée would find out, that for once in his life he was going to try to be loyal. Please, don't tell her."

"What did Livingston tell you about his family?"

"He loved his sister and hated his parents, especially his mother. He kept giving them money for their dumb wellness centre and they kept losing it. He called them hippie losers. After he got engaged, he told them that he was going to stop funding them and cut them out of his will." She started to tear up. "That's all I know."

He passed her a napkin, and she thanked him before rushing off.

32

Greene drove along College Street and glanced over at the Kensington Gate building site. As he'd hoped, there wasn't a heavy police presence at the scene.

To be sure, he drove down Spadina to Oxford and circled back up Augusta. He'd walked up and down this street on his way to and from work all week and hadn't once noticed any signs of life in the house just south of the construction site. He drove past it now and glanced down the alley. A police officer was stationed at the back gate. Another was strolling along the sidewalk. Good, Greene thought.

He kept his speed constant, crossed over College, and parked on a side street. He had a shopping bag filled with vegetables and another with a tall roll of toilet paper sitting on the passenger seat. He carried them with him as he walked back along the route that he'd just driven, down Spadina, along Oxford, and up Augusta. It was Saturday, and the market was packed with shoppers. This made it easy for him to break away from the crowd and, when the officer patrolling Augusta turned in the other direction, to slip along the path beside the house. If anyone saw him, they'd assume he was on his way home from the grocery store.

The backyard was overgrown and deserted. He put the shopping bags down on an outdoor table by the back window, slipped on a pair of latex gloves, and tried the door. To his surprise it was unlocked. He opened it slowly and stepped inside.

He found himself in an old kitchen. No one was there. He closed the door silently behind him and didn't move. He knew that if you are patient and listen hard, you could hear a house. He heard nothing other than the low buzz of traffic on the street. He made his way through the empty downstairs and up the stairs. On the second floor he checked out the empty rooms, including the one in front that overlooked the street.

The room he most wanted to look at was on the north side. The door to it was closed. He knocked on it lightly, like a boat driver tapping on a gas can to be sure it was empty. The only sound coming back to him was the hollow echo of a vacant room.

Inside, the room was dark. It took a few seconds for his eyes to adjust to the lack of light. A thick curtain covered the one window. There was no furniture except a metal chair beside the curtain.

He studied the chair. It was unexceptional. It could have been a year old, or ten. He pulled back the curtain just enough so he could look outside. From his viewpoint, Greene had a clear view of the work shed where he'd discovered Fox's body. Its window was now covered with brown paper. But it didn't matter. The photo of Fox's corpse hadn't been taken on a selfie stick by someone in the alley. Whoever took it had been standing right here.

He slid the curtain back into place and thought about the chair beside the window. Had the person who took that picture, or someone else, used this location to look into the work shed? Spy on the construction site? Follow Fox's movements?

He retraced his steps. He opened the closets in each of the upstairs rooms. Nothing. Same with the living room and dining room on the first floor. In the kitchen he opened up the upper cabinets. They were all empty too.

This was the house that Fox had paid $30,000 to the owners because of the shadow cast by the building crane, and it was totally deserted. The back door wasn't even locked. He had to find out who owned this house and when they'd bought it.

Even though he was sure it would be a waste of time, he started going through the cabinet doors below the kitchen counter. As he expected, there was nothing there. He got to the last one, under the sink, and opened it.

Inside was a yellow backpack.

33

"How did Mr. Fox seem after his lunch with his father?" Kennicott asked Sherani when he was back in the passenger seat of the Rolls-Royce.

She hesitated. "It was always the same. He was angry."

"Did he say why?"

"He said they always fought about the same thing. Money."

Where there's money there's heat, Kennicott's father used to say. He'd been a judge and had seen plenty of family squabbles over money first-hand.

"Was there anything about Mr. Fox yesterday that seemed unusual?"

"No. Except for talking to his father, he seemed very happy. His fiancée was coming home from Japan, and he told me he couldn't wait to see her."

"There's nothing else listed on his schedule. Where did you go after lunch?"

"I'm heading there now."

She drove without saying anything. She was someone who was comfortable with silence.

He looked out the window and watched the city roll by. People were stopping to look at the car. Fox must have loved the attention, he thought. Or did he?

Sherani pulled into a deserted service-vehicle parking lot behind Lord Landsdowne Public School on Spadina Crescent. They were about half a block north of College Street.

"Here?" Kennicott asked.

"Yes. I let him out right at this spot."

"What time was that?"

She checked her logbook. "Two-fifteen."

"Which way did he go?"

She shrugged with practiced indifference. "I have no idea. I drove away."

"Was this unusual? I mean, Mr. Fox getting out of the car in a parking lot and asking you to leave him here."

"He's done this for the last four Fridays. Right here."

"Did you tell anyone about this?"

"Of course not. Mr. Fox was very private."

"I hate to ask you this, but have you seen the photo of his body that's online?"

"I wish I hadn't. It was awful."

"He wasn't wearing the suit he wore when he was at Omni. He had on a T-shirt and shorts. Did he change his clothes after he left the restaurant?"

She shook her head and pointed over her shoulder. "There's a compartment in back that was designed for picnic baskets. Mr. Fox kept his gym bag and a portable cooler there for his water bottles. Yesterday, when he got out of the vehicle he was still wearing his suit. He took one of the bags that holds his water bottles and his gym bag with him."

"What kind of bag was it?"

"A plain black one. Mr. Fox didn't like labels."

"That was at two-fifteen?"

"Yes."

"And you have no idea where he changed clothes?"

"None."

"Did he say anything else to you before you left?"

She started to shake her head, then stopped. "I don't know if this is important."

"Everything is important." At last she wanted to talk, which was always a good thing.

"He said he'd worked out hard at the gym in the morning. It was as hot yesterday as it is today, and he was tired because of the heat. He said he hadn't hydrated enough."

At least Sherani had opened up, Kennicott thought, even if the information didn't lead anywhere.

He got out of the car door on his own. She frowned.

"Where did you go after you dropped him off?" he asked.

"I drove back to the office, parked the car, and covered it as I do every day."

"And after that?" He realized that it hadn't occurred to Sherani that she might have been the last known person to see Fox alive, that she was a possible suspect, and that Kennicott would want to know if she had an alibi.

Her eyes narrowed in anger. Now she understood what he was questioning her about.

"I went to visit my mother. She's in intensive care at Scarborough General Hospital. I've gone there every day for the last month. Go ahead and check with any of the nurses. Ever since she got sick, Mr. Fox never made me work past four."

"I'm sorry. I had to ask."

"You should know that I loved Mr. Fox. I'll do anything to help catch his killer. Why do you think I offered to drive you around today?"

34

Alison saw the subway train approaching the station before she heard it. She walked quickly over to Persad, who lowered her magazine.

"Did you download the footage?" Alison asked.

Persad pulled out a plastic bag with the flash drive inside. "I've never done anything like this before."

Alison stuffed it in her front pocket.

"Thanks for trusting me," she said, and stepped into the train. "I'll be in touch. Very soon."

She took a seat near the back and pulled her laptop and a pair of headphones from her backpack. The subway car was as good a place as any to view the footage. It was heading north, away from downtown. She plugged in the flash drive.

The video loaded quickly. A timer in the corner showed it started at 3:28 p.m. Alison hadn't left the Chinese restaurant until 3:50. She was tempted to skip ahead but made herself watch from the start.

The first images were of the crowd gathering and milling about. Then came Persad, doing practice takes, setting herself up to go live on camera. After that there were shots of babies and dogs and protest signs and the drummer. Alison knew these were cutaways that an editor could splice in later.

The train stopped and started but no one came near her.

She paused the video at 3:50, just before she'd arrived at the demonstration, and hunched closer to the screen. Please, she thought, don't let me be on this tape. She hit play.

Persad was doing a stand-up, taking up most of the screen. This was followed by a panning shot of the protesters. Alison spotted a Blue Jays hat and watched herself weaving through the crowd. She could make out her sunglasses and a flash of the yellow backpack. Bloody hell.

Please, she kept thinking, let me get out of the picture frame. Instead, the camera followed her.

She watched herself break out of the crowd and go up to the TV van. Her backpack stood out like a beacon. The camera caught her walking along the sidewalk toward the house on Augusta and disappearing down the path, before it turned back to film the protesters marching by.

Thank God her hat and sunglasses had hidden her face. But still, this was not good, especially since she'd left the stupid backpack in the house.

She took the video back to the point where the camera had first picked her up and watched it again. She was only on the screen for just one minute and twelve seconds and the whole tape was two hours and twenty minutes long. That was good, wasn't it? What were the chances of someone noticing her?

She closed the computer. She hadn't been paying any attention to what was going on around her but was vaguely aware that as the train went north, the stations were farther and farther apart.

The train was coming to a stop at a suburban station she'd never seen before. The doors slid open and a horde of teenagers rushed in, laughing and joking with each other. Happy. Not a care. Probably none of them had ever seen the body of a murder victim, never mind been foolish enough to photograph it and post it online. They could go on with their lives. But where was her life going?

The train started again. She put her head back and closed her eyes as it entered a long dark tunnel.

35

Kennicott called Darvesh from the parking lot of the public school and told him where he was.

"Get a team of officers over here right away to scour the area, knock on doors, check every back alley and garbage can."

"What are we looking for?"

"Fox's dress clothes. They might be in a black gym bag. When Fox's chauffeur dropped him off here yesterday, he was wearing a suit. He took the bag with him. Then get hold of Adam Lewis at Omni Jewelcrafters on Bathurst Street. He'll send you a picture of Fox in the outfit we're looking for and give you the contact information of everyone at the Friday morning meeting there. Follow up on their alibis."

He hung up. Why had Fox changed out of his suit? Because he wanted to blend in, not stand out. And which way had he gone from here to the back alley? He wouldn't have walked down Augusta, not with the demonstration getting started there. He must have gone down Spadina and cut over somehow.

Kennicott walked to the front of the school and looked across the road. On the other side an old university building was being renovated. A line of trucks was moving construction waste out.

That's probably what he did, Kennicott thought. Changed quickly in an unseen corner of the service parking lot and tossed the bag into one of the bins.

Kennicott was standing beside a huge oblong rock. He'd driven by it hundreds of times but had never stopped to see what it was. A green plaque was attached to its front.

THIS BASIC IGNEOUS BOULDER WAS FOUND AT A DEPTH
OF 12 FEET DURING THE COURSE OF THE EXCAVATION FOR
THIS SCHOOL. THE COMPOSITION IS A VERY RARE TYPE AND
IS ASSUMED TO HAVE BEEN CARRIED HERE FROM CARIBOU
LAKE, NORTH OF PARRY SOUND, BY A GLACIER DURING THE
GREAT ICE AGE APPROXIMATELY 12,000 YEARS AGO.

He put his hand on the rock. The surface was worn down but rough. What a long journey it had made. So many things buried so deep.

He walked around the crescent and past a gruff-looking group of men smoking cigarettes outside a Scott's Mission homeless shelter; the Waverly, a beat-up old hotel; and the Silver Dollar, a rundown bar. Both buildings had been there for decades. James Earl Ray, the man who killed Martin Luther King, had supposedly stayed at the hotel after he fled to Canada.

When he was a university student, Kennicott had gone to the Silver Dollar on many a drunken Saturday night. He'd heard that a developer wanted to demolish the buildings and put up a high-rise for student housing. This being Toronto, inevitably some local residents had protested and right now the project was stalled. Story of the city.

He crossed College and continued down Spadina, counting his strides as he passed a bank, a bar, a board-game cafe, an art supply store, and a souvenir flag shop. He stopped at forty paces, the distance he estimated would put him parallel with the place where the alleyway behind Kensington Gate turned south, then again after another 120 paces, which by his rough estimate lined up with the end of it. He was standing in front of a Chinese restaurant called Huibing. He went in.

A few people were eating at linoleum-topped tables. He sat down and a young Asian woman came over with a plastic menu under her arm, carrying a white teapot and a small white teacup.

"The lunch specials are on the back," she said, passing him the menu. "We only take cash."

"Thanks."

She turned and went behind the counter, picked up her phone, and started tapping away.

He glanced through the menu and then motioned to her.

She returned with a small pad of paper in her hand.

"I'll have the hot and sour soup, and number six, the shrimp," he said. "Where's the washroom?"

She pointed behind her. "Back there."

He waited until she picked up her phone again before he went down the hallway. The door to the washroom was open. He opened and shut it without going in, then walked past it. A bead curtain hung in a doorway near the end of the hall. He glanced back to be sure that no one was looking and went through the beads into a small empty room with a table and two chairs. Back in the hall, he took a few steps to the back door, which was propped open by a red milk crate.

He stepped outside. He was at the end of the alleyway, by the fence with a hole in it. This was the route that he assumed Amberlight had taken.

He slipped back into the restaurant, opened and shut the bathroom door again, and returned to his table. A bowl of soup was there, and he dug in. It wasn't long until the waitress came with his plate of food.

"I've got a question for you," he said before she could get back to her phone.

"What's that?"

"Did you work here yesterday?"

She frowned. "I work here every day. It's my uncle's restaurant."

"Did you see this man?"

He had a newspaper clipping of Fox's photo in his pocket. He unfolded it. She nodded without hesitation.

"The guy who was killed yesterday. Yeah. He was here."

Kennicott took out his badge. "I'm a homicide detective investigating the case."

"Oh," she said, unimpressed. She pointed at the photo. "He comes on Friday afternoons."

"Every Friday?"

"For the last month or so. He doesn't eat here in the restaurant. There's a backroom, and it's reserved for him. Except yesterday. He didn't come."

"Did he usually meet with someone back there?"

She gave him a dull look. "I don't know. My uncle says we aren't allowed to go back there. I'd take in a teapot and two cups before he got here, and he'd come out every half hour for a fresh pot, bring two used cups and get two clean ones. He always gave me a fifty-dollar tip."

"And yesterday?"

"I told you, he didn't come. I wasn't sure what to do, and after a while I went back."

"What time?"

She shrugged. "Probably a few minutes after three-thirty. A woman was there."

Stay calm, Kennicott told himself. Don't ask her any leading questions.

"What did she look like?"

"White. Skinny. She was wearing a Blue Jays cap and sunglasses, which was kind of weird."

"About how old do you think she was?"

She shrugged twice this time. "I don't know. I couldn't really tell. But young, like those rich kids who don't work and hang out in the Market."

The woman wasn't Cassandra Amberlight. Kennicott had a photo of her. "Do you recognize this person?"

"Her, the protest lady. She used to come in here for lunch. She was real loud and rude. She only tipped ten percent. Sometimes less."

"When was the last time she was here?"

"At least a month ago."

Who was the young woman who'd been waiting for Fox? "Anything else you remember about this woman who was here yesterday? The colour of her eyes, her hair?"

"Just that she was wearing a Blue Jays hat and sunglasses."

"Her clothes?"

"I don't know. I think she had on, like, a black T-shirt."

"Tattoos, earrings, piercings?"

"No. You know, she looked like most white girls. She had a backpack."

"What kind was it, do you know?"

"No. It looked cheap. It was yellow."

"Did you talk to her?"

"I brought in the tea and she nodded. That was it."

"What happened next?"

"Nothing. I went back at four and she wasn't there."

"How many cups were used?"

She paused. "I didn't think about it until now. Only one cup. The other was clean."

The waitress looked around the restaurant.

"Can you think of anything else?" Kennicott asked.

"The dead guy was real nice. He once asked me if I was in school. He said I should study architecture, but my uncle wants me to go to business school."

She walked back to the counter and got right back on her phone.

Kennicott picked up the chopsticks and ate a few shrimp, took out a fifty-dollar bill, and left it on the table. He was following Fox's footsteps, but he was getting nowhere.

36

"Good day, Detective Greene. I've already researched your inquiry," Anthony Carpenter said, as he escorted Greene into his well-ordered, second-floor office. "Have a seat."

Greene had been to this law office once before. He'd met Carpenter here when he was trying to find out who had killed Jennifer. It was the day he'd been arrested and now it felt as if that was a lifetime ago.

Nattily dressed, wearing his usual bow tie, Carpenter sat calmly behind his old wooden desk, a single file folder in front of him. Greene took the chair facing him. He was carrying a sports bag, which he placed by his side on the floor.

"Thank you for seeing me on a Saturday," Greene said.

"From June until September I play golf on Wednesdays and Thursdays because it's easier to get tee times, and I work on weekends." He opened the file and slipped on a pair of reading glasses, then handed over a sheet of paper. "This piece of real estate you inquired about is quite interesting."

"What did you find?"

"Conclusion: Seven years ago the detached home located at 329 Augusta Avenue was purchased from its owners, Mr. and Mrs. Halls, and sold to Mr. Birrel Israelite, in trust, for the sum of five hundred twenty-three thousand dollars. There was no mortgage on the property, which the Halls had owned for forty-three years. No liens against the property. It was a cash purchase."

Greene looked up from the memo. "What does it mean that the property was sold 'in trust'?"

"It means that the lawyer, Mr. Israelite, made the purchase and held the property confidentially in trust for his client. Big companies do this all the time when they don't want anyone to know they are gobbling up properties."

"Because the lawyer won't be able to reveal the identity of his client?"

"Exactly. Solicitor–client privilege."

"What do you know about this Mr. Israelite?"

"Only that he's a lawyer in Niagara Falls. But the plot thickens." Carpenter began reading again. "Two years later, the property was sold by Mr. Birrel Israelite in trust to Ms. Alice Robillard in trust for the exact same sum."

"Robillard is also a lawyer?"

"Yes, in Ottawa. Then the house was flipped again six months later to a lawyer in North Bay. Again in trust and again for the same price."

"Presumably the same secret client is behind all of these transactions. Why?"

"I can't read minds. But I'd say they did this to ensure their identity could never be discovered."

"Have you ever seen anything like this before?"

Carpenter shook his head. "For a residential property? No. Not in thirty-three years of practice."

Greene got up and started to pace. "Do you know either of these other two lawyers?"

"No. But I've looked them all up."

An idea occurred to Greene. "Can you check to see what year all three were called to the bar?"

"You're thinking they went to law school together and you could piece together a connection to the owner somehow. I had the same notion. I noted their years of call when I did my original research," Carpenter said, digging into the file. "Let's see, Israelite was called in 1982, went to Osgoode Hall, Robillard was 2001, went to U. of T., and the third one was called in 1994 and graduated from Western. Dead end, I'm afraid."

In other words the lawyers had been chosen at random, the best way to be certain that it was impossible to trace back and find out who the owner was, Greene thought.

"Can you check out other houses adjoining Fox's condo buildings and see if any of them were also purchased in trust? He pulled out a piece of paper. "These are the seven most recent buildings listed on Fox's website."

"Certainly." Carpenter examined the list. "I'll need a day to look into this."

"Thanks." Greene pulled a pair of latex gloves from his pocket and slipped them on. He opened the bag he'd left on the floor and pulled out the yellow backpack and placed it on Carpenter's desk.

"Please deliver this by rush courier to Homicide Detective Daniel Kennicott."

"Certainly."

"Write him a note on your letterhead that says: My client has requested I pass this item to you. It was found earlier today under the kitchen sink in the house at 329 Augusta Avenue."

"You realize," Carpenter said, "that as it's coming from my office, Detective Kennicott will assume it's coming from you."

"Exactly," Greene said, pulling off his gloves. "He'll know it was from me, but he won't be able to prove it."

37

Kennicott strode into the boardroom at the Homicide office. Darvesh was there, waiting for him. He'd laid out several piles of paper, each with a handwritten title page.

"Let's start with the people you met at Omni Jewelcrafters," Darvesh said, handing Kennicott a set of papers stapled at the corner. "We've done a complete background check on each person as well as a summary of their alibis for yesterday afternoon. We've been able to confirm all of them except for Odessa Breaker's. She's on page five."

Kennicott turned to her page. "What does she say?"

"That she was out jogging alone down by the lake. There are no cameras on the trail so we haven't been able to independently verify it yet."

Kennicott peeked at his watch. It was five o'clock. Her note said he should meet her at seven.

"We've been tracking down the original suspects." Darvesh passed him another set of papers and started flipping through his own copy.

"Carol Archer, the angry ex-girlfriend, is in a drug rehab clinic up north."

"Happens."

"George Braithwaite, Fox's former business partner, is on a fishing trip in the Yukon."

"Lucky guy."

"Gary Edwards, the condo board president who is suing Fox. His oldest son graduated yesterday from King's out in Halifax. He's been there since Thursday and isn't coming back until tomorrow."

"Okay."

"Charlie Hicks, the financier who is suing Fox for twenty million dollars. She's into some kind of extreme long-distance bike riding. Her husband says she's currently doing a twelve-hundred-kilometre race out in the Rockies. He sent me a link to the event and I confirmed it. There's a copy there for you."

"Our suspects are falling like flies. What about Fox's father?"

"It's about forty kilometres from the Fresh restaurant to the Fox-hole Wellness Centre. Assuming he rode at twenty-five kilometres an hour, it would have taken him less than two hours. Their lunch ended at two, but he didn't show up until we were there at the Centre at five. That leaves more than an hour unaccounted for. The job site was a few blocks away from Fresh, and the 911 call came in at 4:01:23. He would have had enough time to kill his son. We checked the cameras in stores north of the restaurant."

"Any luck?"

"We got him leaving Fresh, heading north toward Kensington Market at 2:12 p.m."

"Good work. We know he argued with his son about money at their lunch. Where's Fox's estate going to go? To his fiancée? Fox had been supporting his parents for years. Once he was married, was he going to cut them off completely? It'll take time to probate the will; in the meantime check their banking records and credit card debt. I want around-the-clock surveillance on the father."

"You think the wife might have put him up to it?"

"I think we'll investigate them up and down. What about our prime suspect, Amberlight?"

Darvesh handed over another sheaf of papers. "This is her criminal record, her police contacts, and the earlier convictions that she got expunged."

Kennicott started to read through the pages on top.

"Look at the expunged convictions."

Kennicott flipped to the back pages. "Phew, looks like she's got a bit of an anger problem."

"Violence and weapons," Darvesh said. "We searched through her Facebook and Twitter histories. There's lots of vitriol about Fox. But check the page where I've put a yellow sticky. It's a tweet she sent last year."

Kennicott read it out loud: " 'Fox buildings poorly built. I worked construction all thru university. If I had a hammer, guess what I'd do with it!' "

"It gets better," Darvesh said, holding up a last set of papers.

"Tell me."

"I had a rush DNA test done on the water glasses, and . . ."

He passed the papers over to Kennicott.

"We got a match from Amberlight's saliva on the rim," Darvesh said.

"I see why Greene wants her to come in to make a statement," Kennicott said. "She was in the shed on the afternoon Fox is murdered, and we've got the proof."

"What time is she coming in tomorrow?" Darvesh asked.

"At three, if she shows up."

There was a knock on the door.

"Come in," Kennicott said.

Francine Hughes, the receptionist, entered carrying a large package. "I wouldn't normally come back here," she said, "but this was marked urgent, from a lawyer's office, addressed to you personally, Detective Kennicott."

"Thank you, Ms. Hughes," Kennicott said, taking the package from her. It was from the law office of Anthony Carpenter J.D. Why was that name familiar?

"I've got scissors," Darvesh said. He slipped on a pair of gloves, cut through the packaging and pulled out a yellow backpack and a letter.

"Should I read it?" he asked.

"What's the lawyer's address?" Kennicott asked.

"Five hundred Danforth Avenue, second floor."

Now Kennicott remembered who Anthony Carpenter was.

"What's the letter say?"

" 'Detective Kennicott. My client has requested that I pass this item to you. It was found under the kitchen sink in the house at 329 Augusta Avenue earlier today. Sincerely, Anthony Carpenter, J.D.' "

Ari had beat him to the punch again, Kennicott thought. Why hadn't it occurred to him to search that house on the other side of the alley?

"Empty the backpack, Kamil," he said.

Darvesh pulled out a Toronto Blue Jays baseball cap, a pair of sunglasses, a black T-shirt, and a pair of white shorts. He checked all the pockets but there was nothing else.

"Do you know what this is?" he asked.

"It belonged to a young white woman who was supposed to meet with Fox around the time he was murdered."

"I still don't understand. Why is this coming to you from a lawyer's office?"

Kennicott folded his arms.

"It's a message from Ari Greene."

"Detective Greene?"

"It looks as if he's found the Kensington Blogger. Send all this out to see if we can get any DNA, especially from that baseball cap. Urgent request. Get a search warrant for the house at 329 Augusta Avenue. Go through the place top to bottom. And get hold of our legal department. We need to find out who owns that property."

"I'm on it," Darvesh said.

"One more thing. Contact all the TV stations that were at the protest and get a copy of all the footage they shot yesterday. Get some officers to look through it all and see if they caught someone walking into that house wearing these clothes and this backpack. With luck it will stand out in the crowd."

"Done. Are you going to talk to Greene?"

"No need," Kennicott said, unfolding his arms. "We're already having a conversation."

38

Kennicott timed it perfectly. He drove down Parliament Street, under the Gardiner Expressway, the crumbling elevated highway that cut off most of the city from the lake, and onto Queens Quay. On his right he spotted Small Street, a tiny road he'd never noticed before. To his left was an empty abandoned wharf and beyond it the lake.

The steel fence that ran in front of the property was plastered with colourful drawings showcasing the massive waterfront condominium complex that Fox had planned to build here over the next ten years. They depicted a pair of nine-storey office buildings fronting the street, six residential condominium complexes on the water, an athletic centre complete with a pool, rooftop terrace, outdoor dining lounge, solar panels and a green roof. There was an enormous photo of Fox standing at the helm of a yacht under a banner proclaiming "Welcome to Fox Harbour." Another picture showed a scantily dressed, athletic-looking young couple in a shallow pool splashing with the headline "Water, Water Everywhere!" and a third showcased four smiling employees under the banner "Fox Harbour Presentation Centre, Come in and Meet Our Great Sales Team."

A number of runners and cyclists were on the path in front of the fence. Kennicott waited until there was a gap, then drove in, turned down a short gravel road, and parked. He was at the base of a long empty wharf: the future building site. It was exactly seven o'clock.

Odessa Breaker was standing by her car, a sleek Audi 5000. She wore a black-and-white running suit, sculpted to her fit body, and a pair of bright red running shoes. Her cornrowed hair was fastened with black, white, and red clips. She held a red-and-white water bottle in her hand.

As he approached, a flock of seagulls down the wharf began to squawk.

"Right on time, Detective," Breaker said, checking the sports watch on her wrist. She peered over his shoulder and scanned the road behind him.

"Don't worry," he said. "I came alone. Nobody knows I'm here. Not even my partner."

"Brave of you. But I was born suspicious. Let's go."

Breaker started running back up the road. There was loose gravel underfoot, and Kennicott slipped on it, almost falling. He righted himself, and it took him almost a minute to catch up. Breaker was a good runner. She glided along the trail with a long, easy stride. During the fourteen-week murder trial that he'd just finished, Kennicott had only been able to run on the weekends. His legs weren't in shape. Plus he hadn't slept since he'd got up to go to court early yesterday morning. But the evening air was invigorating, and it was cooler by the lake. Don't push yourself too hard at the beginning, he told himself, as he lifted his legs high and found his rhythm.

He was going to let Breaker start the conversation, to use the power of silence the way Greene had taught him. At a curve in the trail, he heard footsteps rushing toward them, and in an instant a group of runners came flying around the corner, forcing them to the side. They stood under a huge concrete pylon that supported the overhead highway as the herd stampeded past. Once they were gone, Breaker put her hand on Kennicott's arm.

"Don't be fooled by those men you met today at Omni," she said. "Believe me, they all hated Fox's guts."

"You saying they were putting on an act for me?"

"Oscar performances."

"Then they weren't upset that he was murdered?"

"Just the opposite. How do you spell relief? I don't trust any of them."

"My partner has checked out their alibis. They're all solid."

"These people are not dumb enough to do something like this themselves. And they're not the only ones. I can think of twenty developers in the city who would have wanted Livingston out of the way. I bet they're all secretly celebrating right now."

"But why?"

She took her hand off his arm. He'd forgotten it was there.

"You don't get it, do you?" She waved her arm at the city behind them. "Toronto is about the hottest real-estate market in North America. Look at all those cranes. No other place is building at the rate we are, and there's way more to come. Do you have any idea how much money is involved in this business?"

"I'm learning."

"I need to run," she said, and took off. He kept pace beside her along the path that took them to the Leslie Street Spit, a long peninsula that stuck out into the lake like a bent finger.

They took the road up the middle of the spit and kept going in silence until they reached the turnaround at the end. Except for the occasional bird watcher, a few cyclists, and one or two other runners, they were alone.

Breaker led him to a rocky beach and they sat, looking back over the harbour at the city. A nearby flock of seagulls squawked in protest at their presence. Out on the water there were sailboats and groups of kayakers and paddle boarders. All normal people leading normal lives.

"This partner of yours," she said at last. "Did he check out my alibi?"

"He said you told him you were running along the lakeshore."

"Running alone. Does that make me a suspect?"

He didn't want to give her a direct answer. This part of the city was remote. There'd be no video cameras, and it would probably be impossible to find a witness who had seen her jogging way out here.

"Adam Lewis called you a public housing czar," he said.

She laughed. "That's Adam being Adam the Ad Man. I'm a consultant."

"You were working for Fox, weren't you?"

She nodded.

"Let me guess," he said. "You two would exchange notes under the table at Omni and then meet in the backroom of the Huibing Gardens on Spadina on Friday afternoons. You'd go in through the alley in back."

A look of admiration crossed her face. "Very good, Detective Daniel Kennicott."

"What were you meeting about?"

"Everyone knows the condo market in this city is a gigantic bubble that's about to burst. The government is freaking out with all the foreign money coming in, jacking up the prices, building condos that no one is even living in. Meanwhile twenty-five-year-olds are stuck in their parents' basements or moving out of town because the prices are going nuts. Fox had to diversify out of the upscale market."

"That's where you come in? Low-cost housing."

"Subsidized by the government. The other developers hate the idea because their profit margins are cut in half."

"And Livingston?"

"Half a loaf is better than owning empty condos with the glass windows falling out five years from now. And he was genuinely inspired to do a new kind of housing for the poor. In the fifties and sixties, the government built tons of public housing. Problem was it was all shit. Ghettos for poor people that became breeding grounds for crime, like where I grew up."

"And you know your way around affordable housing."

"Fox had a serous problem. If he was still the Condo King, the government wouldn't give him a dime. He needed a new image. Credibility. Access. Imagine if he partnered with me, a black woman who grew up poor in Regent Park and put herself through university working as a cashier at a car wash. It was a PR wet dream. I could have walked him into the housing ministry, the mayor's office, introduced him to key cabinet ministers. He would have charmed them all."

She flipped open her water bottle, tilted her head back, and took a long drink. "You didn't bring any water?"

"I should have."

"Here." She passed him her bottle. He shot a spray of water into his mouth without letting the bottle touch his lips, then passed it back.

"What nobody knew was that Fox planned to turn K2, the second development he wanted to build on College Street, into affordable housing."

"You're kidding. His full-page newspaper ads said K2 was going to be the ultimate in luxury condos. If he wanted a new image, why was he promoting it as a playground for the wealthy?"

"He had it all planned out. After the protesters had their big march yesterday he was going to hold a press conference and say, 'My goodness, you're right. I've seen the light.' Like Scrooge waking up on Christmas morning, he was going to be a changed man."

"Smart."

"Smart? Livingston was fucking brilliant."

"How many times did you meet him?"

"Four. Last time was a week ago. He swore me to secrecy."

"Why all the cloak-and-dagger routine?"

"Fox acted rich, but any one of those guys at Omni could spend him under the table in a heartbeat. Everyone in the business thought he'd overextended himself with this Fox Harbour development. He was afraid if the bank or his backers found out about his new plan for K2 before he had the money in place, they'd freak out and call in his loans."

Sweat had formed on her cheek. She wiped it away with her forefinger. It had grown quiet. The seagulls were silent, busy picking away at the pebbles along the shoreline.

"Was there anything unusual about your last meeting?"

"He was real nervous. He was convinced someone had found out about his plan and was determined to stop him. He didn't know who it was."

The sun was lowering. Its rays spangled across the water, lighting up Breaker's skin.

"Why all the secrecy about meeting with me today?" he asked her.

She gave him a long look. "Your brother was murdered. Don't you ever worry that whoever did it might be after you one day?"

The wind picked up, sending a chill across Kennicott's skin. He stared at her. This was something he'd never confessed to anyone. Not even Ari Greene.

She put her hand on his arm. The warmth of her skin seemed to stop the chill. "Don't you see, Daniel?" she whispered. "I thought Livingston was being paranoid. Then look what they did to him."

He could see in her eyes that fear had replaced her usual confidence.

"But with your connections wouldn't another developer want to work with you?"

She took her hand away and wrapped her arms around herself.

"The last thing they want is a new kind of rental housing to compete with their money-making condos. The government is getting wise to what is happening. They are talking about taxing foreign buyers who buy places and don't really live in them. Good luck to them. There are a million loopholes, and way too much cash at stake."

"You really think you are in danger?"

She picked up a rock, tossed it in the water. "Okay, I admit, I'm probably overdoing it. But the way Livingston was acting, something was up. I can't help but feel that this isn't over, and I don't want to be the next body."

He didn't say anything.

"You grew up in a different Toronto than I did," she said. "My mother wouldn't let me outside the house after five o'clock, even in the summer, because of all the drugs and guns and stabbings and shootings. A girl I went to school with was killed by a stray bullet. I bet you think I'm just being paranoid."

He did. But how could he be sure?

"I know it sounds foolish, but that's how I feel. I'm still in shock that this happened."

Her eyes glistened in the light reflecting off the water. He'd seen people in shock before. Their reactions weren't always rational.

"I can get you police protection," he said.

She shook her head and her beaded cornrows swung across her shoulders. "I'm not going home. I packed a bag and left it in my car. I need a safe place where I can disappear for a few days."

She started to shake.

"I have a spare room in my flat," he said, surprised at himself that he'd made the offer. "But I have to warn you, there's only one bathroom."

She grinned. "That's no problem for me. We had one bathroom when I was growing up. And there were six of us."

Why not? Technically she was a possible suspect, but this way he'd know where she was.

She took her water bottle and shot a light spray at his face. They both laughed.

"I'm getting cold, let's go," she said. "And by the way, yesterday I didn't run this way, I went west back into the city. Maybe you should have that partner of yours check the video cameras along Queens Quay."

Before he could respond, she took off at a fast pace. He almost slipped on some pebbles before he righted himself and ran after her. This time it took him about half a minute to catch up.

39

Alison sat on her bed, opened her laptop, turned on her phone, and clicked on the TV. The eleven-thirty news had just begun.

Livingston Fox's murder was dominating the headlines, and her Twitter feed and her blog had lit up with news that the Fox family was holding a midnight ceremony at their wellness centre to honour their son. A few hours earlier, Ari had come home for a few minutes and rushed out again. She was sure this was where he'd gone.

On the TV, Sheena Persad was standing in front of a line of cars pulled over to the side of the road with their headlights and their emergency flashers on.

"This is an extraordinary scene out here," she said. "I'm on Highway 27 north of Toronto, and as you can see behind me, cars are backed up a long, long way." The camera swung to the side and showed a line of lights stretching into the distance.

"TO-TV News has learned that the family of Livingston Fox is holding a midnight candlelit vigil to celebrate the life of their controversial son. Police are continuing their investigation of his gruesome murder and TO-TV News is fully cooperating with the authorities."

Alison sat up in bed.

She was gobsmacked.

"The police are looking for an individual we caught on camera on Friday afternoon."

Oh no, oh no, Alison thought.

The video from the march started to play on the screen.

"You can see this person wearing a Blue Jays baseball cap and sunglasses, with a yellow backpack. Now you can see the individual crossing to the sidewalk on Augusta Avenue where the demonstration took place."

There she was, wearing the baseball cap and sunglasses—and that dumb, yellow backpack. They'd drawn a red circle around her head. The camera tracked her as she zigzagged through the crowd. But Persad had called her an "individual." That meant the police couldn't tell if she was a man or a woman.

Persad was back on camera. "Anyone with information about the identity of this individual is asked to contact Crime Stoppers or the Metro Toronto Police immediately."

Wait a second, Alison thought. Persad must not have told the police they'd met at the demonstration or they would know that Alison was a female who spoke with an English accent. Persad was protecting her. But she wouldn't be able to do it for long.

Alison had to talk to her in person. Right away.

"We've been asked by the police to play this clip a second time," Persad said. "In slow motion."

The video started again. As painful as it had been to watch it first on her laptop, then on TV, now seeing herself for a third time in slow motion was too much. She felt sick. She clicked off the TV and jumped off the bed. She tore her bedroom door open and dashed across the hall. The bathroom door was closed. She flung it open. But she was too late.

Before she could get to the toilet, she threw up all over herself.

40

The cars on the shoulder of the highway had their headlights and flashers on, waiting to drive into the Foxhole Wellness Centre. It was 11:45 p.m. and the night air was still warm. Greene had his window open, as did Bassante, who was sitting in the passenger seat, stewing.

"Fox told me his hippie parents were nut bars," he said. "Now I see what he meant."

"Every family mourns differently," Greene said.

"Yeah. But a midnight candlelight ceremony? Come on. The email says, 'Please observe all legally posted speed signs on your journey, and carpool if possible, so as to lessen the carbon footprint on the planet.' Their only son is murdered and they're worried about the goddamn environment."

Four TV news trucks were parked on the other side of the highway while reporters stood talking to their cameras. They weren't being allowed into the centre.

Greene drove the last few feet to the entrance, where a young woman wearing a white robe bent to his window.

"Welcome to the celebration of Livingston's essence," she said, and handed him two white Glow Sticks. "Please proceed to the lower parking lot. Thank you for carpooling and helping to save our planet."

Greene handed one of the sticks to Bassante.

"Do me a favour," Bassante said, as Greene turned into the grounds. "When I kick the bucket, rent a nightclub and throw a party. That's what Fox would have wanted."

The long driveway was lined with burning torches. At the end of it, a tall man, also in a white robe, directed them past a large old house that had a candle in each window to a road that led to a parking lot below. Two white-robed assistants used their own Glow Sticks to point cars to open spots, and a third directed them to a candlelit path. This took them to a field, which was surrounded by yet more burning torches.

The moon was almost full and high in the sky. It illuminated rows of white sheets that had been laid out on the ground. Most of the spaces were filled with people speaking in muted voices. A wooden platform had been erected in front of the crowd and a white sheet was draped between two trees behind it. Presumably that's where the mourners were waiting.

Bassante nudged Greene and motioned to a clump of trees on a small rise off to the side. "Let's stand over there, out of the way."

"Good idea."

From this vantage point, it was easy for Greene to make out faces in the crowd. He had checked the Fox Developments Inc. website and read the profiles of the people who worked for what they called "Team Livingston" doing finance, sales, marketing, customer service, accounting, and administration. In their photos, most were young, well dressed, and looked enthusiastic. Greene had counted how many times the word *team* was used on the site: fourteen.

Then he'd gone to the website for the Foxhole Wellness Centre. It was much more modest. There were a couple of photos of the buildings and profiles of Karl, Kate, and Gloria Fox, but there was no schedule of classes or treatments, and the rate sheet was a year out of date. He looked at a few travel websites: the latest reviews of the centre were two years old. Most were negative.

A woman playing a flute and dressed in an Elizabethan gown emerged from behind the sheet. A man wearing a doublet and breeches who was carrying a round Chinese gong followed her on the improvised stage. He struck it twelve times. Greene glanced at his watch. It was midnight.

Bassante hissed, "Fox would have hated this shit."

The gong quieted the crowd. Six more robed people came from behind the sheet.

Bassante identified all of them for Greene. The older couple were Fox's parents, Kate and Karl; the woman beside them was their daughter, Gloria; the short woman was Maxine, Fox's assistant; and the tall woman was Sherani, his chauffeur for the last year. Finally there was his fiancée, Anita Nakamura, whom Fox had met this past winter. She was crying uncontrollably. Sherani put her arm around her. Gloria looked unsteady on her feet. Maxine was beside her, clutching her hand and holding her up.

Greene fixed his eyes on Fox's fiancée. The poor woman's life and dreams had been brutally shattered. Then on his assistant. "The short woman, Maxine, would she know where Fox was yesterday afternoon?"

"Max was the captain of the ship. She did everything for Fox. But Friday afternoons he'd turn off his phone and disappear for a few hours. It drove her nuts."

"You have any idea where he went?"

"None, until he showed up at the job site."

"Do you think he had some secret that was big enough that someone wanted to kill him?"

"Why you asking me? You're the homicide detective."

On the makeshift stage, Kate Fox came to the front and raised a Glow Stick high in the air. The audience did the same with their sticks, washing the field in a sea of white.

"It's hard to imagine the world without Livingston," Kate Fox said. "He was such a force of nature."

Greene looked at the audience. Many people were crying. He'd been a homicide cop for so long, it was easy for him to forget that most people never have to face a murder in their midst. He spotted Kennicott and Darvesh sitting near the back.

"Put your light away," he said to Bassante.

"Sure."

Greene put his stick in his back pocket and Bassante did the same.

"You know many of these people?" Greene asked.

"Some. Fox's staff. Builders and contractors. Banker types. Probably some of his ex-girlfriends."

Greene returned his gaze to Kate Fox. Something about her seemed unnaturally cold. Removed. Her eulogy felt clichéd. "Livingston was wonderful to his employees . . . Livingston was a doer, never one to sit still . . . Livingston believed in challenges and hard work . . ." She sounded more like a giving a eulogy for someone she'd never met than a mother grieving the death of her son.

Karl Fox's face was stern, as if it had been set in stone at a young age and never changed. He was watching his wife, transfixed by her, and paid no attention to the grief of his daughter and Anita Nakamura, the woman who would have been his daughter-in-law.

"How about Fox's sister?" Greene asked Bassante. "Were they close?"

"He talked to her all the time."

Kate Fox was coming to the end of her speech. "Goodbye, Livingston," she said. "May your spirit find peace at last."

She returned to the rest of her family. The flautist stepped forward and started to play.

"Why didn't Fox get along with his parents?" Greene asked.

"Who knows? Families. They were polar opposites."

The musician finished her solo, and the man with the gong struck it again.

Gloria stepped forward. She took a few deep breaths.

"I loved you, Livingston," she said in a half whisper. "You were more than a brother to me. You were my best friend. My only friend." She stopped, fighting to gain her composure. She looked up and seemed to notice the audience for the first time. "You people thought you knew him, but you didn't."

In a flash, her grief had turned to anger. This didn't surprise Greene. He'd seen many people overcome with grief morph into rage.

"Whoever did this terrible deed, I hope you are caught and that you suffer the way you made Livingston suffer. The way we are all suffering now." She reached inside her robe and pulled out a ceramic urn. She lifted it in the air and spoke to it. "Livingston, my brother, my keeper, my soul mate forever. When I have your remains, I will keep them with me until the murderer is found. Then, I promise, I'll put one handful of your ashes in the garden of every building you ever built. I've always been proud of you."

She sank to the floor. Maxine rushed to her side.

There was a beating sound in the sky. It grew louder by the second.

Everyone craned their necks and watched a helicopter approach and then hover overhead. Greene could just make out the logo TO-TV News. Someone in the chopper turned a searchlight on, and it started to strafe the crowd with its beam.

Fox's father jumped forward and raised his fist to the sky. "Bastards!" he yelled. "Bastards!"

Gloria looked up, confused. Her mother hurried over and pulled her roughly to her feet. Everyone on stage retreated behind the sheet.

The audience was stunned. No one seemed to know what to do. The helicopter started circling, criss-crossing the crowd with its spotlight. People scrambled to their feet and rushed to their cars.

Greene and Bassante waited in the trees until almost everyone had left and the helicopter had flown away. By the time they got to the parking lot, clouds had covered the moon and it was dark.

"Crazy," Bassante said as he got in Greene's car.

Greene was playing Kate Fox's eulogy and the sister Gloria's outburst over in his mind.

"What do you think?" Bassante asked.

"I think," Greene answered, putting his car in gear, "that this family has some secrets."

41

Kennicott's body jerked. His eyes sprang open. Something was ringing. His phone, on the floor.

He rolled over, checked call display, and answered it.

"What's up?" he whispered.

"Sorry to bother you," Darvesh said. "You were right. The subject is moving."

"Okay, okay. Wait."

Kennicott got up and tiptoed down the hallway to the kitchen. It was still dark outside. He closed the door behind him, being careful to not make any noise.

"What's she doing?" he asked Darvesh.

"She's in her car, blue Subaru, licence plate 'PROTEST,' heading down Spadina. I'm a block behind her."

"Is the tracker working?"

"Perfectly."

Kennicott looked at the clock on his microwave. It was 3:20 a.m. "Anyone else on the street?"

"Two or three cars. She's gone east on Lakeshore. Wait, I've made the turn. She's a few car lengths ahead now and taking the ramp up to the Gardiner."

"Don't get too close." Kennicott opened the fridge, took out a carton of orange juice, and poured himself a glass. "If she'd turned west, I'd guess she was headed to Buffalo. East, the closest border crossing is the Thousand Islands Bridge. That's a three-hour drive."

"I'm on the DVP now. She's sticking to the speed limit."

"She's afraid of being stopped by the police." Kennicott's mouth was dry. He took a drink of the juice. "Good thing we had a Plan B. I assume you can see it?"

"Perfectly."

"I'll put in a call to someone I know at the OPP, they patrol the highway. They'll stop and ticket her."

"Nice. What about when she gets to the border? She could go anywhere once she's in the States."

"Yes, if they let her in."

"Very nice. So that's how it's done."

Kennicott finished his juice. "Follow her at a safe distance."

"When she gets turned back, do we arrest her?"

"No, we wait. Keep her under surveillance. She's supposed to come in with her lawyer this afternoon so we can interview her. Call me in an hour."

He hung up and phoned the Durham Regional Police, who patrolled the highways east of Toronto, and American Customs at the Thousand Islands Bridge.

The door behind him opened and Breaker walked in. She was wearing a pair of white shorts and a loose grey T-shirt.

"Police business?" she asked.

"I tried not to wake you."

"The bed in your spare room is comfortable, but I barely slept. I can't stop thinking about Livingston. You know, for all his showmanship, when you sat down with him one on one, he was a true friend. He was sincere. He wanted to change things."

Kennicott lifted the orange juice carton. "Want a glass?"

"I don't want to get in the way if you need to make some more phone calls."

"I'm done for now. I've got a few minutes before I have to go in. I could make you a latte. The espresso machine is loud so I didn't use it."

"I'd love a coffee," she said.

"So would I," he said.

Their eyes met for a moment. She twirled one of her braids with her finger.

"Make yourself at home here today," he said. "I'll get a patrol car stationed outside. You'll be safe; don't leave the house." And, he thought, it's a good thing I let you stay over. There's no question about your alibi for the night.

"I really appreciate it."

"With luck we'll make an arrest later this afternoon."

"You're kidding. That fast?"

"Keep your fingers crossed."

"That would be amazing. You can't imagine what a relief that would be."

"I think I can."

Neither of them had moved.

"I need to grind up some beans," he said.

She grinned. "You do that and I'll froth the milk."

42

Unlike his daughter and his father, Greene had never bought into the romance of Kensington Market. As a cop, he'd seen the overcrowded rooming houses, the hookers who worked the streets after hours, the back-alley drug dealing, the gang activity, and the too-frequent gunplay.

Still, every time he was in the market, Greene tried to imagine what it must have been like for his parents when they first arrived here. They'd met after the war in a displaced persons camp in Austria, when they were both alone in the world. Their spouses, their children, their parents, and all their relatives and friends had been murdered.

Ari's mother was convalescing in the camp's hospital when she met Yitzhak in the cafeteria. She took one look at him and said, "You're handsome. Why don't you marry me?"

"Why not?" he replied.

They were married ten days later.

Then came an excruciating three-year wait to get into Canada. They arrived in the spring of 1948. Back then Toronto was a dull, closed, and almost all-white city. They taught themselves English, scraped out a living and sheltered in Kensington, the city's gateway to newcomers for more than a century.

In those days it was known as the Jewish Market. People there still raised and killed chickens in their backyards and half of the conversations were in Yiddish. As the Jews moved north, waves of immigrants came from Portugal, the Caribbean, Chile, and East Asia to take their places. The Vietnam War brought in American draft dodgers. Then came Africans, Tamils, East Europeans and Russians, and more recently Mexicans and South and Central Americans.

On Sunday morning the streets were sparsely populated with late-night stragglers wandering home and shopkeepers opening their grates and sweeping the sidewalks in front of their stores. Amberlight's apartment was above a cheese shop that had been there through three generations of owners. As Greene walked up the narrow staircase to the second floor, the smell of moulding cheese seemed to ooze from the dingy wallpaper.

Yesterday, he had suggested in the strongest terms that Amberlight stay at DiPaulo's house for a second night.

"No way," she'd said. "I want to go home."

"If you give me your keys, I can pick up anything you need from your place," Greene said.

"I'd like to sleep in my own bed. There's no guarantee that this might not be my last chance for a long time."

Greene had agreed to come get her this morning. That would give Amberlight time to sleep and get organized, then meet with DiPaulo before going into the police station.

Amberlight's apartment was at the far end of the second floor, and even this early in the morning it was warm in the hallway. Greene got to her door and knocked. There was no answer. He knocked again. Nothing. He found the doorbell and pushed it. Nothing.

"Cassandra," he said, raising his voice, "it's Ari Greene."

Still no response. He pulled out his phone and called DiPaulo.

"I'm at her door and she's not answering."

"Holy shit."

"What do you suggest?"

"I'll call her. Hang on, I'll put you on hold."

Greene turned back to the door and was about to knock again when he heard footsteps coming up the stairs. Slow, heavy steps. A cellphone rang and a woman's voice answered it.

"Cassandra Amberlight."

There was a pause, then Amberlight appeared with her phone in one hand and a carry-out tray with two coffee cups in the other.

"I'm fine, Ted," she said. "Stop being such a worrywart. I just went out to get some coffees."

She looked up and noticed Greene.

"Yes, yes, yes. I see him at the end of my hallway. You two are like a pair of old ladies."

She hung up and walked toward Greene. "These godawful stairs are going to be the death of me. And this dreadful humidity." She was breathing hard. "There was a long line up at Jimmy's. I got you a latte. Be careful, it's very hot."

"That was kind of you," he said, taking the tray and the remaining drink from her.

"I bet you're one of those horrid people who are always on time."

"Do you need to pick anything up from your place?"

"No, let's go and get this over with."

"You nervous?"

"Why should I be nervous? I'm facing the prospect of being convicted for a murder I didn't commit and going to jail for the rest of my life. Piece of cake."

At the top of the steep staircase, she hesitated. She clutched the thin metal railing with one hand while holding her coffee in the other.

"I find going down even harder than going up. And to think, at law school I was captain of the women's hockey team." She grunted with exertion at every step. "I hope to hell you're right about me talking to the cops."

"Remember what I told you," he said. They were halfway down. "When you speak to the police, no secrets."

She stopped to steady herself and took a sip of her coffee. Greene saw her take her hand off the railing.

"Be careful," he said.

"You sound like Ted. I've climbed up and down these stairs hundreds of times."

She started down again. The heel of her shoe caught on the edge of the next step and she fell back. A piece of paper flew out of her shirt pocket and she grabbed it. Her feet jetted out in front of her. Her cup went flying over her shoulder and Greene felt the hot liquid smack the side of his face. He shot out his arm to grab her elbow and the tray in his other hand fell. The cup burst open, and coffee splashed over her legs.

"Ouch," Amberlight cried.

She fell against him, and her weight pushed him back. He didn't think he could hold her. They were going to tumble head over heels the rest of the way down unless he could brace himself. He shot out his free arm, trying to reach the far wall, but didn't feel anything. They were falling.

He stretched his arm out, and this time he felt the base of the wall. He used it to brace himself as he let her weight fall onto his chest as he lowered her as slowly as he could until they were safely sitting.

"Ugh," she said.

"You okay?"

She exhaled. Inhaled heavily. Exhaled again. "I think so." She breathed in and out again. "Thanks."

He could feel the coffee burn on his cheek He rubbed it with his bare hand.

She slumped over, her head between her knees. "Why is all this happening?" She sighed. "Everything in my life. Everything is falling apart."

43

Alison made a point of getting to the Toronto Reference Library half an hour before it opened. She was not the first one there by any means. Students with bulging backpacks, raggedly dressed loners, and older couples were already waiting patiently in the glassed-in lobby. She'd found that Canadians were, as advertised, quite polite, and one of the things she'd grown to like about Toronto was that people from all backgrounds seemed to mix here without conflict.

When the security guard opened the door, almost everyone headed to the computers on the ground floor. There were nine rows of them, and they filled up fast.

Alison got one of the last ones. Lucky. This was the only way she could think of to send an anonymous email. And right now, anonymity was the most important thing in her life.

She typed in the email address Persad had given her and then wrote: "This is urgent. Can you meet me at the subway station at 2:30?" and pressed send. She stared at the screen, her mind racing. It was Sunday. Persad said to call her if she didn't respond to email. Okay, Alison thought, but she couldn't use her own phone.

She looked around. A balding librarian was sitting behind a desk, talking on a phone. She looked back at the computer screen. No reply yet from Persad. She took out the reporter's business card and memorized the phone number, then took her wallet and phone out of her jacket, draped the jacket on her chair and walked over to the librarian's desk. He was finishing his call. He hung up and smiled at her.

"Yes, can I help you?"

"Excuse me," she said, exaggerating her English accent. "Could I possibly trouble you to use your telephone for a brief local call?"

"I'm afraid the library phones are not available to the public."

"I'm here for one week with my mum and I have no cell service in Canada."

He looked around. "Okay, but keep it short," he said, turning the phone for her to use.

She dialled Persad's number. It rang three times.

"Sheena Persad," the reporter said, answering on the fourth ring, sounding breathless. Alison could hear a child playing in the background.

"Yes, could I have room 314 please."

"Sorry, I think you have the wrong—"

"No, no. And thank you for directing me to the Rosedale subway stop this morning."

There was a pause on the other end of the line. Alison heard a little girl saying, "Mommy, Mommy, look."

"Hello, Mum," Alison said into the phone. "I was going to leave a voice mail. I didn't think you'd still be in the hotel room."

"Are you at a public phone?" Persad asked.

"Yes. The Reference Library. It's a lovely spot. You must come see it." She looked over at the librarian. He was tapping his pen on the edge of his desk, eyeing her.

"Is someone listening to you?"

"Exactly."

"I did a drawing," the child said.

"And you don't want to use your own phone," Persad said.

"A kind man here is letting me use the library phone. But I have to be fast."

"Very smart of you," Persad said. "But listen, I need to know who you are and you need to go to the police."

"But I—"

"No buts. This is getting out of hand. I'll meet you. But only if you tell me everything and are prepared to go to the police. Today."

Alison glanced at the librarian. He was giving her an anxious look. She turned her back to him.

"I know," she said, lowering her voice. "You're right."

"Good. I'll have to call the sitter. I'll see you in half an hour at the Rosedale subway station."

"Perfect," Alison said. "Ta, Mum. Love you."

She heard Persad hang up. She turned back to the librarian, who already had his hand out for the receiver.

"Many thanks," she said.

"I'm glad you like our library," he said.

"Love it."

She made her way back to the computer and sat down. She felt off balance. There had been a moment there when she'd forgotten she was only pretending to talk to her mother. *Ta, Mum. Love you.* How many thousands of times had she said that to her mother, and what wouldn't she give to be able to do it for real just one more time?

44

Even before he walked into the house, Kennicott knew it would be immaculate. The outside was picture-perfect. The front lawn was so precisely manicured it looked as if each blade had been measured and cut by hand. The perennials in the pristine front flowerbed were arranged beautifully. The stones in the Japanese rock garden to the side of the front porch were smooth and clean.

He rang the front bell and gentle chimes sounded inside. The door opened. Anita Nakamura, Fox's fiancée, stood in the hallway, wearing a simple pair of grey cotton pants and a pale blue shirt. Her black hair was tied back. The air conditioning was on in the house and a blast of cool air hit Kennicott's skin.

"Good morning, Detective. Please come in. My parents are here as well. They have made tea."

She ushered him through the hallway to a formal dining room. A black cast-iron teapot was in the middle of the table. Small matching teacups, each centred on a white place mat, were set in front of four chairs. Nakamura's parents stood at the entrance to the room and stepped forward to greet him. Kennicott had learned a lot about Japanese manners during the year he spent after university teaching English in a small Japanese port town. He stopped and gave them a slight bow. They smiled and bowed back in return.

They all sat down. The Nakamuras looked at him expectantly.

"I know this is a terrible time for all of you," Kennicott said. "I'm sure with the shock and the jet lag and then the ceremony last night, you must be exhausted."

They kept looking at him but said nothing.

"Murder investigations are complicated. I am limited in what I can tell you at this time. But I can assure you, we are working on this night and day. We will do everything we can to bring the perpetrator of this crime to justice."

They continued to stare at him.

He was reciting clichés to a family in grief. All of his police training had taught him to remain objective. Never get too close. Don't personalize things. It was a rule he'd watched Greene break over and over.

"The reason I became a police officer was to help people. Believe me when I say that I know it's hard to wait for answers."

Mr. Nakamura broke off eye contact. For a moment, Kennicott thought he was going to walk out of the room. Instead, he reached for the teapot.

"Detective, would you like some tea?"

"Yes, thank you."

He poured the tea carefully into Kennicott's cup, then the other three. Kennicot knew that tea was important. A guest was always served first but should not drink until his host had done so.

He waited until Mr. and Ms. Nakamura sipped their tea before he did the same. The temperature was perfect. Anita didn't touch hers.

"We have read about you and the tragedy of your family," Mr. Nakamura said. "Our sincere condolences, and we do hope that one day the man who killed your brother is found. We are honoured to have you as the investigating officer on this case. You may ask us any questions."

"I appreciate that," Kennicott said. "How well did you two know Mr. Fox?"

"We were getting to know him and were looking forward to having him as part of our family," Ms. Nakamura said. "Two weeks ago, before we left on our trip, he brought us a beautiful bouquet of flowers and a lovely book about modern architecture. He asked my husband for permission to marry our daughter. My husband said yes."

"He was very respectful," Mr. Nakamura said. "Our daughter is very, very sad."

"Perhaps it is a good idea if I speak to Anita alone," Kennicott said.

They nodded, stood, and left the room.

"Ask me anything, Detective," Anita said when they were alone.

"Why don't you tell me about how you met Livingston. How long you'd been seeing each other. And anything you can think of that might help."

"It's funny," she said, touching her cup now, cradling it in her hands. "We met in September. I was teaching a night class in life drawing at Central Tech. He was a student. He didn't seem at all special. He always wore an old pair of jeans and a hoodie, and he hardly ever spoke. He worked hard at his drawing, and he was good."

Kennicott tried to picture it. Livingston Fox, incognito in an art class, enjoying being out of the limelight.

"One night, we ended up walking out at the same time. It was the first week in December and there was an early snowstorm. I was the one who said, 'Why don't we get a coffee,' not him. He asked me all about myself. Why was I a teacher? What did I like most about my students? How did I prepare my lesson plans? Before I knew it, it was past midnight."

She rolled the cup between her palms. "I asked him where he lived, and he said 'Oh, I have a place downtown.' My apartment is by the Sherbourne subway station. I asked him if he wanted to come over, and he said, 'Okay, if it's not too late.'"

"So you don't live here?" Kennicott asked her.

"I'm staying with my parents for a few days."

Kennicott put his hands flat on the table, making himself stay perfectly still.

"Livingston was shy," she said. "Considerate. That night, we lay on my bed with our clothes on and listened to music. That's all. We woke up about seven o'clock the next morning. He'd set the alarm on his phone. He said he had to get to work. I asked him what he did for a living and he said he had a desk job at a real-estate development company. You know, I had no idea who he was."

"When did you figure it out?"

"About two months later. At that point, we were dating. I was getting my hair done, and I saw the article about him in *Toronto Life*. I was stunned."

"Were you angry?"

"Not really. He told me he didn't want me to like him because of his wealth. Listen, Detective. Just because I'm from a proper Japanese family doesn't mean I was inexperienced. I've been with lots of men, but no one like Livingston. Ever."

She put her teacup down. "When your brother was murdered, did you feel this way?" she asked. "This emptiness in your whole body? Like a piece of you was gone?"

Her eyes were searching his.

"I still have conversations with my brother and my parents in my head. I wish I had some magic words to make you feel better, but I don't. All I can do is catch the killer."

"I know."

"Did Livingston ever tell you he was afraid or worried or anything like that?"

"No."

"Did he ever talk to you about his plans for the second condo project on College Street? The one he was calling K2?"

"That's the one part of his business that he talked to me about. He was obsessed with it. He had this radical idea of building quality, well-designed public housing. He'd come over to my apartment and spend hours working on the architectural drawings."

It was the same thing Breaker had told him.

"Did you see the plans?"

"Of course. But he swore me to secrecy. He didn't want anyone to know about the project but me."

"Do you know where the plans are now?"

"No. But I know he had only one set, and he was very careful with them."

"When was the last time you communicated with him?"

"There was a thirteen-hour time difference when I was in Japan. I'd wake up early and he'd call me every morning."

"Did he call you on Friday?"

She nodded, lowered her eyes.

"Twice. The first time it was four in the morning here in Toronto. He never did that. I said, 'Why are you up so early?' He said he couldn't sleep and that he had to hear my voice."

"And the second time?"

"It would have been twenty after two in the afternoon here. He was getting ready for an important meeting."

"Did he say who he was meeting?"

"No. He said he wanted to surprise me."

"What else?"

"That he was working hard. He said it was hot and he was tired, probably because he hadn't slept very well."

"Anything else?"

"He said one strange thing. He wanted me to be careful. I asked him what he meant. He said he thought people were tracking his movements, trying to steal his drawings for K2. I asked him who, and he said he didn't know but he was trying to find out. He said to make sure I never told anyone about his plans.

"Anything else?"

She shook her head, struggling to compose herself.

"He said that I'd changed his life. That he'd never really been happy before he met me. That he loved my parents. That he couldn't wait for me to get home."

They didn't talk much longer. Kennicott got up to let himself out, but Nakamura insisted on walking him to the door.

"You are very kind," she said.

"I'll do everything I can and more."

She nodded, biting her bottom lip. Something about her body language told him not to leave quite yet. She gestured down the path and started to walk toward his car. He followed her. They stopped at the sidewalk.

She took a deep breath.

"When they read Livingston's will, his parents are going to find that he cut them out. He left them each one dollar."

"That doesn't surprise me."

"He left a third to his sister, a third to me, and a third in trust."

"In trust? For who?"

"I can't tell my parents this yet," she whispered. Her hand went to her stomach. "I'm pregnant."

"Oh my. Did Livingston . . ."

"He knew. We found out a month ago. The last thing he said to me was 'I love you and our baby too.'"

She started to cry. He waited while she wiped away her tears.

"Please find out who did this to us."

She turned and walked back to the house. He watched until she was inside before he got into his car. He sat behind the wheel and stared out the windshield. At the house next door, a group of kids were playing basketball in the driveway. Two houses farther down, a man was mowing his lawn. Two women pushing jogging strollers ran past. He watched a water sprinkler on another lawn rotate back and forth. Back and forth. Back and forth.

He had no idea how long he'd been sitting there when his phone rang. He looked at the display. It was Darvesh.

"What's up?" he said.

"We got the rush DNA results back on the baseball cap."

"And?"

"I think you should contact Detective Greene right away."

"Ari? Why?"

"I don't want to say on the phone. But it's big."

"Okay, I'm on my way." Kennicott turned on the ignition. The basketball dribbled down the driveway and out into the road. He waited until one of the players retrieved it and ran back to his friends before he slapped his car into gear.

45

When Greene arrived at the Caldense Bakery, Kennicott was already sitting in the window seat, a cup of coffee and a half-eaten croissant in front of him. Greene always shook hands with everyone he met. Kennicott knew that, but he made no move to get up. Greene kept his hands by his side and sat down across from him. There was a file on the table with a large CFS stamp on the outside: the Centre of Forensic Sciences.

Greene looked around the cafe. A soccer game was playing on the TV and a group of men and one woman were crowded around it, watching. Miguel Caldas, the proprietor, saw Greene and motioned to him.

"How's your father?" Kennicott asked, when he looked back at him.

"My dad's fine, thanks. What is so urgent?"

"What's he up to lately?"

"The usual. He goes to synagogue every morning to see his buddies and complain about the rabbi."

"What about yesterday?"

Why was Kennicott asking about his father?

"Ari, do you know where he was?"

This was absurd. "Daniel, what the hell is this about?"

"You're not answering my question."

"He's renovating my basement. I think he was buying some drywall."

"You think but you don't know for sure, do you?"

"Daniel, are you cross-examining me?"

Greene heard footsteps behind him. He turned in his chair.

"Detective Greene," Caldas said. "Lovely to see you again so soon. A croissant for you. What else? Cup of tea? Maybe some soup?"

He put a plate in front of Greene with a croissant on it and a glass of water.

"That's fine for now, thanks, Miguel," he said.

"Enjoy," Caldas said, and walked away.

Greene looked again at the CFS file on the table. What was going on? "Daniel, why am I thinking I should tell you to fuck off?"

"Did your father know Livingston Fox?"

"My father repaired shoes for his whole life. You know that. How would he know Fox?"

"Is that a no?"

"Yes, that's a no."

"Does he have a computer?"

"You think because he's older he's not on the Internet?"

"So that's a yes?"

"He has a computer. He has a cellphone. He used to have a Russian girlfriend who he met online. He's on Facebook. He's even got a Twitter account."

"We know that."

"You know what? You're investigating my father? You know about his Twitter account?" It took a lot to get Greene angry, but Kennicott was so calm it made him furious.

"Does your dad have a blog?"

"My father? Enough." He pointed at the folder. "What's with the CFS file?"

"You should know, Ari."

"Know what?"

"Come on. You know that yesterday I got a yellow backpack from a lawyer named Anthony Carpenter. You know it had a note on it telling me that it had been retrieved from the house across from the Kensington Gate building site."

Greene kept staring at Kennicott. There was no way he was going to admit what they both knew. But what did this have to do with his father?

"And you know there was a baseball cap and a pair of sunglasses inside. And you know the unknown person in the crowd who was caught on TV leaving the protest march and heading in the direction of the house was wearing the same clothes and hat."

Greene kept his face neutral. He'd seen the video. There was no way that person was his father.

"We got a DNA sample from the inside band of the ball cap," Kennicott said. "What I can't figure out is if you knew this hat belonged to a member of your family who was tied up with all this, why did you send me the backpack?"

"What are you talking about? I know my father better than anyone. That unknown person in the crowd who they showed on TV wasn't him." Something didn't fit. Kennicott would not be meeting him like this unless he had something. What?

Kennicott broke off eye contact, pulled out the file, and passed the report over to Greene. "Ari, the DNA is a fifty percent match for you."

"Fifty percent," Greene repeated. He felt numb.

"It's a female."

The crowd around the television erupted in cheers.

"Female," Greene said, hearing the hollow echo of his own voice despite the noise.

"Ari, I know your mother is dead and you don't have kids. But I never knew you had a sister. Or a half-sister perhaps. We started following your dad online because we thought maybe he could lead us to her. We have a preliminary description of her from a witness of the person with the backpack and baseball cap."

Oh no, Greene thought. Oh no. How could he have been so naive?

Kennicott started reading from the report. "Female. Caucasian, brown hair . . ."

"Grey-green eyes," Greene said.

Kennicott stopped reading and looked at him. "That's not in the report. She was wearing sunglasses."

"Eyes like mine," Greene said. He thought back to Alison's text to him on Friday afternoon. *Just heard the news.* Making it sound as if she were at school. He thought back to her time in university in London, how she couldn't sit still for classes. The same thing had happened again. It was less than a year since her mother died. He should have seen this coming.

"Did your witness say the woman had a British accent?" he asked.

"Don't know. Witness says she didn't say anything. Ari, what's going on? You know I'm breaking police protocol big time by coming to you with this first. Your sister is probably the one who took the pictures and posted them. She's almost certainly the Kensington Blogger we've been looking for."

Then, Greene remembered, she had texted: *Someone murdered at K. Gate?? So relieved u r okay!!* As if she knew nothing about what had happened.

"Ari?" Kennicott said.

Greene thought back to when Ted DiPaulo and Cassandra Amberlight came to his house. How Alison had dropped the lilac when she'd seen them, then picked it up and kept it in front of her face when they got to the porch, and how quickly she'd gone inside. She was the Kensington Blogger. She'd probably spent weeks and weeks hanging out in the market and must have been afraid Amberlight would recognize her. He remembered their brief conversation.

"They should charge the person. Young lady, this is your generation. All these cellphones and selfie shots. What do you think?"

"I guess sometimes people just get carried away."

"Ari?" Kennicott was talking to him. "Are you okay?"

Greene focused back on Kennicott. "My father had nothing to do with this. I don't have a sister or a half-sister. It was my daughter."

"Daughter?"

"Yes, Daniel, I have a daughter."

"Since when? How old is she?"

"Twenty. She came back with me to Canada from England, where she grew up. That was in December. I told you I wasn't ready to talk to you yet. That was why. She wants to be a journalist. I thought she was in school, but instead it looks as if you are right. We've found the Kensington Blogger."

46

Alison looked at the text she'd sent her father twenty-five minutes ago. "Dad, I really, really need to talk 2 u. When will u b home??? Allie."

"Walking home, I'll be there in about half an hour," he'd texted back. "What's up?"

"Hurry," was all she'd written.

For the last ten minutes she'd been standing at the end of the street, waiting for him to arrive. Despite the hot sun and the humidity, Alison was shivering. What would Ari say when he found out what she'd done? That his daughter was a liar? That she was the Kensington Blogger who'd posted the photo of Livingston Fox's body online? He was going to be extremely disappointed in her.

The hot weather had brought people outdoors. Along Dundas Street, a rainbow of colourful awnings and umbrellas had sprouted on the patios of the restaurants and bars like a field of tulips in spring. Everyone looked happy.

"Hi there."

Alison turned. Ari was standing right in front of her. He wasn't smiling at her the way he always did. "What's up?" he said.

"I need to tell you something, and it's really bad."

He nodded, not saying anything. He was maddeningly quiet sometimes.

"I . . . I haven't been honest with you. I quit school in April. I couldn't handle it. I've been pretending to go for months."

He gave her one of his slow nods. She wished he'd say something. Anything.

"And, well, I started hanging out in Kensington Market. It's the only place in this city where I feel at home. It kind of reminds me of Portobello Market in London, where I went on Saturdays with Mum, and Grandpa Y loves it there. It's not as clean and neat and modern like everything else in this city of yours."

He still wasn't talking. But she had to tell him. She had to.

"You see. I still want to be a journalist. And, well, like . . ."

"You started the *Kensington Confidential* blog," he said. His tone was flat, lifeless.

Wait. Had he known this all along?

"You knew?" she demanded.

"I just found out."

"How?"

"Yesterday I went into the house on Augusta beside the building site. I found your backpack and got it to the police. Your DNA was on the band of the Blue Jays cap and I'm a fifty percent match. Detective Kennicott told me half an hour ago."

What did this mean? The police had identified her. Was she going to be arrested?

"Am I in trouble?"

"The police want to talk to you."

"I want to talk to them. Are they going to arrest me?"

He shook his head. "For what? Breaking into an empty house? Posting the photo? You won't have a problem, as long as you tell the police everything."

"Of course I'm going to tell them everything," she said. To her surprise, Alison felt a surge of anger at her father. "Okay, I didn't tell you the truth about dropping out of school, but do you really think I'd lie to the police?"

"I didn't say that."

She wasn't shivering anymore. She was furious. And she didn't really know why. "You sure as hell implied it. It's not like you've been honest with me."

"What do you mean?"

"What do I mean? You know exactly what I mean. We've been dancing around this since that day I met you in the solicitor's office."

"Dancing around what?"

She wiped the perspiration off her forehead. She'd been holding back all this time, but to hell with it. "Ari, I don't believe you never knew I even existed for twenty years."

He looked taken aback.

"There I said it."

"But I didn't," he said.

"Twenty years! Come on. You told me yourself you kept all of Mum's Christmas cards."

"I did. But I didn't—"

"You knew. You didn't care. Big deal that you had a daughter somewhere. You didn't give a damn. But then you lose the woman you were in love with and suddenly you remember me? Come on, Sherlock, I thought you were the great Canadian detective. Do you really think I'm that stupid?"

He looked blank. She'd never seen that expression on his face.

"Alison, I didn't know."

"You're lying! And now you say you care so much. Where the hell were you when I was growing up?"

He blinked. "Maybe I was hiding the truth, even from myself."

"See, you're not perfect."

"Clearly, I'm not."

"What am I doing living here in Toronto anyhow? I don't know this place. I stand out like a sore thumb. Sometimes I hate it here. Sometimes I want to go home."

He was nodding. "I don't blame you."

Her whole world felt upside down. Home. Where was home?

"Why did you make me come here anyway?" she demanded.

"As I recall it, this was your idea."

She remembered how he'd grinned at her that night in the restaurant when she'd told him she wanted to move to Canada. "Yeah, well, maybe I did it just to make you happy."

"If you want to move back to England, I'll move there with you. But only if you want me to."

"What about Grandpa Y?"

He shrugged. "Tell me what you want."

"What I want . . ." She hesitated, not sure what to say. She had to stop sweating. She had to get out of the sun. "I want to talk to the police. I want to apologize to Livingston's family. I want to help find the killer. And I don't want your help with any of it."

She tore away from him and marched off. She could bloody well get to police headquarters on her own.

What she'd really wanted to do was to hug her father for the first time in her life, but she couldn't do that until she'd untangled the mess she'd made of things. Besides, she didn't want him to see her cry.

47

The intercom on Kennicott's office phone buzzed.

"Detective Kennicott," Francine Hughes said, "there's a young lady out here who is most anxious to speak to you."

Greene had called Kennicott a few minutes ago to say that his daughter was on her way.

"She looks just like her father," Hughes whispered.

"I'll be right out," Kennicott said.

When he saw Alison in the reception area, he could tell right away she was Greene's daughter. She had her father's eyes, a beguiling grey-green with flecks of yellow. There was the confident way she held her broad shoulders back, the direct way she reached out to shake his hand.

"Nice to meet you," Kennicott said.

"Nice to meet you as well, Detective Kennicott," she said. "My father has told me many things about you. I hope I am not imposing, but it is very important that I speak to you as quickly as possible. I should have done this right away."

He was taken aback by her voice. Greene had told Kennicott that Alison was British, but it still seemed incongruous for this Ari Greene look-alike to have an English accent.

Hughes popped out of her chair. "Lovely to meet you," she said. "Ari is fortunate to have you."

"I'm the one who is lucky to have him," Alison said.

Kennicott guided her to the video room, where Darvesh was waiting. He turned on the camera, the commissioner came in and swore her in, and then, without any prompting, Alison told her story: how she'd come to Canada, enrolled in journalism school, dropped out without telling her father, discovered Kensington Market, started the blog, contacted Livingston Fox and met with him once at his office and then for the next three Friday afternoons in the backroom of the Huibing Gardens restaurant.

Through it all Kennicott kept thinking how remarkably poised she was for a young woman her age.

"You were the one who broke the story about Mr. Fox getting engaged."

She grinned. It was a warm and winning smile, like Ari's. "Mr. Fox made sure I got the story before anyone else. It was my first scoop, and it gave my blog a huge boost."

"Did you ever meet his fiancée?"

"No. I never met anyone in Mr. Fox's life after the time I went to the office and talked to his assistant, Maxine."

She told him about her planned meeting with Fox on Friday. "I waited and waited but he never arrived. He had made me promise not to call Maxine or anyone else if he didn't come."

"What did you do?"

"After a long time a waitress brought in a pot of tea. It was awkward. I didn't say anything to her because I didn't want her to hear my accent. I waited a while longer before I left. I had to get to the demonstration."

"Do you know when you left?"

"Yes, because I kept checking the time. It was exactly ten to four. The demo was starting at four."

She kept talking. Kennicott listened without taking notes. When she finished, he said, "Take me back to when you were at the window of the house you broke into. What exactly did you see?"

"Fox's body."

"Anything else? In the alleyway? The building site?"

"I was stunned. I almost threw up."

"Think hard."

"I only saw two other people."

"Who?" Kennicott asked. This could be the lead he was searching for.

She looked at him with her Ari Greene eyes. "I saw you, Detective, and a policeman who was with you come out of the gate. I didn't want you to see me so I closed the curtain. I was afraid."

Kennicott remembered the moment. He'd looked up at that window. Had he seen the curtain move a little? Maybe. He couldn't be sure. He tried to picture the alley again: the hockey sticks, the locked bike, the puddle of dog pee that Lindsmore had almost stepped in. There had to be a clue.

"Did you see anyone with a dog?"

She shook her head. "No. I feel awful that Fox's family found out about their son's murder because of me. I wish I'd never posted that photo."

"It was very foolish. Think again, was there anything you saw that can help our investigation?"

She pulled out her phone. "I took two more pictures from the window. I don't think there's anything there, but you can have them."

Kennicott nodded at Darvesh.

She tapped on her phone and showed them both photos. They were almost the same as the one on the blog. One was aimed lower and showed more of the hoarding and the pavement below it, the other, higher, showed more of the building site past the shed.

"Okay, Detective Darvesh will copy them when we finish the interview. But now, is there anything else at all that you can tell us that might assist our investigation?"

She closed her eyes and leaned her head on her cupped hand. "I keep seeing Livingston's body. He was kind to me. I'd never even seen a dead person before my mother died, and now this."

Kennicott watched her shake her head.

"All I want to do is help," she said. "I wish I could. I wish I'd seen something."

48

"Detective Kennicott," Francine Hughes said through the intercom. "Ms. Cassandra Amberlight has arrived with her lawyer, Mr. DiPaulo, and Detective Ari Greene."

"Thanks, we'll be there in a few minutes," Kennicott said. He clicked off the intercom and turned to Crown Attorney Albert Fernandez, who had joined him and Darvesh half an hour earlier to prepare for the interview. It was hard to believe it had been less than forty-eight hours since Kennicott and Fernandez had been in court together about to get the guilty verdict in their murder trial. It felt more like forty-eight days ago.

It was highly unusual for a prime suspect to come to the police to make a statement, and they had no idea what Amberlight would say.

"Do you think she's going to confess?" Darvesh asked. "We've got her DNA in the shed."

"My bet is that DiPaulo wants to work out a deal. A quick plea to manslaughter," Fernandez said. "He'll say that his client and the victim argued about the new condo plan. Amberlight lost her temper, pushed him, he fell."

"What about the rebar through Fox's heart?" Darvesh asked.

Fernandez shrugged. "Done in a fit of anger."

"And the concrete blocks?"

"A feeble attempt to make it look like this was some kind of satanic ritual to throw us off track."

Kennicott shook his head. "Not in a million years will she confess. Watch. She's going to be in total denial. My bet is that she never even told DiPaulo or Ari about her run to the border last night. Let's go."

They walked down the short hallway to the reception area. Amber-light was slumped in a chair. She looked exhausted. No surprise, Ken-nicott thought. She'd spent most of the night driving to the border and back. Ted DiPaulo looked apprehensive. Only Greene looked relaxed, his usual unflappable self.

Kennicott went straight up to Amberlight. "My name is Detective Daniel Kennicott."

"Nice to meet you." There was a note of sarcasm in her voice.

"With me are Detective Kamil Darvesh and Crown Attorney Albert Fernandez."

"'When sorrows come, they come not single spies but in battal-ions,'" she said, as she got slowly to her feet.

He'd read that she was a big woman but hadn't realized how tall she was. "We won't bite, I promise," he said.

"Well then, neither will I."

There was a twinkle in her eyes. He sensed that she liked all the at-tention.

"Everything is set up in the video room. We're ready to go."

Amberlight stepped forward, but DiPaulo put his hand out to hold her back, like a crossing guard stopping a pedestrian from stepping off a curb. "First, we need to set the ground rules," he said. "Let's be one hundred percent clear. My client is not under arrest."

DiPaulo was a good lawyer. He didn't waste any time getting right to the point.

"Correct. She's not under arrest at this time."

"Let's hope she's not at any time. I want it clearly understood that Ms. Amberlight has no legal obligation to speak to you."

"None at all."

"Since this is a voluntary statement, not a police interrogation, she has the right to have her lawyer present. If that is not agreeable, there will be no interview."

Kennicott had expected this. Although he'd prefer to interview her alone, it might be good for DiPaulo to hear some of his questions.

"You can be present during the interview, but I insist that you not speak," he said.

"Fair enough. And again, to make absolutely certain there are no misunderstandings, Ms. Amberlight can terminate this interview at any time."

Something caught Kennicott's eye. Amberlight was waving her long arms in the air. "Hello. Knock, knock. Remember me?" she said, a mocking look on her face. "Are you two finished talking about me in the third person while I'm standing here in the first person?"

There was something about Amberlight's bravado that was oddly appealing, Kennicott thought. "The door in the video room will not be locked. You are free to leave at any time, unless we place you under arrest."

"Well then, I suggest you not arrest me."

Everyone chuckled.

She was arrogant but gutsy, Kennicott thought. A jury would either love or hate her. Hard to tell. He turned back to Greene. "Ari, I can't allow you to sit in. There's a chair for you in the video-link room. That's where Albert will be watching from as well."

"Fine," Greene said.

There was a pause. Nobody seemed ready to make the first move.

"Well then, let's get this over with," Amberlight said. "It's not as if we're negotiating the Versailles Peace Treaty."

She marched down the hallway to the video room with her head held high. Kennicott and Darvesh sat across from her and DiPaulo. While the commissioner was swearing her in, Kennicott took out his notebook, turned to a new page, clicked his pen, and wrote out the date, time, location and listed everyone who was present.

"Before you start with your questions," Amberlight said, staring at

Kennicott until he looked back at her, "I want to tell you, Detective, that I appeared in front of your father in court many times. Justice Kennicott was an excellent judge, and his death was a great loss to the bar. My sincere condolences."

"Thank you," Kennicott said. It took him aback. His parents had been killed in a car accident years earlier. Over time, he had come to suspect that the crash was related in some way to his brother's murder. But he didn't know how. Was Amberlight being sincere or trying to manipulate him? Or both?

"And one more thing before you begin your questions," Amberlight said. "I want you to know that I did not kill Livingston Fox."

There goes Fernandez's bet that Amberlight was going to confess, Kennicott thought. DiPaulo gave him a half shrug, as if to say, *What can I do? She's my client.*

"Let's start at the beginning," Kennicott said. He wasn't going to let her take control of his interview. "Did you know Livingston Fox?"

"Yes. It's no secret that I hated everything he stood for. He was tearing the heart out of the city, and I was the only one standing up to him."

She doesn't like to give straight answers, Kennicott thought. She prefers to defer to political statements.

"A month ago he sent me a letter, handwritten, asking me to contact his assistant to set up a time to talk to him. He ended with a quotation. 'If you want to make peace, you don't talk to your friends. You talk to your enemies.'"

"What did you do?"

"Nothing, for about a day. Then I thought what the hell. I went to his fancy office down on Front Street and met him for the first time. After that, we got together for the next three Fridays. Our meetings were secret, or at least that's what I thought, until this happened."

"Where did you meet?"

"At a Chinese restaurant on Spadina. He had it all arranged."

"In the backroom of Huibing Gardens?" Kennicott asked. Normally he wouldn't ask a leading question such as this. But he wanted to signal to Amberlight right from the get-go that he already knew a lot about her and Fox. Let her wonder how much.

"You've done your homework, Detective."

"What about the last time you saw him?"

"Friday. The day he was murdered. Livingston wanted to meet me at the work shed at the back of his building site. I'd never been there before."

Interesting that she'd called Fox by his first name and she was squarely putting herself at the murder scene. DiPaulo was smart enough to make sure she didn't deny the undeniable.

"Did anyone else know about your meetings?"

"No. He insisted they be secret, and I agreed. I sure didn't want anyone to know I was breaking bread with the devil."

"What were you meeting about?" Kennicott was pretty sure he knew the answer.

"He'd decided to turn his next building, K2, into an innovative kind of community housing project."

So far, Kennicott thought, Amberlight has been telling the truth. "Why was he talking to you about it?"

She stuck a thumbnail between her teeth and gnawed on it. Kennicott noticed her fingernails were bitten down to the quick.

"He was hoping I'd publicly endorse his plan," she said at last. "No one on this planet was more surprised than I was."

"What did you think of his plans?"

"I was shocked. I have to admit, they were fantastic."

"Then why did you organize the protest march against it?"

She put her elbows on the table and leaned forward. "The whole thing was his idea."

She described the plan Fox had to shock the public by doing a 180-degree turn. It was exactly what Breaker had told Kennicott. And if a jury believed her, they'd think she had no motive for murder and they'd find her not guilty.

"Why would I want him dead?" Amberlight asked, seemingly reading his mind.

Or was it too neat and tidy? Kennicott wondered. What if Fox had told her at their final meeting that he'd changed his mind and wasn't going ahead with their deal?

49

Greene had always been at the centre of murder investigations, but here he was, watching Kennicott run the show. Following the interview on a video link was frustrating but fascinating.

"You have my DNA and my fingerprints," Amberlight said to Kennicott. "They were all over the shed. Obviously, I didn't try to hide anything. Did I?"

As Greene had expected, Amberlight was trying to run her own interview. But Kennicott had managed to keep control. They were like two boxers who had finished a few warm-up rounds. Now the main event was about to begin.

"Why the change in location for this last meeting?" Kennicott asked.

Smart, Greene thought. Don't get sucked in to answering her question.

"It was his idea. I got the sense he suspected that someone had found out about our meetings at the restaurant."

"What made you think that?"

"The last time we met at the Huibing, he kept asking me if I'd told anyone about meeting with him or his new plan for K2. Then on Friday he was different."

Greene was watching Amberlight closely on the monitor. Her tone had changed. She'd stopped lecturing and putting on a show. She seemed to be genuinely recalling the moment, going back in time in her memory.

"I can't point to anything specific. But he was quiet, slow, not his usual hyperfocused self. He said he was dehydrated from this heat and kept drinking from one of his water bottles. He was such a neat freak, but at one point he dropped a pencil on the floor and I bent down to pick it up and he told me not to bother. I know it sounds trivial, but it was out of character."

Greene remembered seeing the pencil on the floor of the shed. He looked at Kennicott. Was he skeptical? Convinced?

"How did you get into the construction site?"

"He told me he'd leave the back gate open. I walked up the alleyway and went right in. I felt as if I was entering enemy territory."

"Did you see anyone?"

She threw up her hands. "That was the whole point. The meeting had to be secret."

"Is that a no? You didn't see anyone?"

Greene had heard that Kennicott had been an excellent young lawyer, but this was the first time he'd seen him in action. He wasn't letting Amberlight get the upper hand, no easy task.

"No. I didn't see anyone. And no one saw me."

DiPaulo was frowning. He must be imagining Amberlight on the witness stand, where her theatrics would make her seem defensive and unlikeable.

"Do you know what time you arrived at the shed?"

"I know the exact time." She crossed her arms in front of her chest, defiant, like an angry teenager. Greene saw DiPaulo's frown deepen. No matter how hard you tried to prepare a witness, their true colours always shone through when they were questioned by a skilled cross-examiner.

Greene looked over at Fernandez. "We can't choose our clients or our witnesses, can we?" he said.

"That's what makes our jobs interesting."

They both turned back to the monitor. Kennicott kept his cool. "What was the exact time you got there?"

"Two-thirty. He was totally rigid about time. Obsessed."

"And what did you talk about?"

"He'd added a greenhouse to the design. He wanted to give residents a place to grow vegetables and flowers. I remember exactly what he said. 'Just because people are poor, that doesn't mean they should live in an ugly place or eat unhealthy food.'"

"You thought he was being sincere?"

"I did."

"Did you argue with him?"

So that was Kennicott's working theory. It was a good one. With Amberlight's criminal record for assaults and her extreme personality, it wasn't too hard to imagine that her mood could turn on a dime.

Amberlight thrust her face closer to Kennicott. "Believe it or not, once in a while I actually get along with people."

Kennicott grinned.

"She might not be such a bad witness," Greene said.

"Possibly," Fernandez said.

Something in his voice gave Greene pause. Did he know more about Amberlight than he was letting on?

"When did you leave the shed?" Kennicott asked her.

For the first time in the interview, Amberlight hesitated. She sat back, shook her head. "I don't know exactly."

"We've learned that Mr. Fox set the alarm on his phone before every meeting, and that he kept them to either fifteen or thirty minutes."

Amberlight stared at Kennicott with what appeared to be an honest look of recognition. "That's right. We always met for half an hour. When I got there I asked him if he'd set the alarm, and he said he was too tired to bother. I didn't think of it until now, but it was strange."

"When you left the shed, did you leave the door open?"

"I don't remember. I think it was on a spring, and it shut on its own."

She was right about that, Greene thought.

"Which way did you go from there?"

She gave him a withering frown.

"What do you think, Detective? I went back the same way I came in. I wasn't going to parade myself through the construction site."

Here it comes, Greene thought, the key question. Did she shut the back gate? He sat forward, tensed up. This was hard to watch from the sidelines.

"Did you go through the gate by the shed?" Kennicott asked.

Amberlight waved a hand casually, completely unaware of how important her answer would be.

"Of course I did. I closed it behind me," she said. "Fox asked me to."

50

Kennicott clicked his pen a few times. Her answer about the gate seemed genuine.

Seemed. That was the operative word. Some people could convince themselves that they were telling the truth even when they were lying. That's why lie-detector tests couldn't catch pathological liars. Is that what Amberlight was?

"After you walked through the gate, where did you go?"

"I walked home the same way I came."

"Did you see anyone?"

"No. Everyone was at the demonstration. I went up to my apartment and lay down."

"Do you live with anyone?"

She gave a hearty laugh. "Detective Kennicott, I'm sure you've looked into my personal history. Two divorces, seven kids, and none of them want anything to do with me. My vagabond lifestyle. As you can see, I'm impossible to live with."

Instead of giving a straight answer, she thought she could charm her way out of it.

"I take it that's a no. You don't live with anyone."

"No cats, no dogs, no people. And no, no one saw me go into my apartment."

She was getting nervous and trying hard to hide it. The key was not to get taken in by all her drama. "What did you do at home?" he asked.

"I was tired. I guess it was this terrible heat. I took a short nap. Then I got up, picked up my megaphone, went down the awful stairs that I fell on this morning, and walked over to Augusta Avenue."

"How long did all of this take?"

"I honestly don't know."

Bingo, Kennicott thought. When witnesses told you how honest they were, it was often a sign they were lying.

"You are very active on social media. Did you email or text anyone in this time period, post anything on Twitter or Facebook or Instagram?"

Darvesh had checked all of this, and Kennicott knew the answer.

"No, no, no, no, and no," she said.

"Why not?"

"My whole life I've been a rebel, an outsider. It's cost me a great deal, personally, financially, emotionally. Really, in every way. But that's who I am. And now I was going to join the other side. I was afraid people would think I was a sellout."

"Why, if you believed that Fox had genuinely changed?"

She shook her head and heaved a sigh.

"It was more than that. Fox wanted to hire me as a full-time consultant and I'd have a job and a salary, benefits and paid vacations for the first time in my life. And—this is something that was supposed to be kept secret—he was going to give me an apartment in the new building for one dollar a year. It meant no more worrying every month if I could make the rent. And no more living in that shabby apartment with those terrifying stairs. I've never lived in a place with an elevator, and I'm sixty-seven years old."

She sat back in her chair and covered her face with her hands. The room fell silent, the only sound was the low hum of the air conditioner. After what seemed like a long time, Amberlight let out a deep, lonely moan.

She seemed broken.

Seemed.

51

Greene watched Amberlight on the monitor. Transfixed. Whatever opinions people had of her, you had to admire the woman for the strength of her convictions. But he could see that despite the brave face she always presented to the world, she'd become trapped in her public persona, and that beneath all her bravado she was alone and vulnerable.

She lowered her hands from her face. For the next few minutes she talked about how she'd joined the demonstration, heard the news about Fox, called DiPaulo, and gone to his place with Ari Greene to talk before falling asleep in DiPaulo's spare room.

Kennicott was listening intently, nodding, taking notes, encouraging her to talk. It was Witness Examination 101. Get people talking. The more details the better, because the more information she gave him now, the greater the chance she'd contradict herself at a later date.

"And what did you do yesterday?"

Greene knew Kennicott very well. He was trying too hard to seem uninterested.

"I stayed at Ted's all day."

"Last night too?"

"No, I wanted to get home and Ari drove me back."

"I see," Kennicott said. He unclicked his pen and clipped it to the back page of his notebook, sending a signal to Amberlight that the interview was almost over. But his manner was too casual. Kennicott knew something about Amberlight that he wasn't letting on. Greene could feel it.

She hesitated. "Last night?" Her voice was weak. She was stalling, answering a question with a question.

DiPaulo, who had been diligently keeping notes, looked up for the first time. Greene could see he'd caught it too. Something had changed in the interview.

Greene glanced at Fernandez, who was glued to the monitor. "What do you guys have on her?"

Fernandez's face was a mask. "Let's see how your client answers the next set of questions."

Greene looked back at the monitor. Kennicott clasped his hands on top of his notebook, as cool as a cucumber. "After Detective Greene dropped you off at home, what did you do?"

"To tell you the honest truth, I was exhausted," Amberlight said.

Uh-oh, Greene thought.

Kennicott said nothing, using silence to force her to speak.

"I fell asleep," Amberlight said.

"And after that?"

"I woke up."

Amberlight was trying too hard. Overthinking. She sounded like a comedian whose jokes were flat. Greene remembered how she'd insisted on going back to her apartment last night, despite his advice to remain at DiPaulo's place. What foolish thing had she done after he dropped her off at her home?

"About what time did you wake up?"

"I don't know. I didn't look at the time," she said.

Greene felt helpless and he could see DiPaulo did as well. In his gut he could feel that Amberlight was about to make a drastic mistake. And Kennicott had set this up perfectly.

52

Kennicott's heart was racing. Breathe, he told himself. Take your time. He'd manoeuvred Amberlight into a corner. Now was the time to move in for the kill.

He picked up his notebook and tapped it on the edge of the table. "What did you do after you woke up?" He didn't dare look at Amberlight. Instead he examined his fingernails, trying his very best to act bored.

Amberlight cleared her throat.

A stall. She was weighing her options: tell the truth or hope that the police had no idea about her midnight run.

"Well, I went down to Jimmy's and got two coffees. One for me and one for Detective Greene. He was coming to pick me up at ten."

He almost had her. Now he had to sink the hook before he yanked hard and reeled her in.

"That's it? You didn't do anything else last night?"

"That's it," she said.

He smacked his notebook on the desk. It rang out like a cracked whip.

Amberlight's body jerked.

He stood up abruptly and motioned to Darvesh.

"We'll be back in a few minutes."

Amberlight looked astonished.

"As soon as we leave this room we'll turn the video camera off so as not to intrude on your solicitor–client discussions." He opened his notebook, took out two folded pieces of paper and slid them in front of her. "You might want to discuss the ticket you got at 3:51 a.m. last night in Oshawa for driving with a broken tail light, and the report from American Customs at the Thousand Islands Bridge when they turned you back at 6:05 a.m. after you attempted to cross the border and flee."

Now Amberlight looked terrified.

Kennicott joined Darvesh at the door and turned back to her. "I suggest you talk to Mr. DiPaulo, who I assume knew nothing about this," he said.

She looked as if she was about to collapse.

He walked out the door and made a point of slamming it behind him. To put an exclamation mark on it.

53

The last image Greene saw on the screen before it went blank was Amberlight's face, her expression void of all emotion.

"Shit," he said.

He should have seen this coming. The piece of paper that Amberlight had reached for on the staircase that made her fall was a traffic violation ticket for a broken tail light. She hadn't wanted him see it because she didn't want him to know she had tried to cross the border in the middle of the night.

"Besides not having an alibi for her whereabouts between three and four on Friday afternoon," Fernandez said, "your client has a small problem with telling the truth."

"Is Kennicott going to arrest her?"

"Come on, Detective. Wouldn't you?"

Greene had to admit that all the evidence against Amberlight now fit. She had been shown to be a persistent liar, incapable of facing her shortcomings, constantly trying to hide the truth. And the truth was ugly: she had a terrible temper and a criminal record that included violence. She was financially, professionally, and personally at the end of her rope. If Fox really had planned to reinvent the K2 condo project and guarantee her an apartment in it, he could see how she would have grabbed it as a life raft. Then, if he'd tried to back out of the deal or they'd fought about the details at their Friday afternoon meeting, she could have been angry enough to kill him.

DiPaulo must be livid. Greene could imagine the wrath he was raining down on Amberlight right now. Despite Greene's warning that it was crucial that she not lie to the police or hide anything from them, she'd done just that.

Greene stroked his cheek, which was still tender from where her coffee had hit him when she'd fallen on the stairs. That fit too. She'd fallen because she was worn out from driving all the way to the border and back in the middle of the night.

The door to the video-link room opened, and Kennicott and Darvesh walked in. Kennicott's face was solemn. He was classy enough not to gloat.

"I assume you and Ted had no idea about Ms. Amberlight's late-night adventure," he said.

"You know I can't answer that," Greene said.

"I don't think you have to," Kennicott said. "Terribly bad luck for your client. With the rise in petty crime these days in Kensington, sounds as if someone kicked in one of her back lights. She told the officer who stopped her she had no idea it was out."

Kennicott was keeping a straight face. But they both knew what he was saying. This time he'd outsmarted Greene. Probably had an undercover officer kick in the tail light and then Kennicott notified the OPP to stop her.

"Must have been a very vigilant cop to stop someone on the highway in the middle of the night for such a minor infraction," Greene said.

"I guess we just got lucky."

Kennicott pulled out a chair and sat down across from Greene.

"I'm sure the Fox family would appreciate it if Ms. Amberlight could tell us where she put Livingston's plans for the K2 condo that she took after . . ."

He didn't need to spell out after what.

"Don't beat yourself up for bringing her in for this interview, Ari. We would have arrested her anyway, even if she hadn't tried to do a runner. Now that we have her on tape, under oath, caught in a bald-faced lie, this is her one-time chance to make a deal. She can make a quick guilty plea and put everyone out of their misery. It's not hard to imagine that at the last minute she and Fox had a disagreement about their deal and she lost it. We could put together a joint statement of facts and agree that there was no planning or deliberation on her part. She acted in rage and now she deeply regrets it. She came here today to police headquarters to confess and get it off her chest. We'll both propose a sentence of, say, eight years, she'd be out in a third of that time, easy."

Kennicott was holding out the carrot. Now here comes the stick, Greene thought.

"But if we don't get a confession today, all bets are off. She'll be charged with first-degree murder. Given her propensity to lie about everything, including telling us she closed the gate when she knew she'd left it open; it's transparent that she was trying to make it look as if someone else came in to kill Fox after she'd left. This is a brutal murder. My bet is the jury would convict her and she'd be looking at twenty-five years, minimum."

Greene waited. He knew these three men very well, and right now they were all staring at him.

"She's sixty-seven years old, Daniel," he whispered at last.

"I know," Kennicott said. "That's why we're offering her this."

"Shouldn't you be having this discussion with her lawyer?" Greene asked.

"Normally yes, but in this case I think it's better coming from you."

Greene got up slowly. He walked to the door and paused.

"What, Ari?" Kennicott asked. "Do you still have your doubts? She lied to you and Ted. She lied under oath. She had motive. She has no alibi. She tried to flee."

Illogical as it seemed, despite the mountain of evidence, Greene still couldn't see Amberlight as a killer. Something occurred to him. "This revised plan for K2. It must have been the big story Fox wanted to tell my daughter."

"We'll never know."

"Maybe Fox was killed because someone didn't want these new plans to go public."

Kennicott shook his head. "Maybe it was the same gang who O. J. Simpson says killed his wife, Nicole."

They stared at each other. The silence in the room grew heavy.

"Ari, go talk to her," Kennicott said. "We both know what's at stake here."

But Greene could see it in Kennicott's eyes. It was there. Uncertainty.

"Thanks," Greene said, before he walked out.

What were he and DiPaulo going to do, he wondered as he went down the hallway, if after all this Amberlight still denied she'd murdered Fox?

54

"You are going to arrest her, aren't you?" Fernandez asked as soon as Greene was gone.

As the lead detective, it was Kennicott's decision to make. "You mean if she doesn't confess now?" he said.

That was the problem. Was he ready to arrest her without a confession and take her to trial? There were other suspects still out there. What about Fox's father? He wasn't in the clear. What about one of Fox's ex-girlfriends? A former employee? And what Greene had said. Why had Fox been acting paranoid lately, and what made him so concerned about keeping this plan secret? If he had been making a deal with Amberlight, then she wasn't the person he feared. Breaker had warned Kennicott that Fox's competitors were smart and ruthless. She was convinced one of them had hired a hit man to take him out.

"You're the prosecutor," Kennicott said to Fernandez. "Is what you've heard today enough to go to the jury and get a conviction?"

"It would be an extremely strong case."

"What do we lose by waiting a few days? Putting her under twenty-four-hour surveillance?"

"Do you really want to let her go back to her apartment?" Fernandez asked.

He had a good point.

"I've held off searching it because I had a hunch she'd try something like she did last night and try to take off," Kennicott said. "If we'd gone into her place with a search warrant earlier, it would have tipped her off. Now we can get one. If she killed him, she could still have some blood on the clothes she wore on Friday."

"There could be more," Fernandez said. "We might find something on her computer, in her garbage can, her filing cabinet. It always amazes me how criminals don't get around to throwing out incriminating evidence."

"In this case, she didn't have much time."

"Neither do we," Fernandez said. "You let her walk out of here now, even if we put her under surveillance around the clock, we lose control."

Come on, Daniel, Kennicott thought, time to decide. He turned to Darvesh. "What do you think?"

"My vote is with Albert. I say we do it now."

Kennicott picked up his notebook and tapped it on the table a few times. He stood and the two men stood with him.

"Are you going to arrest her?" Darvesh asked.

Kennicott felt a flash of anger. "It's the easiest thing in the world to arrest someone. But trust me, Kamil, one day when you're the lead detective, you'll think you have the perfect suspect. Someone with motive, opportunity, background, who acts suspiciously after the crime. You make the arrest, you put the person on trial, and you are wrong. Dead wrong."

Darvesh nodded. "I'm sorry. I wasn't trying to—"

"You charge someone with murder. Even if they are totally exonerated, their life is never the same." And neither is your own life, he thought.

"What are you going to do if Amberlight doesn't confess?" Fernandez asked.

Kennicott tapped the table again with his notebook. He didn't want to give them an answer because he didn't have one.

"Let's go," he said, "and talk to our prime suspect."

55

Greene had known Ted DiPaulo for more than twenty years, and he'd never seen the man as angry as he was now with Amberlight.

"You will not take instructions from anyone," DiPaulo yelled, pounding the table hard enough to make it shake.

"I know. I know," Amberlight cried. "I was so frightened."

"But I told you, running away would be the worst possible thing you could do."

"You don't understand."

"No, you're wrong. I've been a criminal lawyer for a very long time. I understand perfectly well. I know when I have a client who has no concept of the truth or the consequences of lying. And that's you, every time."

Amberlight put her head in her hands and shook it hard.

"I'll tell you what happens with clients like you," DiPaulo said through gritted teeth. "They get convicted. They go to jail. I lose. I hate to lose. When I lose, I don't sleep for days. And I like to sleep. How can I possibly represent you now?"

"I messed up."

"Messed up? *Messed up?* You destroyed the whole case. Kennicott played you like a fiddle. All you had to do is what Ari told you to do and what I told you to do."

"How was I supposed to know that some kids in the market kicked out one of my back lights? And what was I supposed to do, tell the cops that I tried to get across the border in the middle of the night?"

DiPaulo jumped up in frustration, kicked back his chair, and walked over to the window. He folded his arms as if somehow they could contain his anger. "Yes. It's something called the truth. If you'd said to Kennicott, 'Last night I panicked. It was a stupid thing to do. I tried to drive across the border to go see my sister because I couldn't take the pressure.' If you'd just said something like that, then we wouldn't have a problem."

DiPaulo was really going at her. Greene almost felt sorry for Amberlight.

"I know, I know," she said.

"You lied to the police. You lied to me and Ari."

"And now no one will ever believe me. But I didn't kill Fox. I didn't. I didn't."

"I hope that's true," DiPaulo said. "But after this, you need to find another lawyer."

"What?" Amberlight said, looking up at him. "But Ted—"

There was a loud rap on the door.

Amberlight and DiPaulo froze.

Greene turned his back to them and opened the door. Kennicott, Fernandez, and Darvesh walked in. Their faces were grim, like a jury returning with a guilty verdict.

Enter the executioner, Greene thought.

Kennicott's phone rang. Loud. It was a hotshot.

He jerked his head toward Greene.

They both knew what this meant. Another murder in the city.

Down the hall someone was shrieking. Greene peered out the door. It was, of all people, Francine Hughes. Running toward them.

"Detective Kennicott, Detective Kennicott!" she was yelling.

The hotshot rang again. Everything seemed to be happening at once. This whole afternoon had turned into a disaster.

Greene turned back to the room. Kennicott was answering his phone.

"Kennicott," he said. "What have we got?"

"Detective Kennicott," Hughes said rushing up to him.

Kennicott put his palm up to stop her. His eyes never left Greene as he listened. He was turning pale.

"Okay," he said at last. "We're on our way." He hung up.

"There's been another murder," Hughes said. "Same place where Livingston Fox was killed, the Kensington Gate building site."

"What?" DiPaulo said, stepping forward.

"Daniel?" Greene said to Kennicott. "Who?"

"Ari," Kennicott said, holding Greene's gaze, "I'm sorry. It was your friend Claudio Bassante. He was stabbed through the heart with a rebar."

"Oh no," Greene said. "Oh no."

"In the work shed. The officer on scene says the blood on the floor is fresh. The body is still warm. It looks as if it just happened."

Behind Greene he heard a chair scrape against the floor. He turned. It was Amberlight. She was on her feet now, her shoulders back, her chin jutting out.

"Well," she said, zeroing in on Kennicott. "I told all of you, I didn't kill Livingston Fox. As you said, Detective, I'm not under arrest and the door isn't locked."

Greene watched in amazement as, before anyone could move, Amberlight strode right past Kennicott, marched out the door, and disappeared down the hallway.

56

Greene had a pad and pen out but instead of taking notes he was doodling. Drawing triangles. Big triangles, little triangles, intersecting triangles. Kennicott and Darvesh were sitting on either side of him in the backroom of the Yuens' Tim Hortons. The table was covered with coffee mugs, plates of breakfast sandwiches, and stacks of paper.

They'd arranged to meet here at nine this morning, instead of at the office, to avoid having to deal with the bureaucracy. Greene wasn't officially back on the force, but they all knew he had to be involved, especially since his old friend Claudio Bassante had been murdered. The formalities could wait. The investigation couldn't.

Yesterday afternoon, after Kennicott got the hotshot call, the three of them had rushed to the Kensington Gate building site. They'd split up after seeing the murder scene and now they were reporting in.

Darvesh had done a full background check on Bassante, developed a timeline of his known movements from Friday to Sunday, made a list of key facts and suspects for Fox's murder. He passed copies of his findings to Greene and Kennicott along with copies of the photos from the crime scene.

The pictures were hard for Greene to look at, even though he'd already seen Claudio's body first-hand. Bassante was lying on his back near the entrance to the shed, a rebar stuck through his heart. The front of his face had been bashed in and blood was spattered across the door and the walls. There were also photos of the back gate, open with the combination lock hanging from the handle, as it had been on Friday, when Fox was murdered.

Though Bassante had been killed the same way Fox had been, it was obvious that this murder was not as well planned. It seemed improvised, done in haste. It looked as if Bassante had opened the shed door and the killer had taken him by surprise and smashed him in the face with a flat, blunt object.

A cursory search of the building site had turned up a two-by-four hidden behind a pile of debris. Someone had made what looked like a feeble attempt to clean the blood off it, but Greene could easily see the dried residue. Kennicott had sent it and a hair from Bassante's head out for rush DNA testing, and a few hours later got confirmation that it was a match.

Greene put the photos down. "Daniel, what have you got?"

Kennicott opened his notebook. "At 4:08 I contacted Bassante's ex-wife. I went to see her. His daughters were there too, and I informed them. At 5:30 I put out the press release. Then I followed up in person with everyone I'd met at Omni and they all had alibis that Kamil and his troops checked out. At 10:12 I attended the emergency autopsy, which confirmed our initial theory. Bassante was first hit and then stabbed after he fell. He was probably unconscious when he was killed."

Greene closed his eyes. "I hope so," he said.

"I went back to the office to assist Kamil. At 6:00 this morning I got a call from Fox's sister, Gloria. She wants to meet with me. I'm going to the bus station at 10:05."

"Do we know where Fox's parents were yesterday afternoon?"

"I've had surveillance on the place running twenty-four/seven since Friday. Yesterday afternoon at 1:07, Karl Fox went for a bike ride. He headed northwest, away from the city. He was followed at a safe distance. An undercover took a photo of him in the parking lot outside a bookstore in Orangeville at 3:15, where he bought a book and had a drink in the cafe next door. He rode back home, arriving at 5:35. His wife never left the property."

Greene hadn't written a word. He was still doodling triangles. Long skinny ones. Wide short ones. All sorts of odd-shaped ones. "Did Gloria Fox say what she wants to talk to you about?"

"No, she didn't want to speak on the phone," Kennicott said. "It's an odd family."

"Especially the mother," Darvesh said.

Greene turned to him. "What else have you got?"

Darvesh checked his notebook. "Yesterday afternoon officers went door to door throughout the area around College and Spadina and collected security videos from all the nearby stores and found nothing. We checked the empty house on Augusta and it was clean."

"How about the person who found the body?" Greene asked.

Darvesh flipped to a new page in his notebook. "Earl Moffat, twenty-nine years old. Calls himself a freelance musician and part-time barista. He lives in a communal house in the market. He was walking the house dog, a big husky named Fahrenheit, up the alley. Apparently they don't believe in leashes, and he walks the dog there every afternoon."

That accounts for the puddle of dog pee in the alley on Friday, Greene thought.

"He said when they got near the construction site, the dog started barking like mad and ran through the back gate, which had been left open. Moffat followed the dog, found the body, and called 911."

"Does he have any known connection to Fox?"

"No, except he was at the protest on Friday. One of the officers went through outtakes of the TV crews and found him there, with the dog."

"What about Amberlight?" Greene asked Kennicott.

"We put a tail on her yesterday when she walked out of the station, and we've had her under surveillance ever since. She went home and hasn't come out."

Greene's triangles were getting denser and denser, piling one on top of the other until he'd filled almost every inch of empty space. "Okay," he said, turning to a fresh page. "We have to be missing something. Back to square one. Why did Claudio go to the shed?"

"To talk to someone who turned out to be the killer," Kennicott said.

"And this person," Greene said, putting his pen down and looking at Kennicott. "It had to be a someone who Claudio knew because . . ."

"Because Bassante must have unlocked the back gate and then left it open for the murderer," Kennicott said.

"Exactly." Greene turned to Darvesh. "And why did this person want Bassante dead?"

"Because they'd killed Fox," Darvesh said.

"And?" Greene asked.

"Maybe Bassante had come close to figuring out who the killer was," Darvesh said.

"And why this murder of Claudio was done in such haste," Greene said. An idea occurred to him. It seemed so simple. "Maybe," he said, "we've been looking too far afield. Maybe we need to start looking closer to home."

He picked up his pen again. "Do you remember what Fox's sister said about her brother at the midnight ceremony?"

"That she would always love him," Darvesh said.

Greene wrote the words out that Claudio had said to him when they'd met at his condo. They'd been echoing in his head for hours: *Follow the money.* "What else did the sister say?"

"That she'd spread his ashes after he is cremated."

"Where?"

"At every building he'd ever built and that his company ever would build." Kennicott's eyes lit up. "I hadn't thought of that."

Greene closed his notebook.

"I don't understand," Darvesh said.

"The website," Greene said. "It lists every Fox building and the ones still in the planning stage, doesn't it?"

"It does."

"Do you have a printout?"

Darvesh passed him some papers. "Yes, right here."

"Good work, Kamil," Greene said.

Darvesh looked back and forth between them, confused.

"Daniel, go meet with Fox's sister and find out what she has to say," Greene said. "There's someone I've got to see right away."

57

"Thank you for coming to meet me," Gloria said when Kennicott greeted her at the bus station. Even though it was still warm out, she was wearing a bulky sweater. "I have something important to tell you. Is there a place where we can talk alone?" Her voice was soft.

"There are a few coffee shops nearby. We can find a quiet one."

She shook her head. "No, thank you. Is there a park or someplace where we could go? I don't like the city. Too many cars and people."

Kennicott thought for a moment. There weren't any parks nearby in the downtown core, and the nearest open space was Nathan Phillips Square in front of city hall, which, even at this time of day, would be filled with people.

"I know a bench that's tucked away. Quite private. It's just a few minutes from here."

"That sounds fine."

She didn't say a word as they walked. The bench was in the side courtyard of the Faculty of Dentistry on Edward Street. Kennicott had stumbled on it when he'd last met with Jo Summers, a Crown attorney whom he'd come close to getting romantically involved with. It was on this bench that she'd told him she was moving to Vancouver with her new boyfriend.

"I have to tell you a secret. Can you promise me you won't tell my father?" Gloria said when they were seated.

It was a strange question for a woman in her forties to ask. "Of course."

"He knows I came down to talk to you but he doesn't know that I'm leaving Foxhole."

"Leaving?"

"Yes, finally. I have to. Maxine convinced me. She's going to take me to a safe place. She's picking up Livingston's ashes this morning. I'm meeting her at the office at noon. She's going to drive me around to every one of his buildings and I'm going to spread a little handful at each one."

Her eyes were unfocused. She kept looking around.

"Are you okay?" Kennicott asked her.

"Then Maxine is going to drive me to a place where I will be safe at last. My father doesn't know anything about it, of course. He would be mad if he knew what I was really up to. I didn't even pack a bag."

"Is he the only one who knows you are meeting with me?"

"Nobody else, except Maxine."

"How are your mother and father doing?"

"Kate is not our mother." Gloria's voice took on a new, firm tone.

"Oh. I didn't realize."

"Our mother died in childbirth, when Livingston was born."

"I'm sorry."

He remembered Karl Fox's first words when Kennicott told him the news about Livingston: "He's *my* only son." Not "He's *our* only son."

"Kate seemed very unemotional about your brother's death."

"Kate is very unemotional about everything. She came to work at Foxhole as a masseuse when I was a little girl. It turned out she and my father were having an affair even before my mother died. She hated Livingston and she resents me."

Gloria balled her hands up like a frustrated child.

"When Mom died I stopped eating. I was twelve. I got down to eighty-one pounds. They thought I was going to die. Maxine saved me. She doesn't have kids and she treated Livingston and me as her own."

"And your father?"

"He's totally dependent on Kate. She's ruined the centre. It was my mother's dream. We used to be full all the time, even in winter. After she died, things were okay for a long time because my father was in charge, but bit by bit Kate took over. He could never stand up to her. Look at the place now. It's a total failure."

"Is that why you are leaving?"

"Livingston kept pleading with me to move into one of his buildings. But all the noise and the traffic here in the city, I just, just couldn't do it."

"I understand. Is that why you wanted to meet, to tell me this?"

She gave him a quizzical look. "No, no. I need to tell you about my father. You were kind when you came to talk to us at the centre. I thought you were the only one I could trust."

"Anything that can help us find who killed Livingston is important."

"That's what I told Maxine. She didn't think I should get involved. But when I insisted, she said I should ask if you were close to making an arrest."

It was the question homicide detectives were asked all the time and never wanted to answer. He'd learned from Greene that the best response was *All I can tell you is that we are working full out on this, and as soon as we can we'll tell you first.* It was the answer he'd given Kennicott when he was investigating Michael's murder. And Kennicott was still waiting.

But Gloria seemed so vulnerable that he decided to tell her a white lie.

"You can tell Maxine we are very close to making an arrest," he said. If only it were true, he thought.

She smiled for the first time since they'd met. "I'm sure she'll be glad to hear that. She's so upset. Livingston was like the baby she never had."

Kennicott held himself still. Wait for her to talk, he told himself.

She unfolded one of her hands and smacked her fist into it. "You see," she said, "last night, after the foolish midnight ceremony that Kate organized, my father confessed to me."

"Confessed? What did he say?"

"He doesn't want Kate to find out. You won't tell her, will you?"

"Ms. Fox. This is a murder investigation. I can't promise you that."

She looked taken aback. "Detective," she said, "I told Maxine I needed to talk to you before I leave because you need to know that my father is a weak man but he's not a murderer. He loved Livingston in his own way and despite everything, I still love him. I know for certain that he didn't kill my brother."

"We've been told"—Kennicott spoke—"that he argued with Livingston when they had lunch on Friday."

"They argued every time they had lunch. You don't understand. When you came to our place he didn't tell you this because Kate was there."

"Tell me what?"

"After they had lunch he got on his bike."

"We know that," Kennicott said. "We found a video of him leaving the restaurant and heading north toward the building site."

"But then he turned."

"Turned?"

"Yes, that's what I wanted to tell you. He told me to tell you he turned west on Queen Street and went to his favourite bike store, Duke's."

Kennicott knew the place. It was one of the oldest bike shops in the city. And not on the way to Kensington Market.

"Daddy had ordered this really expensive new saddle from England, and it had just arrived. And he bought new panniers and a new helmet. He said he was there for at least half an hour and then he rode home."

"This could very helpful," he said.

"He said you can talk to Gary, the owner. And look, I have the proof. He made a copy of the receipt for me to show you."

She reached into her pocket and pulled out a photocopy of a Duke's Bike Shop receipt. Kennicott examined it. It was time-stamped

2:35 p.m. This evidence, easy to confirm, would provide Karl Fox with an alibi.

"He hid everything he'd bought inside his old panniers," she said.

Kennicott thought back to Karl Fox bursting into the room at the centre, carrying two old panniers and a beat-up helmet.

"Who was he hiding it from?" he asked, although now he knew the answer.

She shook her head. "Kate, of course. She despises cycling, and he rides all the time. Livingston and I used to joke that he does it to get away from her. He was always asking Livingston for cash."

"Cash?"

"It had to be cash. Kate started monitoring his credit cards years ago, right down to the last penny. This was the only way he could stop her from finding out how much he spent on his cycling equipment. That's what Daddy and Livingston used to fight about all the time. Amazing, isn't it? My father thought nothing of cheating on my mother, but he is afraid to spend ten cents without that woman's approval."

58

"Please excuse me for barging in like this," Greene said to Anthony Carpenter as he strode into the lawyer's office. A silver-haired woman, wearing a polyester dress and white gloves, was sitting across the desk from Carpenter.

Carpenter looked stunned. Apoplectic.

"And excuse me, ma'am," Greene said. "I am a police officer, and I have some urgent business with Mr. Carpenter. It could be a matter of life and death. I need about fifteen minutes of his time."

"But Mr. Carpenter is my lawyer."

"Yes, I know. And an excellent one too."

The woman made no move to leave her seat.

"Detective, you don't have an appointment," Carpenter said.

Greene took a deep breath. "I know that. I'll be happy to pay all the lawyers' fees today for Ms.—" He turned to the client.

"Mrs. Natalie Xynnis," she said. "If you are prepared to cover my legal fees for today, I'll step out, but only for ten minutes."

"Thank you. And again, I apologize."

She picked up a worn leather purse from the floor beside her and walked out.

Carpenter closed the file he had on his desk, crossed over to the cabinet in the corner, and put it inside. It seemed to take him forever to pull out another file and return to his desk.

"I've done the research as per your request," he said.

"And?"

Carpenter took out the list of Livingston's properties that Greene had left with him. Then, one by one, moving a ruler down at a snail's pace, he silently read the address of each property and made a little pencil mark beside it. Greene looked at his watch. By the time Carpenter got to the last one, five and a half minutes had gone.

At last, Carpenter spoke. "If a purchaser somehow had foreknowledge that Fox planned to build a condominium at a certain location, then if he or she was able to buy the said neighbouring property in advance, that would be an excellent investment."

"Exactly. And charge the builders extra because the cranes were casting a shadow over their property."

"It took me three point one hours to do this research. Take a look."

"What did you find?" Greene asked, scanning the printout.

"In the last five months, all seven houses adjoining Fox construction sites, either presently under construction or planned to be under construction, have been purchased in the exact same manner. Flipped three times in trust, always with different lawyers."

"Amazing," Greene said.

"I would say there is a distinct pattern here. I had planned to contact you once I finished my meeting with Ms. Xynnis, by the way."

"This means it had to be someone with inside knowledge?"

"It certainly appears that way."

"I can't thank you enough," Greene said, grabbing the file.

"Be sure to pay for Ms. Xynnis's ten minutes."

"Happily."

"You might like to know that her husband left her three stores on the Danforth and four houses in the neighbourhood that have doubled in value in the last five years. She's worth approximately twenty million dollars. And her biggest complaint is that the cost of parking on the street has just gone up."

59

When he got home, Kennicott found Breaker waiting for him in the kitchen, tearing lettuce and making a salad. She was wearing a pair of his red shorts and a black T-shirt and was drinking from her ever-present water bottle. He'd called her yesterday afternoon after they'd found Bassante's body and told her what had happened.

"Oh my God," she'd said. "Daniel."

"It's horrible."

"Claudio was such a lovely man. He has two beautiful daughters."

"You knew him?"

"Of course. Everyone knows everyone in the construction business. He was one of the best site foremen in the city. Now you see why I'm afraid?"

"Yes, I do."

"Do you have any idea what's going on?"

"We don't know yet. Don't leave my flat. The squad car will stay outside my place and you'll be safe there."

In the background he'd heard another voice. And wind. What was going on? It sounded as if she was outside.

"Did you leave my apartment?"

"I'm in the backyard with your landlord, Mr. Federico. We've been planting tomatoes all afternoon."

"You should know that Detective Darvesh tracked down a video from a store on Queens Quay of you jogging past it on Friday afternoon," Kennicott said. "You don't have to worry about your alibi."

"I never worried about my alibi," she said, her voice cold. "Did you?"

He paused. "I didn't worry about it. But I had to do my job."

"Is that why you're letting me stay here? So you can keep an eye on me?"

It was hard to tell if she was angry or amused.

"That wasn't the only reason."

"Fair enough," she said. Then she laughed.

"We need to plant now," he heard Mr. Federico say in the background.

"Hey, Daniel, your landlord wants me to get back to work," she said.

"Good idea. He's a slave driver. I'll see you later."

Later in the evening he'd called her again.

"How you doing?" he'd asked.

"Going a bit stir-crazy, stuck here like this, not being able to run. The Federicos insisted on having me over for dinner. How are you doing? You must be exhausted."

"Too busy to be tired. Thanks for asking."

Early this morning, he'd called for a third time.

"How was your night?" he asked.

"A bit lonely. And yours?"

Kennicott grinned. "I could think of more enjoyable ways to spend my time."

"You'll have to let me know some of them one day. What's going on with the investigation?"

"We're going back to square one. Sometimes you overlook obvious things when you're charging around. I have a favour to ask you. You knew Livingston very well. Can you make a list of the ten words you would use to describe him? We can go over it when I get home. Who knows where that might lead."

"Sure. Anything I can do to help."

A few minutes ago he'd called her a fourth time to tell her he was on his way. His heart was thumping when he walked in the door.

She gave him a hug. They held each other for a long time.

"It's awful," she whispered at last, holding him tight. "I keep thinking of Claudio's girls."

"So do I."

She kissed him on the side of his neck and let go of him.

"Can you tell me anything about what happened?" she asked.

"Not yet."

She had a pad of paper on the counter. "I made my list," she said. Her handwriting was extremely neat.

"Here are my top ten Livingston Fox characteristics," she said. "Smart, ruthless, inventive, obsessive about time, obsessive about order, funny, engaging, secretive, warm when he wanted to be, and tireless."

He stared at the list. Something he'd heard about Fox in the last three days didn't fit with what she'd written. He thought back to Fox's office. The work shed. How everything was in order. What Amberlight had said about the stray pencil they'd found on the floor of the shed. How he'd said not to worry about it.

"Obsessive about order," he asked Breaker. "What exactly do you mean?"

"Everything always in place. It used to drive Adam Lewis nuts at the Omni. Adam can't get through a morning without spilling something on himself. Fox was always perfectly groomed. And at the table he'd be cleaning up, stacking the dishes, wiping the table with his napkin. His office was like that too."

"If there was a pencil on the floor of the shed, and he'd told someone not to bother picking it up—"

"No way."

"A lot of people have told us about his obsession with time. If on Friday he had a meeting and didn't set the timer on his phone to end it—"

"Fox? Impossible."

Kennicott kept looking down the list. What else? What else? "Tireless," he whispered.

"I could have put that as number one," Breaker said. "Fox had more energy than anyone I've ever known."

"He told his fiancée when he spoke to her in Japan that he was tired. That was on Friday afternoon a few minutes before he met with Amberlight. She said that too. Think, on Friday morning at Omni did he seem off?"

"It really didn't occur to me until now but he was much quieter than usual. He told me he was worn out. He'd got up early to talk to his fiancée in Japan. I remember he was yawning when Adam was taking the group photo. Then he had his eyes closed. Adam had to take five or six shots to get a good one."

Kennicott thought back to Lewis flipping through the photos on his phone, looking for the best shot because Fox's eyes were closed in almost all of them.

"Did he eat anything unusual?"

"No. Just the mushroom soup, like we all do. Lewis insists. And he was drinking from one of his water bottles the way he always did."

She picked up her own bottle and shook it. Kennicott could hear it was almost empty. "Hydrating, like I've been doing all day especially with this heat wave."

Kennicott stared at her water bottle. He thought about the water bottles Fox kept in the back of the Rolls-Royce. How could he have missed it?

"What, Daniel?" Breaker asked. "What?"

He felt her hand on his.

"What time is it?"

"It's eleven-forty, why?"

He pulled his phone out and jabbed Greene's number.

He kissed Breaker on the top of her head. "Thanks," he said, then ran out the door.

60

Alison was upset and she was scared.

Yesterday afternoon, Grandpa Y had told her the terrible news that Ari's friend Claudio Bassante had been murdered in the same place and in the same way as Livingston Fox. Ari called and said he'd be working all night. He'd asked Grandpa Y to sleep over at the house, and he'd arranged for a police car to be stationed outside.

This was unbelievable.

She'd checked her blog. It had gone crazy. People were posting all kinds of theories about who the killer was, speculating that it was one of the developers who was competing with Fox, or one of the condo board owners who was suing him, or one of the protesters from the march on Friday, or some criminal gang who were using his condos for dealing drugs or money laundering.

She'd stayed up all night making notes, reading the new blog posts as they arrived, eating bowl after bowl of granola, more as a distraction than from hunger.

Now it was morning. She couldn't think of anything else to do, so she reloaded the two hours of raw TV footage of the demonstration on Friday. Maybe there was some clue she'd missed. She changed her settings to play the video at maximum speed and started to watch it again. The protest flew by. The marchers, the drummer, the people with babies, the people with dogs, the police marching down the sidewalk, making sure the protesters stayed on the street. All except her, sneaking across the sidewalk to the house on Augusta.

Wait a second.

On her phone she pulled up the three pictures of the shed she'd taken from the second-floor window. Detective Kennicott had looked at them and hadn't seen anything significant. That was because no one had thought of this.

She looked at the photo that showed the hoarding and the alley below it. She zoomed in on the spot she wanted to see.

Wait, wait.

She went back to the picture she'd posted, the one with the clear view through the shed window. Instead of focusing on Fox's dead body, she zoomed in on the water bottles on the desk. There were two, one blue and one orange. There should have been three. Where was the yellow one? Fox always had his three-pack of bottles with him when he met her at the restaurant.

She hadn't seen Fox on Friday. But Ari said the other people who saw him had remarked that he'd been very tired.

No wonder.

She grabbed her phone and called her father.

He picked it up before the first ring even ended. "Alison, you okay?"

"I'm fine," she said.

"What's wrong?"

"Nothing. But I think," she said, "I might have figured something out."

61

"I've got an assignment for you," Kennicott said to Officer Sheppard, as she whipped her squad car through the city at her usual nerve-racking speed. She had just zoomed past a streetcar.

"When?"

"Now."

"Great."

He told her what he needed her to do, and seconds later she deposited him in front of Fox's office.

Greene pulled up in his car and walked quickly over to him. A squad car arrived and Darvesh jumped out. Kennicott checked his watch. It was 11:55.

Kennicott quickly explained the situation to them. That he'd told Gloria that they were closing in on the killer and Gloria had told him that Maxine was taking her away at noon.

Greene pointed to the top floor. "They must be in her office. Daniel, you're the only one who's been up there."

Kennicott described the layout: the receptionist with the half-shaved head and how the door to Fox and Maxine's offices was tucked away behind Fox's private elevator.

"How do you get inside?" Greene asked.

"The receptionist waits ten seconds, then buzzes you in."

"Can she see you on a camera?"

"No. Fox set it up this way. He was a privacy nut. He hated security cameras."

"So no one could see him come or go," Greene said.

"That's how he planned it," Kennicott said. "Ari, Maxine and Gloria have met me and Kamil before but they won't know who you are. Go up the main elevator and ask for Maxine."

He turned to Darvesh. "Kamil, you cover the lobby in case they walk out that way before Ari gets up there. I'll cover the staircase."

"If the receptionist needs to buzz me in, who should I say I am?" Greene asked.

Kennicott hadn't thought of that. "Why don't you say you're a real-estate agent?"

Greene shook his head. "She might not let me in." He turned toward the shops across the street. "Give me a minute." Without saying another word, he took off, dodging through traffic to the other side of the road.

"Where's Detective Greene going?" Darvesh asked.

Kennicott pointed. "To that flower shop. Not a bad idea."

62

Greene charged into the flower shop and threw two fifty-dollar bills on the counter.

"I need the biggest prepared bouquet you have," he said, "right now."

"We have a plentiful selection for you to choose from, sir." The man behind the counter pointed to his standing refrigerator. "They vary in price from—"

"It doesn't matter." Greene yanked the fridge door open and snatched the nearest large bouquet.

He whirled back at the stunned-looking man. "Thanks," he said.

Greene was almost at the door when he remembered something. He rushed back to the desk. "A card, quick. I need a condolence card."

The man gestured at a countertop rack of greeting cards. "We have a number of very lovely ones for you to choose—"

"I'll take that one." Greene seized a card with a black border. "And give me a pen."

The man started scrounging around on the counter.

Greene spotted a pen and reached for it. "I'll keep the pen. You keep the change."

He ran back across the street, took the steps to Fox's office building two at a time, yanked the glass door open, and rushed across the lobby. The elevator doors were closing. He jumped in and pushed number five. As soon as the elevator began to rise he pulled out the pen, wrote a few words on the card, and wove it into the bouquet.

The elevator stopped at the third floor, and a well-dressed young woman got in, tapping on her phone. She pushed the already-lit number five.

"Nice flowers," she said.

"They're for Mr. Fox's assistant."

"Poor Maxine. She's amazing. The whole team is still in just, like, total shock about Livingston."

The door opened again on the fourth floor. Two more employees got in, both glued to their phones. One of them pushed the lit number five.

"I hope you don't mind," Greene said, cutting in front of all of them when the door opened on the fifth floor, "but this is a rush delivery." He strode up to the woman with the half-shaved head at the reception desk.

"I have some flowers to deliver to, let me see now"—he squinted through the flower stems at the card—"someone named Maxine. Is she here?"

"She is," the receptionist said. "She's in a meeting now. You can leave them with me."

"No, I can't do that. The order specifically says they must be delivered by hand." He looked at the card again. "They are from Kate and Karl."

She smiled. "Mr. Fox's parents. Okay. Go to the door around the back of the elevators and wait ten seconds. I'll buzz you in."

Greene walked around the elevator bank and waited. Kennicott had told him that Maxine's office was inside to the left. The moment he heard the buzzer, Greene whipped the door open and dashed in.

Maxine's door was partway open. He tossed the flowers on the floor and flung it open the rest of the way.

63

Kennicott was on the third-floor landing. Pacing. The phone in his hand rang. It was Greene.

"They're in the private elevator, going down."

"What?" Kennicott started running down the stairs. "Darvesh is covering the elevator on the ground floor. Call him."

"Won't help. I'm looking at the elevator lights. It just passed the ground floor and landed at B1. What's down there?"

"The Rolls-Royce." Kennicott was taking the steps down two at a time. "I'm headed to my car."

On the ground floor, he hit the bar on the exit door and raced out onto the street. Sheppard was parked exactly where he'd asked her to with both front windows open.

"Did you see anything?" he yelled, as he ran up to the car.

"A Rolls convertible. Older woman driver, younger woman passenger. They flew out of the parking garage."

"Which way did they go?"

"East on Front."

Kennicott jumped in beside her.

"Seat belt," she said.

He laughed and buckled up fast. The car rocketed forward, throwing him back against his seat. He called Greene. "They're in the Rolls, heading east on Front."

Sheppard was zipping through traffic. Kennicott heard a police siren behind them.

"There she is!" Sheppard cried.

Up ahead, Kennicott saw the car driving erratically. At Parliament

Street, it took a sharp right turn, almost skidding out of control. "What the hell?" Sheppard said. "She's headed south." Sheppard took the corner at a perfect angle and accelerated with force at just the right moment.

The Rolls was about a block ahead. Sheppard grabbed the mic for the roof-mounted speaker. "Police, stop! Police, stop!" she shouted.

The Rolls wasn't slowing down. It passed under the elevated Gardiner Expressway and followed the road along the lake.

"I know where she's going," Kennicott said as Sheppard ran a yellow light at top speed. "On your left, Fox Harbour!"

He saw a group of joggers rounding a curve and heading right into the Rolls-Royce's path.

"Hit the siren!"

The siren roared.

The joggers, half of whom were wearing earbuds, looked up and grabbed each other as the Rolls shot past, missing the leaders by inches. Sheppard flew in behind it.

"Oh no," he said. "I see where she's headed."

"Where?"

"The water."

"Is she crazy?"

The Rolls raced through a small parking space and headed down a long wharf. The water was straight ahead of them, shimmering in the midday sun.

"Not on my watch," Sheppard said. She jammed her foot on the gas and Kennicott was momentarily pinned to his seat by the force. Sheppard's siren was wailing. Her lights were flashing. She was gaining on the Rolls and had almost drawn up beside it. "Stop, police! Stop, police!" her voice boomed over the roof-mounted speaker.

Rat-a-tat. Rat-a-tat. Gravel was battering the undercarriage like gunfire.

Sheppard pulled even with the Rolls. Maxine was in the driver's seat staring straight ahead. Unwavering. Beside her, Gloria was screaming. She had something in her hand. It was the urn she'd had at the midnight ceremony.

"Hold on tight," Sheppard shouted to Kennicott.

She was pulling ahead of the Rolls now. They were seconds away from the water.

"When I say duck, duck!"

Kennicott felt the car in full flight.

"Duck!" Sheppard screamed.

She slammed on the brakes and whipped the wheel around, swinging the squad car into a sharp turn. The rear of the car skidded out behind him. Kennicott buried his head between his knees.

The Rolls smashed into the squad car inches behind his seat. The car rocked up, and for a moment he was sure it was going to flip over.

"No you don't!" Sheppard shouted. "No way, no way."

The car stopped. Kennicott looked up. The right front of the Rolls had hit the rear door of the cruiser. It was stuck there.

He unlocked his seat belt and threw open his door. Sheppard had timed the collision perfectly, leaving his door intact.

Gloria was in the passenger seat, hysterical. But there was no sign of Maxine. Kennicott motioned to Sheppard to take care of Gloria, then rushed behind the squad car. He spotted Maxine running down the wharf toward the water. She had a long tube in one hand and it was churning up and down with her arm, like an oversized baton carried by a sprinter. She had a good lead on him.

He took off. Don't start too fast, he told himself. He didn't want to slip on the gravel again. He kept his legs high, his arms rotating fast. He was gaining on her but she was determined.

The poor, deranged lady. What she'd said at the end of their first meeting came back to him: "Please leave the door open on your way out. I like the fresh air. It comes from growing up by the sea." She hadn't closed the back gate after she'd murdered Fox and Bassante. She hadn't locked the door to the house she'd bought on Augusta Avenue. Old habits die hard.

He was running full out now. Gaining on her, but the water was so close. Seagulls at the end of the wharf flew up. Screeching.

"Maxine! Stop! There's no point," he yelled.

He saw her shake her head. She didn't look back. Two, three, four more big strides. It was now or never. He flung himself in the air and reached for her legs. Her feet. But he felt nothing but air.

Then his fingers touched something. It was round. The tube. He grabbed on to it as he slammed into the ground. The loose stones dug into his chin and his elbows but he held on to the tube. Maxine wouldn't let go and he felt her weight tumble beside him.

He scrambled to his feet. She lay on the ground, curled up in the fetal position, clutching the tube to her breast, steps away from the edge of the wharf. He rushed around to place himself between her and the steep drop to the water, which this time of year would still be very cold.

He crouched down to be at her eye level and placed his hand on her shoulder, expecting her to recoil.

She didn't flinch.

"Are you hurt?" he asked her. "Can you sit up?"

She nodded. "Why did you stop me? Why? Why? Why?" she moaned.

He took her arm and raised her until she was sitting.

Her face twisted in anger.

"Livingston was my boy. My baby boy. That woman. Kate." She spat the name out, as if saying it would infect her with a fatal disease. "She was no mother, no stepmother, no nothing. And Gloria. Poor Gloria was a prisoner there. I had to get her away. I had to save her. She loved Livingston almost as much as I did."

Her voice deepened.

"I changed his diapers. I ran his business. I hid all his girlfriends."

Her eyes narrowed.

"But then she came along. That Japanese one."

"His fiancée?"

"I showed you his calendar for the month. Didn't you see? He was in love with her. It was clear as day. Every week, more and more of his damned private time. She had it all planned out, to steal my boy from me. Livingston was going to leave me all alone."

Kennicott heard the sound of tires on gravel. He looked back down the wharf. A squad car pulled up and Greene got out. More cruisers were piling in behind it.

He held up his free hand to signal Greene to stay back.

Greene gave him a thumbs-up.

He looked back at Maxine. Her eyes were closed. She was shaking her head as if she were in a trance. He put his hand on her shoulder and her whole body crumbled in defeat. She wasn't going anywhere.

64

"**D**ad!"

Greene whirled around. Another police cruiser had pulled up and Alison bolted out of it. She ran straight to him.

"How did you . . . ?"

"I talked the officer outside the house into driving me down here."

Dad. She'd never called him Dad before.

She threw her arms around him. He held her. They'd never hugged before either.

"It's awful about Claudio," she said.

"I know," he said, holding her tight. "I should have figured this out sooner."

"I wish I had too. Did Detective Kennicott catch Maxine?"

"Just in time."

They untangled, and Greene pointed to the end of the wharf.

"Maxine was trying to drive into the lake, and she had Livingston's sister, Gloria, with her. It's a long drop. If they'd gone in, she would have killed them both."

Alison shook her head. "Oh my God. Where's Gloria?"

"She's okay."

"Thank goodness. Why are the police standing here?"

"Kennicott signalled me to hold everyone back."

"Is he arresting her?"

"He will. But right now he's letting her talk. Often the best time is the moment you apprehend a suspect. The urge to confess is very strong, and it's best done in private."

Alison tilted her head. "I bet you taught him that, didn't you?"

He shrugged. "Maybe he picked up a few pointers from me along the way."

"Maybe?" she said with a smile, then gave him one of her playful punches on the arm. "What's going to happen now?"

"We wait until Daniel gives me the signal. You should be proud of yourself for figuring out that one of Livingston's bottles was missing, and that the puddle by the gate was water from the missing bottle, not dog pee."

She shrugged. "I never realized how easy it was to be a detective. All you have to do is count."

They both laughed.

She seemed relaxed standing beside him.

"Why did Maxine do it?"

"The two oldest motives in the world. Jealousy and greed. She was jealous because she was losing her baby boy to Fox's new wife. And greed. She was buying up properties beside Livingston's new condo developments, extracting huge fees for the shadows the cranes cast over them, then making a fortune selling the homes once the neighbourhood's property values went up."

"Such a horrible waste," Alison said. "But why was she trying to drive Gloria into the lake?"

"I think the only logical explanation is that she's crazy."

Alison took his hand. Another first.

"Claudio has children, doesn't he?" she asked him.

"Two daughters. I'm going to get Ted DiPaulo to make sure they are taken care of. Same for Livingston's child."

"Livingston? I didn't know he had children."

"He doesn't. Kennicott told me this morning that his fiancée is pregnant."

"Oh my." She rested her head on his shoulder.

Greene didn't move.

"I want you to know," Alison said, as she wrapped her arms around his waist, "that I'm working up to say I love you."

He put his arm around her shoulder. "There's no hurry," he said. "I'm not going anywhere."

65

M axine stopped shaking her head and opened her eyes. She looked dazed.

"The tube," Kennicott asked her gently, "are those Livingston's plans for K2?"

"I needed to destroy them. Livingston was always spending, spending, spending out of control. Can you imagine now he was going to build low-income housing? It was that fiancée of his. She infected his mind."

"Why was that such a bad idea?" he asked, putting his hand on the tube in case she tried to hurl it into the water.

"Low-income housing?" she scoffed. "The profit margins are much too low! Fox Harbour, this place was his dream. But he owed his creditors millions. And the banks? If they'd heard about this K2 plan of his, they would have pulled the plug in a minute. Livingston would have been ruined. *Ruined.* How could I let that happen to my child?"

She reached in under her sleeve and fished out a crumpled tissue.

"You bought houses next to his new construction sites so you could spy on him."

She jolted back, as if she'd been slapped in the face. "I had to watch over my boy. I needed to protect him."

"The money you got for your building crane fees and from selling the houses at a profit. What did you do with it?"

"For goodness' sake. You yourself gave a twenty-dollar donation. Someone has to take care of the children."

"The Daley Youth Shelter," he said, remembering the painting in her office and the donation box on her desk. And how she'd referred to youth then as children.

"I couldn't let them grow up the way I did. With nothing."

"You realized that Livingston was getting suspicious of you. That's why you . . ." Kennicott stopped to let her end the sentence.

"My baby was being a bad boy. I was the only one who could discipline him. Not that horrible Kate, and his father was useless. Don't you see? I had to protect him from himself. That's what a good parent has to do. I knew in his heart he still wanted to be with me, and now he can rest in peace."

"What about Claudio Bassante?"

Her face turned red. She ground her teeth in frustration. "Claudio. I was the one who told Livingston to give him a job when no one in the business would have anything to do with him."

Now it made sense.

"You knew he'd be anxious to succeed because of his past," Kennicott said, "and that he'd approve the payments for the cranes."

"Livingston didn't care because Claudio always came in under budget. But why did he have to be so curious? I told him that Cassandra Amberlight was the killer. Still, he was having his doubts, thanks to that friend of yours, Detective Greene. Claudio told me Greene hired a real-estate lawyer to try to trace back the owners of the properties beside the building sites."

"And you had him meet you at the shed yesterday—so you could eliminate him."

"Claudio was going to ruin everything. You don't understand. No one understands. It was all for the children."

"There were only two water bottles in the shed," Kennicott said. "But Livingston always carried three. You took one of them, didn't you?"

"Waste not, want not."

"Like your mother always said. And you poured out the whole bottle of water in the alleyway outside the gate. You'd added heavy sedatives to all the bottles to make Fox more and more tired as the day wore on."

She had a faraway look in her eyes. "Blue. Orange. Yellow. It was our little secret code. *BOY*. Livingston was my little boy. He could be so forgetful, this way he knew which order to drink them in."

And how much sedative to put in each one, Kennicott thought.

"I've given him a bottle since the day he was born," she said. "We had such a beautiful afternoon together, just the two of us. He was tired out and he needed his nap. He lay down in my lap and I combed his hair with my fingers the way I always did. I sang him a lullaby. When he fell asleep he looked so peaceful. He didn't even flinch when I put the concrete blocks on his hands. And then . . ." Her voice drifted off.

He could picture it. Maxine standing on the chair in the window in the second floor of the house on Augusta, spying on Amberlight and Fox in the work shed, seeing Amberlight leave the construction site and close the gate behind her. Then going into the shed, Fox falling asleep on her lap, then setting it up to make it appear that someone big and strong was the murderer before she killed him.

"Cassandra Amberlight was the perfect suspect for you, wasn't she?"

"That terrible woman, trying to make a public housing deal with my boy. She was violent and strong. Why didn't you arrest her? I gave you every reason."

"But you forgot to close the back gate, and you even left the back door to your house unlocked."

"I'm a Newfoundlander. We never close our doors. I told you that the first time we met. You weren't listening."

She held out the tube to Kennicott and he took it from her.

"Where is my baby girl, Gloria?" she asked him.

"We're taking care of her."

"I had to get her away from that witch."

"Kate?"

"She was starving the poor girl to death. With Livingston gone, Gloria was all I had."

He thought back to Maxine bursting into the room on Friday afternoon, running up to Gloria. How at the candlelight ceremony she'd been the one to comfort Livingston's sister.

"I wanted her to see the water."

She hoisted herself up, and gazed out across the harbour. Kennicott stood up beside her. The seagulls had returned and were screeching louder than ever. A ferryboat was churning toward Ward's Island, and a pair of sea kayaks passed by close to the shore. She put her hands behind her back, clasping them in a pose of surrender.

"It's time for you to take me, isn't it?" Her voice was so soft that he had to bend forward to hear her.

"Yes, it is." Gently, he put his free hand over her crossed wrists.

"The doors are going to be locked from now on, aren't they?"

"I'm afraid they will be."

"Please, may I have one more minute to look at the water?"

"Of course."

"I've always loved being next to the sea," she said. Her voice had turned childlike. "It's calm today. The tide is in, and I hope we'll see some whales. Mother said Father will be returning soon. I wish I could wait for him. I wish I could."

She turned to Kennicott. Her eyes were misty, distant.

"Uncle Horace, nice of you to come be with me."

He didn't know what to say.

"I was hoping Daddy's boat would come back this morning. Do you think it will come tomorrow?"

He nodded. "I think so."

"I've been waiting such a very long time. We must go now, Mother is tired. I have to take care of the children."

"Yes," Kennicott said. "The children."

He looked over her shoulder back along the wharf. A line of squad cars was there, their flashers whirling, uniformed cops standing in front of them at the ready. TV trucks had arrived, their antennas raised in the air. In the distance, he saw the TO-TV helicopter heading toward them. Officer Sheppard was cradling Gloria, whom she'd wrapped in a heat blanket. Darvesh was waving one arm in the air as he talked fervently on his phone.

And Ari Greene, walking his slow, homicide-detective walk, was coming toward him. A set of handcuffs was dangling from one hand and his other arm was extended, reaching out to shake Kennicott's hand.

NOVEMBER

66

Alison bit her lip. "Was that good?" she asked.

"It was perfect," Sheena Persad said.

"Can I try it one more time?"

"No, there's not enough time. We're going live in fifteen seconds."

"Okay, I think I'm ready," Alison said.

"Move the mic a little lower. Remember to breathe."

Alison hadn't realized she'd been holding her breath.

"In five, four, three, two, one." Persad counted the numbers down with her fingers, then pointed to Alison.

"Good afternoon, this is Alison Gilroy-Greene reporting live for TO-TV News. I'm standing on Spadina Avenue in front of one of Toronto's landmark buildings, the Waverly Hotel."

As they'd rehearsed it, the camera shifted to Alison's left.

"With me now is well-known lawyer and activist Cassandra Amberlight. Ms. Amberlight, I understand that two months ago you actually moved into the hotel."

Amberlight stepped forward, taking up most of the space in front of the camera. This had not been planned.

"Yes, I took a room on the ground floor. When I formed the Save Southern Spadina Coalition, I believed it was vital to show my personal commitment to the cause."

"And the goal of the coalition is?"

"To save historic buildings." As she spoke, Amberlight cast her hand behind her. The camera followed. "The Waverly is one of the oldest hotels in Toronto, opened in 1900. Next door we have the storied Silver Dollar bar, home of the blues in Toronto since 1958."

"Thank you, Ms. Amberlight." Alison pivoted to her other side. The camera followed her and zoomed in for a headshot. "Also with me now is Ms. Anita Nakamura, the president of Fox Cityscape Foundation, and Odessa Breaker, president of the newly formed Toronto Public Housing Forum."

Nakamura was wearing a loose coat. She was clearly very pregnant and had asked that her extended belly not be displayed on TV.

"Ms. Nakamura," Alison said, "I understand that your company has worked very closely with the Spadina Coalition and the Housing Forum."

"Yes, we have," Nakamura said. "I'm pleased to announce today that an historic agreement between these wonderful stakeholders and our great company has been signed. We are putting up a modern rental building with affordable housing and student residences, and we're going to restore the Silver Dollar and preserve its iconic facade."

"Ms. Breaker, your thoughts?" Alison asked. Keep the mic down, she told herself. Don't talk too quickly. Breathe.

"This is a crucial step toward ending the ghettoization of communities in our city," she said.

Alison turned back to Nakamura. "What can we expect in terms of the look of this new building?" she asked.

"Spadina Gate will feature a world-class design the whole city can be proud of," Nakamura said. She pulled the cover off a drawing that was resting on a tripod stand. "We are paying homage to the late Livingston Fox. He loved fine architecture. Innovative, mixed-use, integrated, quality housing was his vision for the city."

"He was a fan of Bauhaus design, was he not?" Alison asked.

"It was his favourite, and you can see its influence in this design, which is based on some of his own architectural drawings."

The camera moved back to Alison.

"And so, yet another new building, preserving the old and celebrating the new, is going up right in the heart of the city. For TO-TV News, this is Alison Gilroy-Greene reporting live from Spadina Avenue in downtown Toronto."

She remembered to lower the mic and smiled for what seemed to be the longest few seconds of her life until the red light on top of the camera went off.

She exhaled loudly. "Phew!"

Persad ran up and hugged her. "That was perfect."

"Thanks to you." Alison turned to Breaker, and Nakamura. "Thanks, You were both terrific."

"Good luck in your new career," Breaker said. "Sorry, but I've got to run." She shook Alison's hand and rushed off.

"All the best," Nakamura said.

"I want you to know that Livingston was a great help to me in my career," Alison said. "He always made me feel special."

"Only the people who knew him understood what a generous man he could be," Nakamura said, clasping Alison's hands.

"Good luck with the baby."

"It's a girl. I'm going to call her Liv. Means 'life.' "

Alison watched Nakamura walk away and saw her put her arm around a thin woman who had been waiting on the sidelines. It was Fox's sister, Gloria, holding an urn in her hand.

"So you really are going to be a journalist," Amberlight said behind her.

Alison turned. "Well, that's the plan for now," she said.

"Funny, isn't it?" Amberlight said. "They never did find out who the Kensington Blogger was, did they?"

Alison stole a quick glance at Persad, who winked at her.

"No, I guess they didn't," Alison said.

"Whoever it was, she was a good reporter." Amberlight took a few steps and then turned back and pointed down Spadina. "By the way, did you see that the Huibing Gardens closed down?"

"I did," Alison said. "It's too bad."

As soon as the words were out of her mouth, Alison realized the mistake she'd made.

Amberlight grinned. "I thought so," she said.

Alison looked at Persad, then back at Amberlight, and shrugged.

"Don't worry, your secret's safe with me," Amberlight said. "Maybe one day people will learn how you and me and Breaker changed the city because of our meetings with Fox in the little backroom of that restaurant. Maybe they'll put up a plaque."

"Livingston deserves it."

"Hold your head up high, young lady," Amberlight said. "You had nothing but good intentions. I'll see you at the next demonstration."

Before Alison could respond, Amberlight turned and walked toward her latest home, in the historic Waverly Hotel.

Acknowledgments

It is a joy to write contemporary novels about Toronto. The city is so rich and complex and I work hard to get all the little details right. But there's a downside to writing about a real, not a fictional, place. Once in a while I take literary licence and change things around, and it seems my readers always catch me out.

In my first novel, *Old City Hall*, I went to Vesta Lunch, a classic downtown Toronto diner, to find a location for an important scene. It was perfect, except there were no booths for customers—or my characters—to sit in, which was key. So, I added them. Soon after the book came out I got an email from a reader telling me: "I often eat at the Vesta Lunch, and have never seen the booths that you describe there."

In *The Guilty Plea*, my third book, I had the name of the conductor on the Ontario Northlands train, "Hamish," embroidered on his shirt with red thread. I took the long train ride north twice while doing my research and, I confess, I knew there were no stitched name tags. But it felt like such a nice touch. Inevitably, I received an email from a retired conductor who had worked the same rail line. He informed me that employees' names "are not embroidered on their shirts."

Perhaps my most egregious bit of literary liberty taking occurred in my second book, *Stray Bullets*. I had the nerve to put the famous Tim Hortons Roll Up the Rim to Win contest in September, even though I knew it was the wrong month. I just couldn't resist—the phrase is too great not to makes its way into one of my novels. I got the following email: "Roll Up the Rim to Win is mentioned in the book. The contest is in April not September, other than that a great book. Thanks."

I am most grateful that so many people write to me and take the stories and the characters to heart. After my fourth novel, *Stranglehold*, came out, I received this email from an anxious reader: "My mother and I would like to know why Ari went away for a year. My mother says do not get rid of Ari or she won't buy your books."

Fortunately, Ari is back. But I'll leave it as a mystery which small literary liberties I've taken this time around. I'm sure I'll hear from you.

Huge thanks, and sincere apologies, to my wife, Vaune Davis, and my three children for their endless support and patience.

And thanks to my agent, Victoria Skurnick, as well as all the people at Simon & Schuster Canada. In particular, Amy Prentice, my publicist and cheerleader through all five books; Dinah Forbes, the freelance editor who never lets anything slip (she did warn me about the Roll Up the Rim); and Nita Pronovost, any writer's dream editor: inspiring, brilliant, and wise.

Special mention to Kevin Hanson, president of Simon & Schuster Canada. The first day we met, I promised him twenty books in this series. I'm passing the quarter mark with this fifth novel and I appreciate more than ever how Kevin's belief in me and his unwavering support have made all the difference.

Toronto
January 31, 2017

P.S. Do keep those cards, letters and emails coming. I respond to every one.